WHAT HAPPENED TO
THE CORBETTS

Nevil Shute was born in 1899 and educated at Shrewsbury School and Balliol College, Oxford. Having decided early on an aeronautical career, he went to work for the de Havilland Aircraft Company as an engineer, where he played a large part in the construction of the airship R100. His first novel, *Marazan* (1926), was written at this time. After the disaster to the R101, he turned his attention to aeroplane construction and founded his own firm, Airspeed Ltd, in 1931. In the war Nevil Shute served in the Navy, doing secret work for the Admiralty. He still found time to write, however, and during this time produced several novels including *Pied Piper*, *Pastoral* and *Most Secret*. These were followed in 1947 by *The Chequer Board* and, in 1948, *No Highway*, which became a great bestseller and an extremely popular film. In 1948 he went to Australia for two months, a trip that inspired his most popular novel, *A Town Like Alice*. He returned there for good with his family, and remained until his death in 1960. His later novels include *In the Wet*, *Requiem for a Wren*, *On the Beach*, and *Trustee from the Toolroom*.

D1331607

Nevil Shute

What happened to
the Corbetts

Pan Books in association with
Heinemann

First published 1939 by William Heinemann Ltd
This edition published 1965 by Pan Books Ltd
Cavaye Place, London SW10 9PG,
in association with William Heinemann Ltd

9
ISBN 0 330 10380 6
Printed in Great Britain by
Richard Clay (The Chaucer Press) Ltd, Bungay, Suffolk

Good luck have thou with thine honour: ride on, because of the word of truth, of meekness, and righteousness; and thy right hand shall teach thee terrible things.

—Psalm 45

PREFACE

THIS book was written in the year 1938 and published in April 1939, five months before the outbreak of the Second World War. At the time when it was written it was thought probable that war with Germany would come before long, and there was much activity in England over Air Raid Precautions. Most of these activities at that time were directed to countering bombing attacks by gas bombs, and there was little realization by the public of the devastation that would be caused by high explosive or by fire.

At that time I was connected with the aircraft industry and so, perhaps, better informed than most authors on the potentialities of the various forms of air attack. I wrote this story to tell people what the coming bombing attacks would really be like, and what they really had to guard against. I was right in my guess that gas would not be used and in the disruption of civil life that would be caused by high explosives. I overlooked the importance of fire. I would like to think that the publication of this novel at that time did something to direct attention to the danger of disease. In this the publishers, William Heinemann Limited, did a good job for the country, for they distributed a thousand copies free of charge to workers in Air Raid Precautions, not as remainders but on publication day.

In this edition I have retained the Author's Note printed at the end of the book, because it seems to me to be of some historic interest.

NEVIL SHUTE

TOWARDS DAWN Peter Corbett got up from the garage floor and, treading softly, moved into the driving seat of the saloon. Presently he fell into a doze, his head bowed forwards on his arms, upon the steering-wheel.

He woke an hour later, dazed and stiff. A grey light filled the little wooden building; it was early March. The rain drummed steadily upon the roof and dripped and pattered from the eaves with little liquid noises, as it had done all through the night. He stirred and looked around him.

Behind him, in the rear seat of the car, lay Joan, his wife, sleeping uneasily. She was dressed oddly in an overcoat, pyjama trousers, and many woolly clothes; her short fair hair had fallen across her face in disarray. On the seat beside her was the basket cot with little Joan; so far as could be seen, the baby was asleep.

He moved and looked out of the window of the car. Beside the car Sophie their nurse was lying on a Li-Lo on the oil-stained floor, covered with an eiderdown, sleeping with her mouth open and snoring a little. Beyond her there was another little bed, carefully screened between the garden roller and a box of silver sand for bulbs. From that the bright eyes of Phyllis, his six-year-old daughter, looked up into his own; beside her lay John, his three-year-old son, asleep.

Moving very quietly, he got out of the driving seat and stood erect beside the car; he had a headache, and was feeling very ill. From her bed upon the floor, Phyllis whispered:

'Daddy. May I get up?'

'Not yet,' he said mechanically. 'It's not time to get up yet. Go to sleep again.'

'Weren't they *loud* bangs, Daddy?'

'Very loud,' he said. He moved over to the garage window

and looked out. Everything seemed much the same, but he could not see beyond the garden.

'Daddy, were the bangs loud enough to be heard in London?'

'Not in London.' He was feeling sick; his mouth was coated and dry.

'Would the bangs have been heard in Portsmouth, Daddy?'

'No. I don't know.'

'Anyway, they'd have been heard *all over* Southampton, wouldn't they, Daddy?'

'That's right,' he said patiently. So much, indeed, was evident. 'But now, try to sleep again and don't talk any more, or you'll wake Mummy and John. There won't be any more bangs now.'

He stepped carefully across the Li-Lo to the corner, and stooped over the little bed. He pulled the rug across her. 'It's not time to get up yet. Are you warm enough?'

'Yes, thank you, Daddy. Isn't it fun, sleeping in the garage?'

'Great fun,' he said soberly. 'Now, go to sleep again.'

He moved quietly down the garage past the car, opened the door, and went out into the garden. His raincoat had half dried upon him in the night. He had no hat; the rain beat on his face and ruffled hair, and this refreshed him.

He lived in a semi-detached house, a large house in a good suburban road. It had a well-kept garden stretching out behind to the back road; the wooden garage was at the end remote from the house. He lived comfortably in a fairly modest style; he was the junior partner of Johnson, Bellinger, and Corbett, solicitors, in Southampton. He ran a medium-sized car which he had bought second-hand, and a nine-ton cutter yacht which he had bought sixteenth-hand; these, with his three children, absorbed the whole of his income. He was thirty-four years old, a pleasant, ordinary young man of rather a studious turn.

He stood for a few moments in the garden in the rain, looking around. His house looked much the same as usual, so did the houses on each side of it. There was a window broken in a house a few doors down the road; otherwise he could see nothing wrong. He moved up the garden, opened the garden door, and went into his dining-room.

A sudden draught of cold air blew into his face, fluttering the papers on a table where the telephone was standing.

He frowned. There was a window open somewhere in the house. Someone had left it open in the confusion of the night – and on a rainy night like that! It was too bad.

He passed through the hall into the drawing-room in the front of the house. In fact, the windows were still open, but they had not been left open by the maids. The glass in every pane was cracked and shattered. Most of it had fallen inwards from the frames, and was lying on the floor. The rain streamed in through the great apertures, trickling down the furniture and making little pools upon the carpet. The settee, and Joan's easy chair, were drenched and sodden. Before the window the chintz curtains blew about, sopping and forlorn.

His lips narrowed to a line. 'Christ,' he said very quietly.

There was nothing to be done, and if there was, he was feeling too ill to do it. He turned from the ruined room, and went upstairs. A short inspection of the house showed him the extent of the damage; it was practically all confined to glass and damage from the rain. In the front of the house every pane of glass was shattered on the first and second floors; a few windows at the top remained intact. The back of the house was quite undamaged; the windows were unbroken and the rooms dry.

A clanging bell brought him to the nursery window in time to see a white ambulance go past the house at a considerable speed. He heard the brakes go on with violence as it passed him; it seemed to draw up down the road out of his sight. There was a commotion down there, noises of people and sounds that he could not place.

He turned from the window, went downstairs to the bath-room, opened the medicine cupboard on the wall, and took a couple of aspirins to ease his headache. Then he went down to the front door, opened it, and looked out.

The rain blew down the street in desolate great gusts; low over his head the grey clouds hurried past. Something peculiar about the houses opposite attracted his attention; he stared for a moment while a dulled, tired brain picked up the threads. And then it came to him. Practically every window within sight was shattered like his own, and the rooms stood open to the rain.

He walked to the front gate, bare-headed in his raincoat, and looked down the road. A hundred yards away the ambulance was halted with a little crowd of people round it; they were putting a stretcher into it with care. It seemed to him that there were ruins there, as if the garden wall had fallen down on to the pavement. He knew what must have happened and it interested him; he went out of the gate and started down the road.

The ambulance moved off as he drew near. He knew the house, of course. He did not know their name. He knew them as an elderly couple who drove a very old Sunbeam car, with a married daughter who stayed with them intermittently with her children. As he came up the little crowd turned to disperse, and Corbett saw for the first time the results of a bomb.

It had fallen in the front garden. There was a shallow crater there, three or four feet deep. Bursting before it had had time to penetrate far into the ground, the force of the explosion had gone sideways. The garden wall of that house and the next was nowhere to be seen; it was obliterated, lying in heaps of mould and shards of broken brick and mortar scattered the road. The front wall of the house had collapsed and had fallen in a great heap into the front garden, blocking the door and exposing dining-room and bedrooms to the air with all their furniture in place, much like an open dolls' house. A portion of the roof had slipped and now hung perilously, swaying and teetering in the wind; from time to time a slate crashed to the ground.

His next-door neighbour was there, Mr Littlejohn, a

builder of houses out at Sholing. Corbett knew his neighbour fairly well over the garden wall, and liked his comfortable manner. But now the broad rubicund face was drawn and tired, and very serious.

Corbett asked, a little foolishly: 'Is anybody hurt?'

The builder turned to him. 'The maid. It's her they've just taken away. But I don't know if it was the explosion, or whether she had a fall getting down from her room. That's her room, the one at the top with the wash-stand. Doesn't look as if it had been touched now, does it? – barring the wall, of course.'

'Where was she?'

'Lying out in the garden here, all messed up.'

Corbett blinked. It seemed incredible. 'What happened to the old people?' he inquired.

'They're all right – but for the shock, of course. The blast must have been terrific in the house. See what it's done to all our windows. But they sleep at the back, so I suppose they were all right.'

'Are they in there now?'

Mr Littlejohn shook his head. 'Mrs Wooding's got them in her house – her that lives at Number 56. They'll be all right.'

He turned away. 'I tried to telephone the hospital, but my line's out of order. Is yours working?'

'I haven't tried it,' said Corbett. 'It was all right last night.'

'I bet it's not now.'

They turned, and walked together up the road towards their houses. 'Well,' said the builder heavily, 'I got enough of this in the last war to last my lifetime. I didn't never want to see it again.'

'I was too young,' said Corbett. 'I've never seen anything like this before.'

'Let's hope you'll never see it again.' They walked on for a few paces in silence.

'I didn't know what to do,' said Corbett. 'Where did you go?'

The builder laughed shortly. 'Soon as I realized what it was I got my missus out of bed and we went down to the cellar. And then I thought, maybe there'd be a sort of slanting hit – like that one – and the house would fall on top of us. So then we went upstairs again, and sat on the stairs outside our bedroom, because that way we got a room and two walls between us and the outside – see? But there – whatever you do may be wrong.'

'I know,' said Corbett. 'We went out to the garage.'

'To the garage?'

'I was afraid of the house coming down. But if the garage walls blew down on us – well, it's all light wooden stuff, and besides, the car would keep it off you. So we lay on the floor beside the car.'

The builder nodded slowly. 'That's all right. But when all's said and done, there's nothing to beat a trench. A seven foot trench so that your head gets right beneath the ground, but not so deep you may get buried in it. That's what you want to get – a trench dug in the garden.'

They paused for a moment by the builder's gate. 'What's it all about, anyway?' asked Corbett dully. 'Are we at war?'

The other shook his head. 'I dunno.'

'Who do you think it is we're fighting?'

'Blowed if I know. One or other of 'em. I suppose.'

Corbett went back into his house; before going out to rouse his family he poured himself out a whisky and soda. He stood for a few minutes in his dining-room drinking this, a weary and dishevelled figure in his sodden raincoat. Before him on the table was a copy of the *Evening News* of the night before, wide open at the centre page. His eyes fell on the cartoon. It represented the Prime Minister, very jocular, dangling a carrot before two donkeys separated from him by a wire fence. One of the donkeys had the head of Hitler, and the other, Mussolini.

Corbett remembered how they had laughed over it at dinner-time. It did not seem so very funny now.

He stared at the paper. He had bought it from the boy

on the corner, on his way back from the office, as he always did. He had had an interesting day, and not too tiring. He had got home about half-past six and had been to see the children in their beds before they went to sleep, and played with them a little. Then he had gone down with Joan, and before dinner they had planned a new position for the sweet pea hedge, taking it off the wall and putting it between the garage and the lilac tree. She had shown him that the magnolia was coming out; they had talked about the errors of omission of the gardener, who came once a week. Then he had read the paper for a little; he remembered having heard during the day that all leave had been cancelled for the Fleet over at Portsmouth, because of the tension on the Continent. But there was always tension on the Continent, and leave had been cancelled many times before. There didn't seem to be anything particularly alarming in the paper.

So they had gone in to dinner and talked about their holiday, wondering if it would be nice to take the car to Scotland this year, for a change. And after dinner there had been a concert of chamber music on the wireless; they had listened to that until the news came on at nine o'clock when they had switched off, having read the evening paper. Then they had played a game of cards together and had gone to bed a little after ten, to lie reading in their twin beds till half-past eleven. It was about that time that *Murder in Miniature* had slipped from his hand, and he had rolled over and put out his light.

The first bomb fell soon after that, before midnight.

The concussions were considerable – they must have been, because he could remember nothing from the time that he put out his light and settled down to sleep till he was standing at the window with Joan, his arm around her shoulders, peering out into the rainy night. The bursts, distant as they were, were rocking the house and setting things tinkling in the room.

'Peter, what can it be?' she had asked. 'They wouldn't be firing guns for practice at this time of night, would they?'

He had shaken his head. 'Not on a night like this. There's nothing for them to see.'

And suddenly she had cried: 'Oh, Peter! Look!'

He had looked, and he had seen a sheet of yellow flame perhaps a quarter of a mile away, outlining the roof-tops in silhouette. With that there came a shattering concussion, and another, and another, nearer every time.

'Oh, Peter!' she had cried. 'It hurts my ears!'

He had hurried her from the window; they crouched down on the floor beside the wardrobe at the far side of the room. 'Keep your hands pressed tight over your ears,' he had said. 'I think this must be an air-raid.'

That salvo passed; as soon as it was over she had insisted upon going upstairs to quieten the children and the nurse.

There was a lull, but the concussions continued intermittently in other parts of the city. He had to do some quick thinking then. Like most Englishmen of that time, he had read something about Air Raid Precautions in the newspapers. He knew, vaguely, that he had been advised to make a gas-proof room, and he knew with certainty that he had done nothing about it. There had been something about buckets of sand for incendiary bombs, and something about oilskin suits for mustard gas. And there had been a great deal about gas-masks – in the newspapers, at any rate.

Quickly his mind passed in review the relative safety of the top room of the house, the cellar, and the garage. He did not think of staying on the stairs, as Littlejohn had done. It was more by instinct than by reasoning that he had decided on the garage, and hurried to the nursery to tell his wife.

The children had been terrified at the concussions, screaming at the top of their voices. In the turmoil he had given his orders to the woman in a firm, decisive manner, and had gone to carry rugs and bedding down the garden to the garage. A fresh salvo fell near at hand and set him cowering by the kitchen stove; in the middle of all this all the lights in the street and the house went out. He heard, somewhere near at hand, the crash and rumble of falling masonry and the wailing of a siren on some ambulance or police car.

That salvo passed. In the lull that followed he went groping around in the pitch darkness, and got Joan and the nurse with the three children and all their bedding out of the nursery and down the garden in the rainy night to the garage. There he had made a bed for the two older children on the floor, protected by the garden roller and the box of silver sand. Then he lay down upon the floor himself with the two women and the baby in the basket cot. He had brought a bottle of whisky from the house; he opened it and gave Joan and the nurse a drink. It made them feel a little better.

They had lain there all night on the damp, oily floor. The raid had gone on continuously till after three o'clock, the explosions sometimes distant, sometimes very near at hand. The children had been crying for much of the time; the nurse had cried softly to herself most of the night.

It was over now. Corbett put his empty glass down on the table and stretched himself erect in the morning light; he was feeling more himself. It had been bad while it lasted. Now he must get the family indoors again and start cleaning up the mess, try and do something about the windows. After that, he must go down as soon as possible to see if everything was all right at the office. If he had time, it would be nice to find out if the country was at war and, if so, who the war was with.

He went first to the kitchen, to put on the kettle for a pot of tea before he brought them from the garage. The hot-water boiler was alight, and the water was hot. That was a good first step; things weren't so bad, after all. He raked the boiler out and filled it up with coke. Then he filled the electric kettle at the hot-water tap and switched it on to boil while he went out to fetch them from the garage.

The indicator showed that no current was flowing to the kettle.

He jerked the mains switch once or twice without result; his lips set to a thin line. This was very bad. He did the whole of his cooking on an electric range; there was no gas in the house. He tried a light switch and a radiator plug; then he went to the front door and tried the bell. He looked at the main fuse in the box, which was intact. Very soon he had proved that there was no electricity supply at all.

He went into the dining-room and tried the telephone, to ring up the supply company. Like Littlejohn, he found the line was dead.

He searched around the kitchen but could not find an ordinary kettle in the house, though there were three electric ones. He filled a saucepan with hot water, took off the cooking disc from the hot-water boiler, and put the saucepan on; it would boil slowly there. He stood then for a minute thinking hard; there was the breakfast to be cooked. Finally he shrugged his shoulders; there were only two alternatives for cooking, the dining-room or drawing-room fire. The drawing-room was uninhabitable with no windows; he went into the dining-room, laid the fire with paper, wood, and coal, and lit it.

Then he went out to fetch his family indoors.

A quarter of an hour later they were all in the dining-room, the children dressing by the fire, Joan beginning to consider breakfast. She had made a quick trip through the shattered rooms with him, and had retired to wash her face in warm water. She came down to find him wrestling with the fire, which had gone out and filled the room with smoke.

Sophie, their nurse, went straight up to her room and came down half an hour later, glum and silent.

He was half through lighting the fire for the second time when the front door was pushed open, and Mr Littlejohn came in. 'Thought I'd just come in to see if you were quite all right,' he said. 'I did ring, but the bell's out of order.'

Corbett stood up, wiping his coal-stained hands. 'That's very nice of you,' he said. 'The bell works off the main. I've got no current in the house at all.'

'Neither have I,' said the builder, ' – nor gas, either. Is your telephone working?'

Corbett shook his head. 'That's off, too. I tried to ring

them up about the electricity. We do all our cooking by electricity. That's why I'm mucking about with this fire.'

The other nodded. 'It's the same with us. Got any water?'

The solicitor looked startled. 'Oh, yes. It's running at the tap all right.'

'Ah, but is it coming into the tank from the main, up at the top? That's what you want to watch.'

'I don't know. I never thought about that.'

The builder smiled. 'First thing I thought about, the water. But then, I been in the trade, you see – all my life. Let me go up and have a look at the cistern, and I'll soon tell you.'

'Is yours off?'

'Aye.'

They went up to the attic; Corbett watched anxiously as Mr Littlejohn depressed the ball-valve. 'Not a drop,' he said cheerfully. 'Just the same as mine. Dry as a bone – see?'

He got down from the cistern. 'That's what I came in about, really and truly,' he said. 'I wanted to be sure you knew about it, and not go lighting up the hot-water boiler, or having a hot bath, or anything of that. I been in the trade, and I know what to look for – see? So I thought I'd just pop in and see if things were all right. Hope you don't mind.'

'It's awfully good of you,' said Corbett. 'As a matter of fact, the boiler's going now. I keep it in all night. I'd better let it go out, hadn't I?'

'It's all right so long as you don't draw off any more hot water – or not very much. I wouldn't make it up again – let it go out natural.'

They went downstairs, looking at bedrooms and the drawing-room as they went. 'These windows are just terrible, of course,' said Corbett. 'I'll have to try and do something about them. I wish this bloody rain would stop.'

The builder nodded. 'I'm going down to my place, soon as I've had a bite to eat,' he said, 'to get a couple of my chaps up with some matchboarding to put over them temporarily till I get some glass cut. Do yours the same, if you like – while they're here.'

Corbett thanked him.

'Well, I'll be going along,' said Mr Littlejohn. He paused by the door. 'One other thing,' he said. 'You haven't had no trouble with the drains?'

'Not that I know of. I haven't looked.'

They went to look. The downstairs water-closet pan was about half-full of a black liquid that undulated and changed level as they watched.

'That's bad,' said Mr Littlejohn, regarding it, fascinated. 'That's very bad, that is.'

'Isn't yours like that?' asked Corbett.

'It may be now. It wasn't when I looked a quarter of an hour ago.'

'What ought I to do about it?'

The builder scratched his head. 'Don't see that you can do anything about it, really and truly,' he observed. 'It's flooding does that – pressure and flooding in the sewers; that didn't ought to be there at all. But there – I suppose it's all you can expect.'

He turned to Corbett. 'I wouldn't let any of them use this place,' he said. 'Not for an hour or two, till I find out how things are. You've got another one upstairs, haven't you?'

They satisfied themselves that that one was all right.

Corbett walked with him to the door; the builder made him step outside into the rain. 'Just between you and me, Mr Corbett,' he said: 'there's no sense in alarming people – ladies, and that. But what I mean is – the electricity and gas, they're just an inconvenience, if you take my meaning. A bit of coal in the grate, and a good resourceful woman like my missus or Mrs Corbett, and you're right as rain. But the water – that's different. You want to watch the water and not let them go wasting it, or flushing closets with it, or anything of that – not till we know where we are. You've got fifty gallons more or less in your cold cistern and another thirty in the hot-water tank, and that's plenty to be going on with. But it's not enough for all the house to have a bath, or let run to waste. Not till we know how things are. I mean, when it's going to start running in again.'

Corbett nodded. 'That's true. Thanks very much for the tip.'

The builder said: 'I just been a walk. You been down Salisbury Road yet?'

'Not this morning.'

'There's a house down there – it's terrible, Mr Corbett. Really and truly. I never seen anything like it – not even in the war – not from one shell, that is. Still, what I meant to say was this. Two of them fell in the road, one at the far end and another a little bit this way. Well, the one at the far end, the water main's bust for sure. There's a regular fountain coming up, properly flooding the place. And it's not running away, neither – like it should. That looks as if the surface drains is crushed.'

There was a momentary silence.

'You see, Mr Corbett, a lot of people, they forget about the water. It don't give no trouble in the ordinary way, and you don't think. But once the mains is cracked, they take a power of a lot of getting right again. Water ain't like electricity, where you can string a bit of wire along on poles to the house and everything's all right. Water's water, and it takes a long time to get the mains in order once they're cracked.

'And where one of them bombs has fallen,' he said soberly, 'it'll all be cracked. Water and gas and sewers – all mixed up together.'

Corbett went back into his house and told Joan about the water. She wrinkled her brows. 'We'll have to get it put right before tonight,' she objected. 'There's the children's baths. Phyllis and John could go without, perhaps, but baby must have hers.'

'I should think you might take a little in a basin for baby. The other two will have to go dirty.' He went on to tell her about the drains. 'I'll see if it's possible to do anything about the water today,' he said. 'But in the meantime, we'll just have to go slow on what we've got.'

'I suppose so,' she said wonderingly. 'Seems funny, doesn't it? Here, come and eat your breakfast.' She leant over the smoking fire, and transferred a couple of rather smutty eggs from the frying-pan to a luke-warm plate.

He asked. 'Where's Annie?' They had a daily maid who came in before breakfast.

'She hasn't turned up yet. I hope her rabbit dies.'

She busied herself about the grate; he sat down with the children to the meal. Phyllis asked him:

'Daddy. Are we going to sleep in the garage again to-night?'

He was startled. The possibility had not occurred to him before. 'I don't think so,' he said. 'Not unless the bangs start coming again.'

His answer was digested in silence for a minute. Then: 'Daddy, if the bangs come again, may I take Teddy to bed with me in the garage?'

'May I take Horsey, Daddy?' asked his son.

'Why – yes,' he said patiently. Joan came to his rescue.

'Get on and eat your breakfasts,' she said. 'You've not eaten anything. If you don't eat your breakfasts up, Daddy won't let anybody sleep in the garage tonight.'

That finished them for the rest of the meal. Corbett got up from the table, lit a cigarette. He said: 'I must get down to the office right away. I want to see how things are there. If anything's happened to our files and records – there'll be awful trouble.'

'You can't go down without having a shave,' said Joan. 'Make yourself tidy, dear. This water will be hot in a minute.'

He stared at her in wonder. 'I must be off my head,' he said at last. 'Fancy thinking of going down to work without having shaved. . . .' He rubbed a hand over the stubble on his chin.

She pressed his arm. 'Don't worry. I expect everything will be all right down there.'

Twenty minutes later, spruce and neat in his business suit,

22

bowler hat, and dark overcoat, and carrying a neatly furled umbrella on his arm, he came to her again.

'I'm off now,' he said. 'I can't ring you up because the phone's out of order – I'll try and get that put right. I'll be back to lunch if I possibly can, but don't worry if I'm not.'

She stood for a moment in thought. 'Candles,' she said at last. 'We'll have to have some candles if the electricity isn't going to be on tonight. The milk hasn't come yet, either. We take three and a half pints. If it doesn't come I'll have to go and get it, but I don't want to leave the house.'

He nodded. 'Candles and milk.'

She turned to him. 'I tell you what would be a godsend, if you could get it. A Primus stove – like we have on the boat. And a kettle to go on it – and paraffin and meths, of course.'

'I'll do what I can. I'd better take the car.'

She reached up and kissed him. 'There's sure to be an awful lot of other things,' she said. 'Come back for lunch, if you can.'

'All right. Turn on the wireless and see if you can get any news out of it while I'm away.'

She frowned. 'I'll try, but is it any good? I thought that worked off the mains?'

He had forgotten that.

He went down the garden to the garage, got the car, and drove towards his office in Cumberland Place. He was appalled at what he saw. In Westwood Road he passed a house that had suffered a direct hit; above the first floor there was very little left of it. He went on, sober and a little sick, and stopped once more to inspect a crater in the road where there had been a motor-car. After that he did not stop again.

He had to make two detours to avoid roads that were blocked with bomb-holes.

The streets were full of people. Most of them seemed to be looking around, viewing the damage before they went on to their work. There was a sort of stunned bewilderment apparent in the crowd, and mingled with it the exhilaration of the novelty, a certain thrill and pleasure in the break of the routine. There was excitement, interest, in the streets. People were standing at street corners chatting eagerly to strangers; at other points there seemed to be the apathy of tragedy. Corbett wanted to buy a paper but could see no posters; the newsagents' shops that he passed were closed. A great many shop windows were smashed; in one or two places gangs of men were working nailing boards across.

He reached his office about ten o'clock, and parked outside it. Duncan, the managing clerk, slid from his desk as Corbett came in.

'Morning, Duncan. Mr Bellinger in yet?'

'Not yet, Mr Corbett.' The old man hesitated. 'Wasn't it a terrible night, sir?'

Corbett nodded. 'Pretty bad. Everything all right at home, I hope?'

'Yes, sir. We were spared.'

'Spared? So was I. We've got that to be thankful for.'

'Oh, yes, sir. We have indeed.'

'Has *The Times* come?'

'No, sir. None of the papers have come this morning. Nor the post either.'

'Have we had any windows bust here?'

'No, sir. Everything seems to be quite all right. I think we've been very fortunate.'

'I should say we have.'

He moved over to the telephone switchboard and tried the various lines; it was all dead. He went through into his office.

With no post, no paper, and no telephone, there was only routine work to do; he could not settle down to that. He idled for ten minutes at his desk, waiting for something to happen. Then he noticed Andrews's car parked outside his office next door. Andrews was a chartered accountant, and a member of the same club.

He went out, and into the next office. Andrews, lean and saturnine, was idling as he had been.

'Morn/ng,' said Corbett. 'Have a good night?'

24

'Not so bad,' said Mr Andrews. 'Bit of coal in the bed, but nothing to signify.'

'Do you know if we're at war?'

Mr Andrews said: 'We are now.'

'Who are we fighting?'

Mr Andrews told him in a few short sentences.

'How did you get to know all this?' asked Corbett.

'It's on the wireless. They're broadcasting news almost continuously.'

'My set's passed out. It's on the mains.'

'So is mine. But I've got a set in the car, and that's functioning all right. The King's broadcasting at three o'clock, and the Prime Minister at two-thirty.'

'If we get any current I must listen in to that.'

'If we had some ham,' said Mr Andrews, 'we could have some ham and eggs if we had some eggs.'

'Do you know, has any other town been bombed?'

The accountant leaned forward. 'Has any town *not* been bombed! They've all had it, from what I can make out – just like us. Portsmouth, Brighton, Bristol, Guildford, Bournemouth, Oxford, Birmingham, Coventry, Plymouth – oh, and a lot more. Practically every town in the Midlands and the south of England.'

'My God!' said Corbett.

Mr Andrews leaned back in his chair. 'The real cream of the joke,' he said, 'the part that'll tickle you to death, is that there's no news that any of the bombers were shot down, or interfered with in any way.'

'That's a bad one.

'Of course,' Corbett continued, 'I suppose it came as a complete surprise.'

'Evidently.'

There was a little silence. Corbett frowned. 'I don't under-stand how it was done. I didn't see any aeroplanes, or hear any engines. Did you?'

'No, I can't say I did. I saw a few searchlights, but they didn't seem to be much good. The clouds were too low.'

25

The solicitor got up restlessly and walked over to the window. 'My God,' he said, 'we're in a bloody mess.'

He stood staring out of the window over the little park on the other side of the road. There were craters in it like great excavations. Through the trees he could see the buildings of the Civic Centre; part of it seemed to have come down.

Without turning from the window he said: 'Did you count the bombs?'

Andrews shook his head. 'I had other things to think about, old boy.'

'I wonder how many there were? There's been a frightful lot of damage done.'

The accountant picked up a pencil and held it poised above his blotting-pad. 'On the average,' he said, 'how many explosions did you hear a minute?'

'Lord knows. Sometimes they came quick, and then there'd be a bit of a gap. I heard about fifteen come down one minute.'

'But on the average?'

Corbett thought carefully. 'More than four. Perhaps five or six. But you really can't say.'

The accountant flung his pencil down unused. 'There are a hundred and eighty minutes in three hours. That means the best part of a thousand bombs.'

Corbett nodded. 'I dare say there were that number. But what sort of a force of bombers would that mean?'

'I've no idea.'

Corbett turned back into the room. 'There must have been a lot of people killed,' he said heavily. 'Have you heard anything about the casualties yet?'

Mr Andrews shook his head. 'They didn't say anything about that side of it upon the wireless. There were three people killed in Wilton Road, near by me. Family called Winchell. Do you know them?'

Corbett shook his head.

'Father, mother, and one child,' said Mr Andrews succinctly. 'The other kid got off scot-free.'

There was a little silence.

'I can't stay here,' said Corbett restlessly. 'I'm going out. I've got to buy a Primus stove.'

He went out into the streets. In the half-hour since he had come into the centre of the town there had been a marked change for the better. The idle, gossiping crowds had vanished from the corners, and now the streets were full of busy, energetic people going about their business. The craters in the streets where bombs had fallen were full of men working upon the various mains and conduits, shattered and uncovered by the explosion. In half a dozen places the overhead wires of the trams were down and trailing in the road; he saw several repair gangs working upon those. A great many of the windows of the larger shops were shattered irretrievably; in most of them the assistants were engaged in putting up some sort of barrier or protection to the shop-front. There was a tendency to chalk up such notices as BUSINESS AS USUAL.

Southampton was itself again, busy and enterprising.

He went into an ironmonger's where he was known, to buy a Primus stove. 'I'm sorry, Mr Corbett,' said the man, 'but I'm right out. Haven't got a Primus in the place. Regular run on Primuses there's been this morning, what with the gas being off and all. I'm sorry.'

'Do you know where I could get one?'

The man suggested one or two other places. 'Would you like me to save you a gallon of paraffin, Mr Corbett?'

'Is that short?'

'There's been a great run on it this morning. We shall be out very soon.'

He bought a can, had it filled with paraffin, and took it with him to the office. Then he went out again.

He got a Primus stove with difficulty at a ship chandler's down by the docks. After trying half a dozen stores, he got some very large candles irreverently at an ecclesiastical suppliers. Fresh milk was unobtainable; it seemed that very little milk had come into Southampton that morning. He got a few tins of condensed milk at a grocer's shop.

Towards noon he was in the High Street, walking back

27

towards his office. Quite suddenly beneath his feet he felt a subterranean rumble, and a hundred yards away a manhole cover shot up into the air from the middle of the road, followed by a vivid sheet of yellow flame. The heavy cover fell with a resounding clang upon the road, doing no damage. There was a sudden rush of people from the street; one or two women screamed.

There was an expectant pause.

Nothing more happened, and presently the people ventured out into the street again. A little crowd had collected. A harassed-looking policeman with a grey drawn face and dirty streaks around his eyes appeared from somewhere and stood by the open manhole.

'Move along there,' he said mechanically. 'Don't get crowding round – there's nothing to see. Keep moving on. Come on, there – keep moving. Bit o' gas in the sewer. Nothing to worry about now. Move along, please.'

Corbett went over to the hole; the man recognized him as a police court acquaintance, and saluted. 'Not so good, this,' said Corbett.

'I didn't see it happen, sir,' said the constable. 'I was around the corner, in Fishbourne Street. But there have been one or two of these this morning.'

'Did you say it was gas in the sewer?'

'Town gas from the mains, they say, sir.' He said wearily: 'It'll take a while to get things properly fixed up, after a night like what we've had'

Near the Civic Centre Corbett bought a newspaper still wet from the press, and read about the war.

The war news was quite short, and made up from the news broadcasts suitably filled out by the local editor. There was an account of similar raids which had taken place in other towns, which did not interest him very much. It left him cold to hear in messages sent out from London that London had been more heavily bombed than any other town. On another page there were full details of the emergency programme of broadcasting, of academic interest only in a town where the electric mains were dead. He reflected for a minute. There was a battery set in his old yacht at Hamble, if he could get to that. But probably the batteries would be run down. He had not used it since the previous summer.

The back page of the paper was given over to a stirring patriotic appeal. It seemed that there were a number of ways in which he could enlist to serve his country. All of them involved leaving Joan and his three children to get along as best they could. His brows wrinkled in a frown; he wanted to think over that. It wasn't a thing to be rushed into. If there was going to be another air-raid, somebody would have to be at hand to help Joan with the children. Especially if this talk of gas meant anything. . . .

Back at the office his secretary, Miss Mortimer, was waiting for him with her hat and coat on. She got up as he came in.

'Please, Mr Corbett,' she said. 'Could I have the day off?'

He nodded. 'That's all right,' he said. 'We shan't be doing any work today. I'm going home myself.'

She sighed with relief. 'Thank you so much, Mr Corbett. It's my daddy and mummy, you see. They live all alone, and they're so old now. I can't get to know what's happened to them, or if they want any help, unless I go there myself. I'll be back as soon as ever I can.'

'That's all right,' he said again. 'Where do they live?'

'Just outside Poole, Mr Corbett – between Poole and Bournemouth. I'm not sure how the trains are going, but if it comes to the worst, I could get over on my bicycle. It's only about thirty miles.'

She paused. 'Of course, I went through the Air Raid Precautions course, and I'm supposed to be working at a First Aid post. But I can't think of anything else but how Daddy and Mummy are getting on. I do think the old people ought to come first, don't you, Mr Corbett?'

'That's your own problem,' he said. 'I can't help you there.'

She considered for a minute, and said doubtfully: 'I might be able to get somebody to take my place before I go.'

She left him, and he turned to the old clerk. 'We'll pack up for the day,' he said. 'Lock up the office, and get along home and look after your family.'

'Thank you, sir. But there's only my wife and myself. The children are all out in the world.'

Corbett nodded. 'So much the better for you.'

'I'm sure, sir.' The old man hesitated. 'Did you hear where we could get our gas-masks, sir, by any chance?'

The solicitor shook his head. 'I haven't heard a word about that yet.'

He went out to the car, laden with his purchases. The rain had stopped and the clouds had lifted a little; over his head a couple of aeroplanes made reassuring noises, crossing, turning, and recrossing the city. He watched them for a minute.

'Making a photographic survey of the damage,' he said, half to himself. 'That's not a bad idea, for a start.' He had guessed right.

Outside his office he ran into Andrews, crossing to his car. Andrews said: 'Been down to the docks this morning?'

Corbett shook his head.

'I've got a job going on down there. You never saw such a picnic.'

'There's been a lot of damage?'

'Not a great deal, really. One of the small Cunard boats – I don't know which – she's foundered in the Ocean dock. They were saying that there was another one at Millbrook – a Greek tramp. One or two of the sheds have got it pretty bad. But the trouble is, they're all trying to get away to sea together, on this tide. Evans told me there are thirty-eight ships docking out this morning – most of them just moving down to anchor in the Solent and Southampton Water. The masters won't listen to reason, and they're not giving a damn for anyone or anything. They're getting their ships out of it before tonight.'

Corbett nodded slowly. 'They think there's another raid coming tonight?'

'Everybody seems to think that.' He paused. 'I tell you,

I've never seen anything like it. This wind isn't helping, either. They've had two collisions in the fairway – one quite bad. There aren't enough tugs to go round. There's a Dutch ship beached at Cracknore Hard with her stern right out in the channel – I never saw such a pickle.'

They stood in silence for a moment.

'Heard anything about gas-masks?' asked Corbett.

'Yes. I asked about that at the Civic Centre. They reckon they'll be here tonight.'

They separated, and Corbett got into his car to drive home. As he went, he noted with surprise the progress that was being made in the rehabilitation of the city. Trams were running again northwards from the Civic Centre. In London Road there had been three great craters, half-filled with water. Two of these had already been roughly filled with gravel brought by heavy lorries; in the third a strong gang of men were working on the repair of a sewer. Practically every manhole in the pavements and the roads was up, and occupied by a man working. Clearly it would not be many days before the services would be working again, in that district at any rate.

He drove on into the suburban roads, and there the situation was not quite so good. Most of the houses gaped with broken windows; in the streets the bomb-holes were still streaming water to the gutters.

'There won't be any water in the town, at this rate,' he muttered.

He stopped the car before his garden gate and went into the house, carrying his purchases. Joan met him in the doorway.

'Peter,' she said, 'Sophie's gone.'

'Gone?'

'She lives at Romsey. She was awfully glum after breakfast, and then she said she wanted to go home. I tried to get her to stay out her week, but she wouldn't. She just went and got her things on and walked out.'

'Did she take her clothes and stuff with her?'

'No. She said she'd send for them, or she'd come and get

them. She was in such a state of nerves she didn't know what she was doing.'

'Has Annie come?'

She shook her head. 'She hasn't turned up today. We've got nobody at all.'

He laid his hand upon her arm. 'Never mind. Annie may be in tomorrow. But if she isn't, we'll get along all right till things get settled down. There's nothing doing in the office, so I'll be able to give you a hand in the house for a bit.'

He mused for a moment. 'That's the evacuation of the city, of course,' he said thoughtfully. 'Sophie's one of them. I saw a lot of people going out along the London Road. But I don't know that we've really come to that.'

He thought uneasily of the shipping, of the tramps and liners barging against each other and colliding in their endeavours to get clear of the city before night.

'Oh, and Peter,' said his wife. 'The water closet in the downstairs lavatory has been misbehaving. It sort of overflowed, I think. It's beastly.'

He went with her to look; they stopped outside the door. The floor of the little room was covered in black, liquid slime, with an offensive smell. The pan was full of undulating sludge.

Joan said: 'The Corporation ought to come and put that right for us, shouldn't they? I mean, it ought not to do that.'

He agreed that it ought not. 'But whether they'll be able to spare anyone to come and look at it for the next day or two – that's another matter.'

In this trouble, he went round to see Mr Littlejohn. He found him with two joiners putting the finishing touches to the matchboarding of his drawing-room and first-floor windows, turning the rooms into dark caverns. 'Made a nice job of this,' said Mr Littlejohn. 'They'll be starting on yours after dinner.'

'It's awfully good of you,' said Corbett, and consulted him about the closet.

'Mine did the same,' said the builder wearily. 'Terrible mess it made – all over the place. Unhealthy, too – not what one ought to have about in the house at all. I put down a lot of Sanitas. But see, I'll show you what to do.' He took Corbett and showed him how he had taken up an iron man-hole-cover in the front garden. 'Now if it happens again, it just comes up and flows over in the garden here and soaks into the ground, and don't hurt nobody.'

He thought for a moment. 'Leastways,' he said, 'it's better than having it in the house with you.'

Again Corbett told his story of the episode in the High Street, to an enthralled audience. 'Of course,' said Mr Little-john, when he had finished, 'that explains everything, when you get them sort of goings on. Blew the cover right up in the air, did it? Well I never !'

They talked happily about the drains for a time. And then:

'You thought what you're going to do if they come back again tonight?' asked the builder.

Corbett rubbed his chin in perplexity. 'I did think about a trench,' he said. 'I don't know how long it would take me to dig.'

'Cor,' said the builder, 'that wouldn't take no time, not just a little bit of a thing, like what you'd need. There's only you and the missus, and the children. You'd want to get about five feet down and big enough to take a couple of chairs, just so that your heads was below the surface, sitting down. It wouldn't take more than three hours, or four hours at the most, digging a little bit of a hole like that.'

'Of course,' said Corbett, 'the other thing would be to get out into the country for the night.'

'I been thinking of that,' said Mr Littlejohn slowly. 'But – I don't know. After all, they wouldn't come two nights running, hardly – not to the same place.'

Corbett said: 'I shouldn't think so. At the same time, I'd sleep happier tonight if I'd got a trench to go to.'

'That's right,' said Mr Littlejohn. 'Tell you what. I'll slip along to my place after dinner, and fetch back a couple o' picks.'

2

AFTER LUNCH Corbett started in to dig his trench. The rain held off; before he began he made Joan come with him to the garden to settle where it was to be dug. They debated this for some time. 'You don't want to put it in the lawn,' she said. 'It'll look awful when it comes to be filled in. You'd never get the mark out of the grass. Let's have it in the back bed, along the wall. I don't mind about the dahlias, and you can dodge the plum tree.'

Corbett scrutinized the nine-inch wall, already cracked in one or two places. 'I don't want that wall to come down on top of us,' he said doubtfully. 'I think the safest place is in the middle of the lawn.'

She could not deny that; they stood and looked at the smooth turf. 'It does seem an awful shame,' she said. She turned to him. 'Peter, you don't think we're making too much of this, do you? I mean, I know we had a terrible time last night. But it's not likely to happen again, is it? I remember reading about it in the last war. They never came to the same place twice over, did they?'

He rubbed his chin. 'I don't know,' he said at last. 'I don't see why they shouldn't.' He laid his hand upon her arm. 'I think we'll have it in the lawn,' he said. 'It'll be an awful sweat, but I believe I'd like to have it for tonight – just in case. Look, you go down into the town and see if you can find any milk. I'll look after the children.'

She nodded. 'It's not only milk. There's bread and meat – oh, and all sorts of things. Hardly any of the tradesmen have been this morning. I'll have to take the car, I think.'

She turned to him. 'Baby's asleep in the pram. You will look after her if she cries, won't you? And don't let Phyllis wake her up?'

He smiled. 'Go on down into the town,' he said. 'They'll

be all right with me.' He very much disliked looking after the children, and she knew it; she smiled at him, and went.

He decided to make his trench six feet long, three feet wide, and six feet deep. He marked it out on the grass in the middle of the lawn, and commenced to dig. He was in average condition for a young man working all day in an office, but he was tired and stale from lack of sleep. In spite of his fatigue he went at it doggedly; by the end of an hour he had dug about a foot deep over the area that he had marked.

He rested for a little then, and went on. When Joan returned an hour later he was very tired.

She stood and looked at it. 'It isn't very deep,' she said. 'Is it terribly hard work?'

'Terribly,' he said shortly.

She laid her hand upon his arm. 'Poor old Peter. Come in and sit down for a bit, and I'll make a cup of tea.'

He stared at the trench, dissatisfied. 'It's got to be deeper if it's going to be any good.'

'After tea,' she said. They had tea with condensed milk, reserving what fresh milk they had for the children. She had only been able to get a pint of milk, in an open jug, together with some more tinned milk and a variety of provisions. Most of the latter she had bought from a lorry in the street. 'The shops didn't seem to have anything you wanted,' she said.

He nodded. 'Milk and stuff isn't coming into the city. Everything's very much disorganized today.'

She said: 'The fresh bread only came into the shops this afternoon.' And then she said: 'Down in the town, everything's beginning to smell. I don't know if it's my imagination, but it all seems sort of fusty – like an Italian town. Horrid.'

He laughed shortly. 'Well, look at the drains. Our house isn't just a bed of roses.'

She nodded. 'Peter, what had we better do? I mean, now you've taken up that manhole thing in the front garden?'

He rubbed his chin. 'I'll have to do something about that.'

He did. He took a cane-bottomed chair, a sharp knife, a bucket, and one of the dining-room curtains, and built an edifice behind the garage that would have done credit to Lem Putt. He took Joan out and showed it to her proudly. 'I don't say that the City Engineer would view it with enthusiasm,' he said. 'But till he comes and puts the drains right, it'll have to do.'

Joan was not impressed. 'It doesn't look very comfortable,' she said. 'And it's going to be horrid when it rains. Can't you put a roof over it?'

They went indoors, and made a large tea for the children in the kitchen, their last meal of the day. In the middle of that there came a thundering at the front door; Corbett went and opened it. There was a man there, wearing an armlet.

'Gas-masks,' he said. 'How many in your household?' There was a lorry slowly driving down the street, with men going from house to house.

'Good work,' he said, impressed. 'There's my wife and myself, and three children.'

'How old are the children?'

'Six and three. And a baby.'

The man went back to the lorry, and returned with the masks. 'Here you are – be careful of them. Don't use them unless the gas is really there. When you've used them for ten hours, come to the Civic Centre and exchange them for fresh ones. There. One large for you, one medium for your wife, and two small ones for the children. We can't do nothing for the baby.'

Corbett met his eyes. 'What am I supposed to do with the baby?'

The man looked awkward. 'Everyone asks that. You want to have it with you in a gas-proof room, if you can make one.'

'That's not so easy, with the windows in this state.'

'I know. You might be able to screen off a bit of the cellar with wet blankets, or something of that.'

He moved on to the next house. Corbett went back to the

kitchen, detached Joan from the children, and told her about the baby.

'But, Peter,' she said, 'what are we to do? We can't all sit out in your trench in gas-masks, and the baby not have one.'

He sighed. 'I don't know. There may not be any gas. I'll see if I can think of something.'

He went out to the garden and continued digging in the falling dusk. He dug till he could not see what he was doing any more. Then he stopped, sweating and very tired, and went to have a word with Mr Littlejohn. He found him knocking off work.

'Eh,' said the builder, 'I'm not the man I was. I haven't dug like this for twenty years. Time was, I'd have sunk a little hole like that in a couple of hours.'

He had done about as much as Corbett, about four feet deep, but very much neater. 'I was looking for something to put over it,' he said. 'Make a roof for keeping out the rain. Splinters, too. But I don't seem to have anything up here – unless I unscrewed a door. . . .'

'Drive the car over it,' said Corbett.

'Eh,' said the builder slowly, 'that's a good idea, that is.'

He rubbed his hands together. 'What say if we have a Guinness?'

Corbett smiled. 'That's the most sensible remark I've heard today.'

It was practically dark in the garden. There had been isolated aircraft in the air most of the day; now with the coming of the night there seemed to be a great deal more activity. A squadron of nine machines passed above their heads, flying at a low altitude.

The builder glanced up at them. 'Aye,' he said without rancour. 'There's plenty of them now. But I'd like to know where them chaps were last night.'

With the evening the clouds were rolling away. In the deep blue of the sky the few stars were showing; it was clearing every minute. They stood together in the garden looking up.

'Going to be a clear night,' said Corbett.

Mr Littlejohn nodded soberly. 'That's bad,' he said. 'Clear nights is what they like. Remember how they used to come over, moonlight nights, in the last war?'

Corbett nodded. 'But it wasn't clear last night,' he said.

They moved towards the house. 'That's right,' said the builder. 'Raining cats and dogs, it was – all night.' He paused. 'Did you get to hear anything about the raid – I mean to say, how they done it? I didn't hear any aeroplanes at all, last night. And how did they know what they was bombing at?'

Corbett shook his head. 'I don't know. I've not met anyone who does.'

'Well,' said Mr Littlejohn, 'if they did that to us last night when they couldn't see nothing, we'll cop it properly tonight when they can see what they're doing.' He sighed. 'I ought to try and get a bit deeper with my hole, I suppose.'

They went into the house, and sat down in the florid sitting-room; he produced cigarettes and Guinness. A copy of the paper lay spread out upon the table. The builder laid his hand on it.

'All this it says about enlisting,' he said slowly. 'Are you going to do anything?'

Corbett was silent for a minute. 'I don't see how I can, just yet,' he said. 'I don't know what would happen to my family. Joan couldn't get on by herself, with three kids to look after, and all this going on. I don't know what she'd do, if I wasn't here.' He raised his head. 'It isn't that I've got the wind up. But one's got to see one's wife and kids right, first of all.'

The builder nodded. 'You don't want to think of it,' he said. 'It wouldn't be proper for you to go away and leave Mrs Corbett to struggle along on her own. You don't want to think about enlisting till you've seen them right.' He took a drink of stout. 'I been feeling the same,' he said. 'There's only the two of us, Mr Corbett – just me and the missus. And last time I enlisted right at the beginning, August the 7th it was, and went right through. Wounded twice, I was.

In the fat part of the leg – that wasn't nothing – and one right through here.' He tapped his left shoulder. 'And I'm not that old I couldn't go again. I'm forty-eight.'

He paused. 'I been thinking about it all the afternoon,' he said. 'And I made up my mind, Mr Corbett. I'm not going – not till I can see my way a bit better. It wouldn't be fair on the missus leaving her alone, with raids like that we had likely to happen any night. We've been together all these years, and I'm not going to leave her at a time like this. It wouldn't be right. Of course,' he said, 'if I could get to see her settled and comfy in a little house somewhere where it's safe, then it'd be another matter.'

Corbett laughed shortly. 'Somewhere safe and comfy,' he repeated. 'It seems to me that's going to take a bit of finding.'

The builder stuck his chin out. 'That may be. But till I've got the missus properly fixed up they're not going to get me to go soldiering again.'

Corbett finished his glass, and got up. 'I've got to go on,' he said. 'Let me know if I can do anything to help in the night. And thanks for the drink.'

Mr Littlejohn came with him to the door. 'You been out this afternoon? I took a walk round. They've been getting on fine with all these holes in the roads. I reckon the Corporation have done champion. Another two or three days will see it all cleaned up, the rate they're getting on.' He laughed. 'That's if they don't have it all to do again, after tonight.'

He looked up at the sky, brilliantly clear and starry. 'Good luck, Mr Corbett,' he said soberly. 'Remember that I'm just over the way, if you want any help.'

Corbett went back into his house. Joan came to meet him, looking tired and worn. 'I've got the children into bed,' she said. 'They were awfully disappointed that they weren't going to sleep in the garage. We had tears about it. Peter, do you think they'll come again tonight?'

'It's a bright, starry night,' he said. 'It must be perfect for a bombing raid. I'm afraid they may.'

39

She nodded. 'I thought that, too. I've been looking out what we've got for first-aid, if we wanted it.'

'That's a good idea. How are we fixed?'

'Not so bad. We've got a lot of bandages and cotton-wool, and some iodine and plaster. I keep it for the children, knees and elbows. And one could always make a splint out of something or other. The only thing we haven't got is any sort of sedative – morphia, or anything like that.'

He eyed her. 'Do you think we need it?'

'Well – do you?'

She hesitated for a minute. 'They say the maid at that house down the road lay out in the front garden for three hours before the ambulance came. It's like the war, Peter. I do think we should have something of the sort.'

He nodded. 'I'll have to get it from a doctor. I could go round and see if Gordon's in.'

The surgeon had been godfather to his son. They were great friends, a friendship born of week-ends spent together on the little yacht, fishing and bathing in the Solent. Corbett walked round to his house, a quarter of a mile away, and told his need to Mrs Gordon. 'I'll see if he's awake, Peter,' she said. 'I think he is. But he was up at the hospital all night, and he didn't get back till nearly midday.'

'Don't wake him, Margaret, whatever you do.'

She shook her head. 'I won't do that.'

She went upstairs; in a few minutes the surgeon came down in his shirt-sleeves. 'I was just getting up,' he said. 'My God, Corbett – what a night! Are your people all right?'

The surgeon rubbed his hand across his eyes. 'You never saw anything like it at the hospital,' he said. 'Two hundred and thirty major operations in seven hours. Each of us had two tables going – operating on the one while they were getting the other ready. God help us if there's another raid tonight. We haven't been able to evacuate them yet, and we're in an awful jam. They're lying all along the corridors on mattresses.'

'I'd no idea that it was anything like that. How many casualties do you suppose there were?'

'The inside of a thousand – say one for every bomb. Of those about three hundred must have been killed outright. We had five or six hundred at the hospital.'

Corbett said: 'You must be frightfully tired. I won't keep you.' He explained his need for morphia.

The surgeon scribbled a prescription. 'Get this at the chemist,' he said. 'One tablet only, in water. Not more, in any circumstances. And look, this is important. Get hold of a blue pencil, and chalk a big cross on the patient's cheek if you've given it.'

'What about the children?'

'Half a tablet – not that unless you absolutely must. Don't give it to the baby at all.'

Corbett thanked him, and walked down into the town to find a chemist. Over his head in the clear night the aircraft roared on their patrol; in the distance an occasional searchlight shot a white beam to the deep blue sky. As he went, he saw the progress that had been made with the craters in the streets since morning. There were none now that had not been attended to; those that had not been filled in were boarded over, and the flow of water to the gutters had been stopped.

In one part of the town the electricity was on. The streetlamps were turned out and all lights were subdued by curtains, but the mere fact of the light being there at all gave promise for the future.

He visited the chemist, and got his morphia. As he was leaving the shop he ran into a young man whom he knew slightly, who worked in the office of the Town Clerk at the Civic Centre. He talked to him for a few minutes about the state of the city.

'The electricity is pretty straightforward,' said the young man. 'It's on now over a good part of the town. The telephone should be all right tomorrow – we got a line to London restored this afternoon. Gas – Lord knows when we'll get the gas again. Sewers – well, they work in some parts. But it's the water that's the real difficulty now. There's no water to speak of in any part of the city, and what there is just bubbles up out of the pavements and runs away to waste.'

He paused. 'Good class houses have storage tanks, of course – the sort of house that you live in. But some of the poorer parts are in a terrible way for water, really they are. In Chapel and in Northam, down behind the docks, they've been scooping up the water from the gutters where it came up out of the road, and drinking that. If this goes on we'll have to start carting water in from the country.

'It's not only Southampton,' he said. 'It's the same all over. Every city in the country seems to be the same for water. We're all in the same jam.'

He swayed a little as he stood, and caught at the chemist's door. He laughed shortly. 'I'm about done in, I don't mind telling you. I'm one of the Air Raid Wardens – I was up all last night. And after that, a day like this in the office . . . I hope to God that they don't come again tonight.'

Corbett went back through the dark, unlighted streets to his house. Joan had a hot meal ready for him; they sat down together. 'I'd never have believed the town would rally round so well, and get the mess cleared up so quick,' he said. 'But everyone's tired out. If they should come again tonight – it'll be just too bad.'

Over their heads the sky seemed full of aeroplanes, passing and re-passing in the night.

After his supper, Corbett went out to the garden, and dug for another hour at his trench. He was so tired at the end that he could hardly lift the pick; he got down to a depth of about five feet below the surface. Finally he could do no more. He went and got the car and drove it over the flower-beds into the garden, crossing the lawn till it straddled above the trench. Then he went back to the house, utterly exhausted.

Joan met him in the hall. She had collected in baskets all that they were likely to need during the night: the gas-masks, first-aid kit, food, and whisky. These she had put ready in the hall. Corbett went over to them. 'God!' he said. 'Fancy having to do this sort of thing!'

They stared at each other in wonder. 'It's all happened in so short a time,' said the girl. 'Like being in a different world.'

He nodded. 'Well, there's nothing more that we can do. Now we've just got to wait for it.'

She laid her hand upon his arm. 'You must go to bed and get some sleep,' she said. 'I'm going to sleep upstairs with the children. Get some sleep, anyway, before anything happens. I've put a bottle in your bed.'

He kissed her. 'You'll come and wake me if you should hear anything?'

'Of course I will.'

'I wouldn't take off too many clothes, if I were you,' he said. 'Be so that you can get out in a hurry, if we have to.'

He went upstairs and lay down in his underclothes. Over the house the aircraft droned in the dark night; there seemed to be great numbers of them in the air. 'They're on the spot all right tonight,' he muttered to himself. Then he rolled over on his side, and sank into a heavy dreamless sleep.

When next he stirred and opened his eyes, the day was bright.

He blinked, leaned up on one elbow, and looked at his watch. It was seven o'clock. A shaft of sunlight, nearly horizontal, was streaming into the room; he sat up and rubbed his eyes. Then it came to him that there had been no raid, and that he was sleeping in his clothes.

He got up and went to the window, feeling rather foolish. He saw his garden and the ruins of his lawn, the piles of raw clay on the grass, the car perched drunkenly above the trench, the pick and shovel lying discarded in a rose-bed. He passed a hand over his face, and went to the wash-stand for a drink of water.

He went to have a bath, still half asleep. He remembered the water shortage before turning on the taps, however, and did his best with a cold sponge. Then he went back to his room, and dressed in a dark business suit.

Joan came to him as he was dressing. 'There wasn't any raid,' she said. 'I slept right through. Did you?'

'Never had such a night.' He turned to her. 'I believe we've been making altogether too much of this thing,' he said. 'It's my fault – I should have had more confidence in the defences. I ought to have known they'd never get away with it a second time.'

'You mean, they got through with the first raid just because they took us by surprise?' she said.

He nodded. 'They had perfect weather for a raid last night. But with the aeroplanes there were about, they couldn't possibly get through again. I think we shall be all right now.' He smiled, a little ruefully. 'But just look at the mess I've made of our lawn!'

She came and looked out of the window with him. 'It *is* a mess,' she said, and laughed. 'Never mind, dear – I'll get the gardener to put it right. It was the right thing for you to do.'

'You think so? I've been thinking we got rather carried away.'

'I don't think we did. After all, they might have come again. We couldn't know.'

He nodded. 'I suppose we couldn't. Anyway, you'd better get the gardener for another half day this week.'

'I don't know,' she said thoughtfully. 'I rather like to feel it's there. Don't let's be in too much of a hurry to get it filled in.'

'All right. Go on and get the children up, and I'll start cooking breakfast. What have we got – bacon and eggs? I wish we'd got some maids back.'

'They'll probably be back today.'

Breakfast was a tricky, tiresome meal, complicated by lack of milk and by the requirements of the children. Before it was over tradesmen started to arrive at the back door, among them the milkman. Corbett finished his meal as soon as possible and then, on plea of urgent work, made his escape to the office.

'I'd like to have the car this morning,' said Joan. 'I've got a lot of shopping I must do, and I'll have to take the family with me, baby and all. I can manage if I have the car. Shall I come and pick you up for lunch?'

He nodded. 'Look in about one o'clock. I'll come home if I can.'

He walked down to the office. In the streets the trams and omnibuses were running normally; in spite of the boarded windows and the gravel-filled craters in the roads the city seemed to have regained its usual atmosphere. He bought a paper at the first shop that he passed and stopped for some minutes on the pavement reading about the war. It seemed that we had carried out a great reprisal raid, but the communiqué was short; there had been no time for any great detail.

'Hope our chaps got away with it as well as they did,' he muttered.

He went on to the office. There was a very big mail waiting for him on his desk, two days' post in one. His partner, Bellinger, who lived at Bishop's Waltham, came into the office; they exchanged experiences and discussed the war news for a few minutes, then separated to deal with the arrears of work. They were seriously inconvenienced by the absence of Miss Mortimer, their secretary; Bellinger sent Duncan, the managing clerk, into the town to find and engage another girl. Corbett spent the morning laboriously typing answers to a dozen letters, and in drafting out a partnership agreement.

Towards lunch-time he was startled and pleasantly surprised to hear the telephone-bell ring. He went to the switchboard himself and answered it. It was Gordon, speaking from the hospital.

He said: 'Is that you, Corbett? It's Gordon this end. Thank God this thing's working again. You got that prescription all right? Fine. Look here. I want you to see that every drop of anything your family have to drink has been boiled. Yes – boiled. We're getting posters out about it in the town this afternoon, but I wanted to ring you and tell you personally. It's really important. Tell Joan as soon as you can. She'll have to boil all milk, and especially all water, before she uses it. And try to keep her off raw vegetables and fruit.'

'I'll tell her. But what's it all about?'

'I can't tell you over the telephone. And, anyway, we're not quite certain yet ourselves. But there's a lot of sickness in the Northam district that's come up quite suddenly, and we're a bit worried about it. You'd better tell your staff about boiling the water. Don't make it alarmist.'

'I won't do that.'

'Good man. It's probably nothing at all – just a scare, you know. Doctors who've been out East get funny notions, sometimes. But tell Joan to boil everything she can.'

He rang off, and Corbett tried to settle to his work again. He found he could not concentrate. Presently he went back to the switchboard and tried to ring his house. He heard the ringing tone, showing that the line was sound, but there was no reply; there was no one in the house. He went back to his desk and the consideration of his partnership agreement.

Joan called for him before lunch. He told her about Gordon and his message. She wrinkled up her brows.

'It's diphtheria, I suppose,' she said. 'That's what you get when drains go wrong, isn't it?'

He shook his head. 'I couldn't tell you. If it was diphtheria, I don't see why he should have been so mysterious about it.'

She smiled. 'Everybody's been a bit rattled, Peter. You can't blame them. Do you know, quite a number of people left the city yesterday and went out into the country for the night. The Cummings did that, and the Howards. I met Mrs Howard this morning. She said they just drove out into the country and parked by the side of the road, and sat in the car all night. They didn't sleep a bit well, and when they woke up and found there hadn't been a raid at all they felt awfully sold.'

She paused. 'They asked us to go in for a sherry tomorrow night.'

'Good. I'd like to go.'

They went out of the office to the car, full of parcels and children. As they drove through the town he noticed a great outbreak of recruiting posters on the hoardings, roughly printed and looking very new. And as they drove by one hoarding they saw a man finishing the posting of a placard, in large red block capitals:

BOIL YOUR WATER

Underneath there was some sort of explanatory text.

'They've not been long with that,' he said.

He went back to the office after lunch, and worked all afternoon. In the middle of the afternoon the weather clouded over, and it began to rain a little. His office faced north and grew dark early; mechanically he reached up and switched on the reading-lamp above his desk. To his surprise and gratification, it lit at once. The electricity was functioning.

He was so pleased about it that he went and rang up Joan. 'The lights are working here,' he said. 'Are they with you?'

'I don't know. Wait a minute while I try.'

He waited. Presently she came back to the telephone and said: 'It's all on now. I tried the lights and the cooker, too. It's all working. We'll be able to have a proper dinner to-night.'

He said: 'I give the Corporation full marks for that. They must have worked like niggers.'

She sighed. 'It is good. We'll be able to listen to the wireless now, and find out what's been going on.'

She hesitated for a moment. 'Peter, I was just thinking. Didn't you tell me that the Littlejohns cook on gas?'

'I think they do.'

'The gas isn't on, is it?'

'I don't suppose so, for a minute.'

'Would you like it if I asked them in for supper? I mean, if our cooker's working and theirs isn't? He's done such a lot for us, the last few days.'

'I think that's a very good idea. Have you ever met her?'

'No. I've seen her about once or twice. Sort of mousy.'

'Ask them round by all means. I'd like to have them.'

In the house the girl laid down the telephone and stood for a moment in thought. Then she went out of the front

47

door and round to the next house. She rang the bell, waited for a time, and rang again.

Presently there were steps inside; the door was opened by a pale, faded little woman that Joan had seen in the next garden once or twice, from her bedroom window. She wore a coarse apron over her black dress; she had her sleeves rolled up, and her hands were red and swollen.

'It's Mrs Corbett, isn't it?' she said. 'This is nice, I'm sure.'

Joan said: 'Good afternoon. I just came round to ask if Mr Littlejohn and you would like to come to supper with us tonight. Our cooker's just started working again – we cook on electricity. You use gas, don't you?'

The little woman was flustered. 'Ted wanted me to have one of them electric things when we came here first,' she said. 'But we didn't seem able to make it work right. We had the man in to see to it, but he couldn't make it any different. Sometimes I'd put the kettle on for a cup o' tea and come back in ten minutes, and it wasn't on at all. Other times, it'd be burning away and wasting all the afternoon, and nobody would ever know. I told Ted it was a fair worry to me, and he had it taken out and put in gas.'

'The gas isn't on yet, is it?'

'No, my dear. Isn't it a trial? I was just washing out the net curtains from the sitting-room, because they had to come down, you see, because of the windows. And every drop of water to be boiled on the dining-room fire.'

Joan commiserated. 'It does make things difficult, Mrs Littlejohn. But our cooker's working again now, and I thought it would be so nice if you could come round with your husband, and we'd have a proper hot supper tonight.' She paused, and added with inspiration: 'We could cook it together.'

The mousy little face displayed some animation. 'Oh, my dear, that was a nice thought, I'm sure. I hadn't nothing but a little tin of salmon to give Ted tonight, and I was that worried. Because he likes to have his supper hot, with his bottle of Guinness and his bit of cheese, dear.' She became suddenly flustered again. 'Won't you come inside, Mrs Corbett? You mustn't mind – the house is all upside-down, with the windows and that. But come in and sit down, Mrs Corbett, and let me make a cup of tea.'

Joan declined. 'I want to go down to the shops, and see if I can get a joint. I believe I know where I could get a leg of lamb,' she said thoughtfully. 'There'd be time to cook that, wouldn't there? I wonder, would you mind keeping an eye on the baby for me, Mrs Littlejohn, and I'll go down and see what I can get. I won't be very long.'

The little woman said: 'It would be real nice to have the baby, Mrs Corbett. I seen your family over the wall so many times. It must be lovely to have children like you've got.' She sighed faintly. 'Three of them, and all.'

She raised her eyes to Joan. 'I had a little baby once, but she died.'

'I'm so sorry.'

Mrs Littlejohn said: 'In the war it was, my dear. I was in service in a place at Hove, and Ted was in camp at Shoreham. In 1916 that was, my dear, after he'd been out and come back wounded.' She hesitated for a minute, and then she said: 'He was that masterful, you wouldn't think. And he had to go back to France before I really knew about the baby, but he got three days' leave again, and we were married in Brighton. But the baby wasn't like yours, my dear. She never put on any weight, and then she died. And they told me that I couldn't have another, ever.'

'I'm terribly sorry,' said Joan. It would not hurt to let a dammed stream run for a few minutes.

The work-worn hands pleated a fold in the apron. 'It don't do to complain,' she said, 'only I do think you're ever so lucky to have such a lovely family, Mrs Corbett. But I've been lucky, too. You wouldn't know what a good husband I've got, and Ted's got on so well in the building trade, you wouldn't think. And now we've got this lovely house to live in, and the garden with the flowers, and all. And he wanted me to have servants, too, and we did have them once, but I like doing things my own way. So now the girl comes in mornings just to give me a help out, doing the scrubbing up and that.'

Joan put a sluice-gate gently back into the stream. 'Come along in and see the baby,' she said. 'Then I'll leave her with you while I go down and get the meat.'

They went and fetched the baby in its basket cot, and put it on the kitchen table by Mrs Littlejohn's wash-tub. 'My,' said the little woman, 'hasn't she got a pretty colour? She's ever so like you.'

Joan left them together, and drove down into the town. From every hoarding now the red placards exhorted her to boil her water. 'That's all very well,' she muttered to herself rebelliously. 'The electricity's on now, so one can do it. But when you've got no electricity or gas, and precious little paraffin, it's not so easy to go boiling everything over the dining-room fire.'

In the dusk she called in at her husband's office. 'I came to see if you'd come home with me,' she said. 'I've just been down to get a joint to cook for dinner. Mrs Littlejohn's going to help me.'

He eyed her quizzically. 'What's she like?'

'Like Amy, that old maid we had just after we got married. I like her – she's a dear.'

He looked out of the window. 'What's the weather like?'

'It's starting to rain a bit. We'd better put the car away.'

'Are we going to put it over the trench again tonight?'

'I hadn't thought of that. What do you think?'

He got up from his desk, and tidied up his papers for the night. 'If you ask me what I think,' he said, a little wearily, 'I think that bloody trench ought to be deeper.'

'But do you think we'll have another raid tonight?'

'I don't know. They came before when it was raining.'

They went out of the office to the car. Over their heads the clouds hung low, in grey, wet wreaths. A solitary aeroplane flew over them at about two hundred feet, immediately beneath the clouds; there was no other aviation.

'The petrol's a bit low,' he said as they got into the car.

'We'd better stop and get some more.' But at three filling-stations that they tried in turn there was no petrol to be had.

'We were cleaned right out yesterday dinner-time,' one garage hand told them. 'The tank wagon's coming, but it hasn't come. There's been a proper run on it.'

Corbett asked: 'Why is that?'

'People going out into the country for the night, I suppose. Everybody seemed to want a fill up yesterday.'

Corbett drove back thoughtfully to his house. It was raining in earnest by the time they got there; in spite of that he changed into old clothes and went and dug in his trench. At the end of an hour he had got down to six feet, which he judged deep enough; the bottom of it was a sticky mess of mud and water. Finally he drove the car over it again and went back to the house, hoping very much that he would not have to use it in the night.

Mr Littlejohn arrived as he was finishing. 'Coming on real dirty again,' he remarked, looking at the weather. 'You'd say they wouldn't come tonight. But then, it seems all topsy-turvy. Last night I thought that they'd have come, and they never.'

He mused a little. 'Not so many aeroplanes about tonight.'

'It's early yet,' said Corbett. 'And it's a filthy night for flying.'

The builder grunted. 'That may put our chaps off,' he said, a little sourly. 'It didn't seem to stop them bombers.'

They went into the house. 'I was talking to the Deputy City Engineer today,' said Mr Littlejohn. 'They reckon over two hundred bombs fell in the roads. They haven't half had a job.'

'They've done very well,' said Corbett.

'Aye,' said the builder. 'Wonderfully well, they've done. Over two hundred holes to be filled, and mains repaired, and that.' He was silent for a minute. 'Still, come to think of it, it's what you might expect. In poor parts where the houses stand up close without much garden, if you take me, nearly thirty per cent of the surface must be roads. So with a thousand bombs dropped all over, it's only what they had a right to expect.'

Corbett laughed shortly. 'I bet they didn't expect a thousand bombs,' he said.

They sat down to a supper of roast lamb, tinned vegetables, and Guinness which Mr Littlejohn brought from his house. 'Mrs Corbett doesn't never have no trouble with her electric cooker, Ted,' the little woman said wistfully. 'It cooked the joint a fair treat.'

'Like to change back again?' he asked.

She shook her head. 'No,' she said quietly. 'It's ever so clean and nice, but I like something you can see.'

They talked about the holidays that they were going to take that summer. 'We always go on the boat,' said Joan. 'This year, we thought of having a change. We've been thinking of taking a tent with us in the car, and going to Scotland.'

'Brighton,' said Mr Littlejohn comfortably. 'That's where we go. First fortnight in August, every year the same.'

Joan turned to his wife. 'It must be fun, that,' she said sympathetically.

'It's ever so lovely, Mrs Corbett,' she replied. 'It's where I met Ted in the war – I was telling you. We've been every year since then, nearly. You can sit on the pier and there's such a lot to see – the people all enjoying themselves, and the band, and the pierrots, and that. The time passes so quick, you'd never think. You've hardly got there before it's time to come away again. It's ever such a lovely place.'

Corbett nodded. 'It's good fun, a holiday like that, if you just want a lazy time,' he said. Nothing would have induced him to do it himself.

'That's right,' said Mr Littlejohn. 'You and Mrs Corbett – you like doing things when you're on holiday. We like to sit quiet in a motor-coach, and watch other people doing things.'

Mrs Littlejohn said: 'You can go lovely drives from Brighton. . . .'

After the meal the Littlejohns got up to go. 'Early to bed,' said the builder. 'Maybe we shan't get so much sleep later on.' He looked out into the wet night. 'Still, it doesn't look much like a raid tonight.'

The little woman said to Joan: 'It's been ever so kind of you, I'm sure.' She hesitated. 'If you want the baby looking after any time, Mrs Corbett, it would be a real pleasure. Quite took to me she did, didn't she?'

They went away; Corbett stood looking after them thoughtfully. 'Brighton in August,' he said. 'I just can't understand it.'

Joan shook her head. 'They're such – such genuine people,' she said. 'I don't say that I want to see an awful lot of them, but they're terribly nice in their own way.'

She yawned. 'It will be good when things get settled down and we can get some maids again,' she said. 'I'm sick of washing nappies for the baby.'

Again they got out baskets with the gas-masks, food, and drink, and left them in the hall. Then they went up to bed.

In the dark, rainy night they woke to a shattering concussion, near at hand.

Corbett did not hear it consciously. He found himself suddenly awake and standing near the door of his bedroom, his hands pressed to his ears which were aching with pain. In the nursery upstairs he heard the children begin crying; he ran up to them, to help Joan.

As he opened the door there was a blinding flash outside that lit up the room through the green curtains, and another concussion. The glass from the nursery windows fell tinkling to the floor; the children redoubled their screams. Joan was busy with the baby; he moved forward and touched her on the shoulder. 'Get Baby out into the trench,' he shouted through the din. 'Stay there yourself. I'll get the others dressed and bring them out.'

There was another concussion, this time farther off. Joan slipped on shoes and a raincoat over her pyjamas, picked up the child and wrapped it in a shawl, and ran downstairs. Corbett turned to the other children.

'Come on, Juggins,' he said gently to his screaming three-year-old son. 'Be a brave soldier and get dressed. Big men like you aren't frightened of a few little bangs. Where did they put your combinations?'

Another bomb fell near at hand; he touched both children, thinking to quiet them. Then he picked up a woollen garment from a chair. 'Come on, old man,' he said. 'Get into this, and we'll go and find Mummy.'

Phyllis, his six-year-old daughter, stopped crying instantly. 'That's my combies that you're giving John,' she said, snivelling indignantly.

Corbett forced a laugh. 'I'll give him all your clothes unless you put them on yourself,' he said. 'Then you'll have to wear his.'

He got the children dressed without much trouble after that. Bombs continued to fall in the more distant parts of the city; he hurried the children down through the house and into the garden, only stopping to get a pair of shoes and a coat for himself. Joan was in the trench; he passed the children down to her.

'This is a bloody picnic,' he said sourly.

She laughed shortly. 'You're right. It's terribly muddy here, Peter. If you could get a couple of chairs it might be better.'

He went back to the house and got the chairs, slid them down into the trench beneath the car, and followed them. Then he took the baby from Joan and sent her back into the house to dress; the child was crying steadily, confusing his thoughts. While Joan was away one or two more salvoes fell, not very near at hand, towards the centre of the city. Presently she returned, bringing with her the children's mackintoshes and gum-boots.

Corbett gave the baby back to his wife, went back into the house and dressed himself. Then he went round the house opening what windows still had glass left in them; the wind and rain blew freely through the rooms, soaking beds, furniture, and carpets. He tried the wireless set, but found it dead; evidently the current had failed again, or was cut off from the city.

He went back to the garden. Before getting down into his trench he went and looked over the garden wall; in the dim light he could see the bulk of the Littlejohn's car standing above their trench. 'Littlejohn!' he called. 'Are you all right?'

'Oh, aye,' said Mr Littlejohn. He climbed up out of his trench and came over to the wall. 'Is everything all right with you?'

'So far,' said Corbett. The bombs were still falling in the city; away to the south they heard the sharp crack of guns.

'It's a terrible thing, this,' said the builder. 'There don't seem to be any of our own aeroplanes up, do there? Or searchlights, neither. I suppose them guns are anti-aircraft guns.'

'I suppose so.' They surveyed the sky. 'I can't hear any aeroplanes at all,' said Corbett.

'Wait a bit,' said the builder. 'I can hear some now. Listen – very faint. Hear them?'

The wind sighed and the rain drove across the gardens; they stood in silence for a minute, listening. 'I hear them now,' said Corbett. 'They must be at a tremendous height.'

'Maybe that's why there aren't any searchlights,' said the builder.

'Searchlights wouldn't be much good on a night like this. They'd only show them where the town was.'

'I reckon they know that all right,' said Mr Littlejohn grimly.

Another salvo started to fall near at hand, and sent them hurrying to their trenches.

Corbett struck a match and looked at his watch; it was about one o'clock. He settled down on the chair opposite his wife in the narrow, muddy trench and took a child upon each knee. The baby, tired out with crying, had fallen asleep; the other two children slept intermittently.

Joan asked: 'Peter, whatever shall we do if they start to drop gas-bombs? With Baby, I mean?'

'I've been thinking of that,' he said. 'I think the best thing will be for you to stay here with the other two, and I'll take her up to the nursery and stay there with her. With the windows open, right up at the top of the house like that, I don't believe you'd get much gas. It's fifty feet up from the ground.'

They thought it over for a minute. 'I don't like you being in the house, Peter,' she said. 'I think it's much more dangerous there than it is here.'

'You wouldn't want me to leave Baby up there all alone?'

'I'd rather she was all alone than have you with her in the house.'

He touched her hand. 'I'll take her up there if we think there's any gas about. At present it's all high explosive. There's been no gas dropped yet, or incendiary, either.'

Slowly the hours passed. The rain pattered against the car, and trickled from the wet ground down into the trench. Corbett sat, cramped and stiff, one child upon each knee; they dozed uneasily, waking and crying when the detonations were near to them. The baby slept quietly on Joan's lap undisturbed by the heaviest concussions; they were anxious about her. She seemed utterly exhausted. They got some relief by stuffing cotton-wool into their ears.

From time to time they heard the wailing of a siren on some ambulance or police car. The sound of distant gun-fire was continuous, and very occasionally they heard the droning of aeroplanes. The wind sighed past them and the rain made little liquid noises; no other sounds shared the night with the shattering concussions of the bombs.

At last there came a long interval. Corbett looked at his watch; it was a little after three. He was dazed and stiff. 'It lasted three hours last time,' he said. 'This may be the end.'

Joan stirred beside him. 'How long ought we to wait?'

'We'll give it half an hour.'

Towards the end of that time he got out of the trench and went to the garden wall. Mr Littlejohn was standing on his lawn, looking about him at the sky.

'Seems as if it's over,' he said. 'You'd think they'd give an "all clear" signal of some sort, wouldn't you?'

'They didn't give any sort of "take cover" signal,' said Corbett.

'That's so. Seems like they don't know when it's coming or when it's over, don't it?'

'Do you think it's over now?'

'I don't know. I believe I'll get the missus indoors, and chance it.'

Corbett went back to Joan. 'We'll give it a few minutes longer,' he said. He got out the basket of provisions and gave her a drink of whisky; the children drank a little milk and nibbled a sponge-cake.

Presently they got out of the trench, and went back into the house.

Apart from the windows, no more damage seemed to have been done to the house. Corbett helped Joan to put the children back into their beds in the darkness; they fell asleep almost instantaneously. They did not go to bed at once themselves, being hungry; instead, they went down to the kitchen, lit the Primus stove, and fried a little meal of bacon and eggs. They consumed this in the dim light of an ecclesiastical candle; the electricity was dead again. The food made them feel better.

Corbett lit a cigarette from the candle, and stared reflectively at his wife. 'I don't know what you think,' he said, 'but I'm getting a bit tired of this.'

'You couldn't be more tired than I am. How many more raids like this do you think we're going to get?'

'Lord knows. I think we ought to think about clearing out into the country.'

She nodded. 'I've been feeling like that, too. But where would we go? To the boat?'

'It's the only place we've got.'

He gave her a cigarette, and held the candle for her while she lit it; they sat and smoked in silence over the remains of their meal. 'It'd be awfully difficult,' she said at last, sighing a little. 'I mean, three children on a little boat like that!'

'It would be possible,' he said. 'Put Phyllis and John in

the companion bunks, and rig up a sort of cradle in the forecastle for the baby.'

'Over the lavatory, I suppose.'

'That's right. Then you and I could sleep in the saloon.'

She shook her head. 'It would be awfully difficult. There's such a lot of washing to be done for the baby, and you know what it is, carrying water on board. Besides, what would we do for milk?'

'Use tinned milk. But anyway, we'd be at Hamble. That's in the country. You might be able to get milk more easily there than here.'

'You should be able to.'

'As regards the water,' he said, 'it seems to me that wherever we are we'll have to start carting it before long. I haven't noticed any water coming in here yet, except the rain. I don't know how much there is left in our tank upstairs, but I bet it's not much. We might get better water there than here.'

He paused. 'You couldn't wash the nappies out in salt water, using salt water soap?'

Joan wrinkled up her nose. 'Not much. What about this, though? Suppose we sailed the boat up a river – right away from the sea? Where she'd be floating in fresh water?' She paused. 'We'd have all the water that we wanted, then.'

He sat for a minute, deep in thought. 'It's an idea,' he said. 'I don't know where you'd find a river like that on the south coast, though. A river deep enough to float our boat, where the water wasn't salt.'

He got up from the table. 'Let's sleep on it,' he said. 'We'll make a decision in the morning.'

She lingered for a moment in the dark, shadowy entrance hall as they made their way upstairs. 'It's horrible even to think of leaving,' she said slowly. 'I mean – this is our home.'

He took her hand. 'Never mind. It won't be for long.'

She went up to the nursery to sleep with the children. He turned into his own room and took off his shoes and coat, then he threw himself on the bed in his clothes and pulled the blankets over him. Very soon he was asleep.

He slept late. Joan, taking the children downstairs to cook their breakfast, looked in on him; she did not wake him. It was not till ten o'clock that he awoke, thrust his feet into his shoes, and went downstairs.

'You should have waked me,' he said to Joan. 'I'd have given you a hand.'

She smiled at him. 'Come and eat your breakfast.'

He rubbed a hand over his unshaven chin. 'Have you heard anything of Littlejohn?'

'Not this morning.'

'I'll just go in and see if they're all right. Then I'll come along. You can leave the washing-up – I'll do that.' He had no thought of going to his office.

He went out to his front door. In the street he met Mr Littlejohn returning to his house, grey and troubled. He said: 'You've heard the news?'

'No,' said Corbett.

'Cholera,' said Mr Littlejohn.

Corbett stared at him, wide-eyed.

'There's been an outbreak of cholera, down Northam way. Over seventy cases, so they say. They've got patrols on all the roads. Nobody's got to leave the city till he's been inoculated.'

3

WHEN LIVING dangerously, there comes a time when extra risks are taken as a matter of everyday occurrence; the mind has become inured to them, and they are hardly thought about. Corbett was not particularly upset by the news that he had heard. He questioned Littlejohn about it, but the builder knew no more than the bare facts, which he had got from a policeman that he knew.

Corbett went back into his house and sat down to his breakfast. After a little reflection, he came to the conclusion that there was no point in trying to conceal the cholera from Joan. He finished his meal, lit a cigarette, and asked her:

'Do you know anything about cholera?'

She stared at him, puzzled. 'Cholera? It's a thing they get in India. Black men die of it in heaps. And pukka sahibs go and stop it. Why?'

'We've got it in Southampton.'

She stared at him. 'Cholera?'

He told her what he had heard from Littlejohn.

'What *is* cholera?' she asked. 'Is it catching?'

He said dryly: 'I imagine so.' And then he said: 'This must be what Gordon meant.'

She was puzzled. 'But you don't have cholera in countries like this, Peter. It only happens in the East, doesn't it?'

He shook his head. 'I don't know.'

'Look and see if there's anything about it in the encyclopaedia.'

He went and fetched the volume from the drawing-room; together they bent over it.

Five minutes later, he stood erect. 'Well, that's it,' he said, a little heavily. 'There seems to have been plenty of epidemics of it in this country before. Bunches of them. It comes from water contaminated with sewage.'

'You got to have a case to start it off, though.'

He shook his head. 'Not necessarily.' He laid his fingers on a line; she bent over to read the small print. 'Plenty of carriers in a seaport town like this.'

'Is that a carrier, like a typhoid carrier, Peter?'

'That's right. It might be a Lascar sailor.'

She looked at him seriously. 'You think it's happened just because the drains are broken up?'

'I suppose so.'

She turned again to the book. 'It says here, case mortality, fifty per cent. In plain English, does that mean what it seems to mean?'

He smiled a little grimly. 'I should think it probably does.'

She stared up at him, wide-eyed. 'But, Peter, what ought we to do?'

He laid his hand upon her shoulder. 'Don't worry. We'll have to get inoculated as soon as we can. I'll go and find out what's happening as soon as I've done the washing-up.'

He hesitated. 'I wouldn't let the children go out today, if I were you. Keep them in the garden.'

'You bet,' she said. 'Peter, I've been thinking about the boat. It'd be frightfully inconvenient, but I believe I'd really rather we were there.'

He nodded. 'I know. This puts the lid on it.'

More in hope than in confidence he went and tried the telephone. He found it out of order.

He did the washing-up with Joan, and shaved, and dressed. He went out to the garden and had a look at the trench; there was standing water in the bottom of it. He decided to leave the car over it as some protection from the rain, and walked down to the town. On his way, he was shocked at the condition of the town. The damage was of the same character as after the last raid, but he noticed that there were far fewer people in the streets. The cumulative effect of the damage, coupled with the rain and the deserted aspect of the streets, gave to the town a ruined and a desolate appearance.

He went first to his office. From the street he saw that

there were broken windows; he let himself in with his key and made a quick inspection of the rooms. Practically all the windows had been shattered. The rain streamed in on to his desk; the sodden papers and the broken glass gave to the room an atmosphere of squalor and depression. He set his lips and moved all his documents to an untidy heap at the far side of the room, remote from the window. Then he did the same in Bellinger's office.

There was nothing else to be done. There was no post to go through, no newspapers to be read. He did not think that there was any likelihood of clients coming in. He went out into the street again, locking the door behind him.

Andrews's car was standing outside his office. Corbett went in and found the accountant alone, moving furniture away from the windows in much the same way as he had been doing. Corbett sat down on the edge of a desk.

'Well,' he said, 'we're in a pretty pickle now.'

'Right in,' said Mr Andrews grimly. He offered him a cigarette.

They sat smoking in silence for a minute or two. 'Bloody things seem to come over and do just what they like,' said the accountant at last.

'How the hell do they do it?'

'I met an Air Force chap since I saw you last,' said Mr Andrews. 'He said that in the first raid they came at some colossal height, fifteen or twenty thousand feet, and just bombed through the clouds. No pretence of aiming at anything – they just dumped the stuff. What he couldn't tell me was, how they knew where to dump it.'

They sat in silence again. 'I suppose that's against all the rules of war?' said Corbett.

'I suppose so. Anyway, nobody bothers about that sort of thing these days.'

There was a pause. Corbett said: 'Are your people all right at home?'

'So far. You didn't know the Rossiters?'

Corbett shook his head.

'You've missed your opportunity,' said Mr Andrews.

He stubbed out his cigarette, half smoked, in an ash-tray, hesitated for a minute, and lit another. He flicked the match away, and stepped nervously over to the shattered window. 'I'm not going through another night of it. I'm getting my family out of it this afternoon.'

'Where are you going?'

The other shrugged his shoulders. 'I don't know. I don't suppose one will be able to get in anywhere. I've got a tent. I'm taking that with me.'

Corbett told him about the cholera, and the cordon that had been put upon the roads. 'It's reasonable,' he said. 'If this really is cholera, they want to localize it.'

The accountant's lips set in a thin line. 'Nobody's going to localize me,' he said. There was an ugliness in his manner. 'Inoculated or not, I'm getting out.'

Corbett nodded slowly. 'I'm going over to the Civic Centre to see if I can find out how one gets the inoculation done.'

He walked across the park to the new buildings. He found the centre in a ferment, the car-parks jammed with little air-raid fire engines, lorries, and ambulances. The group of buildings had been hit in one or two places; one wall had slipped, revealing the teeming office life inside like a section of a hive of bees.

He had two or three friends in the Town Clerk's department, and he was well known to the minor officials. He made his way into the corridors and waited till he found an opportunity. Presently he met a young man that he knew, who drew him into an office away from the crowd. Corbett offered him a cigarette.

'I came to see if I could find out anything about this cholera inoculation,' he inquired. 'Where one gets it done?'

The young man laughed, without humour. 'They're hoping to set up a clinic to do the whole city.'

Corbett eyed him keenly. 'A big job. When will that be?'

'When the serum comes.'

'I see,' said Corbett quietly.

The young man explained. 'They've got any amount of

stuff for typhoid – or so they say. And, anyway, that seems to take a long time to incubate. But they've used up what little they had for cholera already, on the patients' families. Now they've got to wait till they can get some more.'

'How long?'

'I don't know.'

'In fact, we've been caught napping?'

'Seems like it. But who'd ever think of cholera? I thought that was a thing you only got in India. Typhoid and diphtheria – yes. But not cholera.'

Corbett shook his head. 'There used to be a lot of epidemics of it in this country.'

The young man sighed. 'Well, it looks as if we've got another one.' He paused. 'Somebody was saying this morning that they've got it in Bristol, too.'

'Seaport town,' said Corbett. 'That might be.'

He turned to the young man. 'This cordon on the roads,' he said. 'Is it still working.'

'I think so.'

'I don't see how they can keep people in the town tonight, to face another raid. They'll have to let them out, inoculated or not.'

The other agreed. 'Well, that's what I think. But they're very keen to keep the cholera from spreading. And if we aren't careful it'll be all over the country.'

Corbett nodded. 'It's difficult,' he said, a little heavily. 'Do you know what they're doing about it?'

'They're having a conference upon it now, in the Town Clerk's office. There's someone down from the Ministry of Health, and the Town Clerk, and the MOH, and General Fitzroy.'

'General Fitzroy?'

'The military have taken over the cordon for the police. Didn't you know?'

Corbett went out into the town. The damage to the houses and the shops was much more extensive than it had been after the first raid. There seemed to have been a certain amount of looting; in one or two places there were constables

64

on guard over badly damaged shops. He tried to sort out the new damage from the old, but found it practically impossible to differentiate. All he could say for certain was that the town now was very gravely injured. It seemed to him that in the centre of the city nearly one building in five had suffered serious damage, apart from broken windows which were everywhere. He did not think it was so bad in residential districts such as he lived in.

Once more the roads were full of bomb-holes; this time, however, little water came from them. Again in the centre of the town squads of men were working at the repair of mains, cables, and sewers; again, parties of workmen were boarding up windows that had been smashed. He got the impression that the work was not so active as it had been after the first raid. The squads seemed weaker in numbers, more dispersed. There did not seem to be the same enthusiasm to get the city right again that he had noticed formerly.

He noticed many soldiers working with the corporation squads. He noticed also, and very definitely, that the town smelled. It was difficult to define the smell. It was not wholly drains. It seemed rather to be an atmosphere of mustiness and squalor, such as you might find in a poor, dirty house with tight-shut windows. Not very nice.

He made his way back home on foot. On his way he passed a garage and saw cars being filled up. He went inside and found the proprietor, whom he knew.

'I'll put six gallons by for you, in cans,' the man told him. 'But you must come and get it before dinner-time, Mr Corbett. I'll be sold right out by that time at this rate, and I may not be able to keep it. Some of the chaps get real nasty if they think you're holding any back.'

He saw the petrol put in cans and placed beneath the desk of the small office; then he went on. He reached his house to find his wife with Mrs Littlejohn, doing the baby's washing.

'It don't take but a minute,' said the older woman, 'rinsing out a few little things like this. Many hands make light work, that's what I say.'

He took Joan into the next room on some pretext. 'She's

been such a help, Peter,' said the girl. 'I'd have been off my head with the children and the washing if it hadn't been for her.'

He told her what he had learned in the town. 'We'll never get to the boat while they keep this cordon up,' he said. 'And Lord knows when we'll get inoculated.' He paused. 'I might creep through alone, or you might, if we thought it was worth while to try. But we'd never make it with three children and the car.'

'I don't want to separate, Peter. There's no point in that. Let's stick together.'

'All right.'

'That means we stay here for tonight, does it?'

'I'm afraid it does.'

She smiled. 'The electricity's off, so the cooker's out of action. Still, we've got the cold lamb to eat.'

He said: 'I've got to take the car down for petrol. I'll look around and see what food I can get hold of.'

'Do see if you can get some milk. Fresh if possible – otherwise get some tins.'

'All right.' He paused. 'I tell you what I'll do. I'll go along and see if I can find Gordon. He might be able to help with this inoculation business.'

He drove the car off the trench and out of the back gate. He fetched his petrol from the garage, and then drove down into the town to look for food. There was very little fresh meat to be got, and what there was was bad in quality and smelling a little. He did not buy any.

'It isn't very nice,' they admitted in one butcher's shop. 'Still, it'd be all right for stewing, or making a curry, or anything like that. It's a job to keep meat good, these times.'

He asked: 'Why is that?'

'The refrigerator downstairs. It's electric.'

He bought a small sack of flour, and a fair quantity of miscellaneous tinned foods. He could not discover any fresh milk in the town at all; at three dairies they told him that none had come in that day. He got six tins of condensed milk, however, and was glad to do so.

Finally he drove to Gordon's house. He hesitated to ring the bell, thinking that the surgeon might be sleeping after his night's work. Instead, he pushed at the front door; it was open, and he walked in.

He stood in the hall and called softly: 'Is anybody there?'

The door of the consulting-room opened, and Gordon appeared. 'Hullo, Corbett,' he said quietly. 'Come along in. I'm just going back to the hospital.'

Corbett said: 'I won't keep you, then. But first I want to thank you for troubling to ring us up that afternoon about boiling water and stuff. It was good of you to think of us.'

The surgeon said: 'That's nothing. As a matter of fact, I very nearly didn't. At the time I didn't really believe that it was cholera. It seemed – incredible.'

'How did it start?'

The other shook his head. 'I don't think anyone knows. The only explanation is, there must have been a cholera carrier in the city. Of course, immediately you get a real case of it it's bound to spread, with conditions as they are.'

'I came to see if you could help us over the inoculations.'

Gordon said wearily: 'I can't, old man. I only wish I could. There's not a drop of serum in the town – for anyone. The pathologists are working on it at the hospital, but it will be forty-eight hours before they get their first batch through. And we want such a devil of a lot of it.'

'I won't keep you, then,' said Corbett. 'But how's Margaret?'

'She's gone back into uniform – you know she was a nurse before we married. She's down in Northam, with the cholera cases.' He smiled. 'So we're both busy.'

'You got a lot of casualties last night?'

'Just about the same as last time – five or six hundred at the hospital. The difficulty is in evacuating them. They've got to be got out of the city. A woman who's been blown up by a bomb doesn't get on well if you keep her in a town that's bombed each night. But with this quarantine cordon things are awfully difficult. And anyway, there's nowhere

we can send them to. We filled the country hospitals bung **full** after the first night.'

Corbett nodded. 'You've been operating all night?'

'Two tables – just the same. It's a bad business, Corbett.'

The solicitor said very quietly: 'You make me feel ashamed of myself. You're working like this for the city, Margaret's nursing cholera, and I'm doing nothing at all. All I do is come and worry you for morphia and serums for myself and my own family.' He got to his feet. 'I'm sorry, Gordon.'

The surgeon said: 'Don't hurry away. And don't be a bloody fool – or not more than you can help being.' He pushed across a box of cigarettes, and lit one himself.

'This thing has been a great disaster to us all,' he said after a time. 'I never thought, if war should come again, that it would be like this. Still, that's the way it is.' He paused. 'I've got my job to do, and you've got yours. Mine's very easy – just hard work at doing what I'm used to.'

Corbett said: 'That's not true. I'm not doing anything. I suppose I ought to go off and enlist.'

Gordon swung round on him. 'Don't think of it. Go on doing what you're doing now.'

'What do you mean by that?'

The surgeon said: 'I mean just this. You've got three strong and healthy children. The country's going to need them presently. Your job is to keep them safe through this, and that's the only job you want to think about. If you get Joan and your three kids through this in safety you'll have done your stuff – and God, man, it's a whole time job if ever there was one! Don't think of anything else until you've done that job properly and well.'

He paused. 'Get them away. Get them to Ireland or America, or anywhere they'll be safe from bombs and from disease. But get them out of this.'

Corbett said: 'I suppose you're right.'

'I know I'm right. I've thought of this all night. I've had young people on the table – kiddies, some of them. Children that I knew, that Margaret knew. And I've been patching –

patching – patching all the time, trying to make the damage that they'd got less onerous for them. And I've been thinking if only I could work at getting them away, out of the danger of it all, I'd be doing a better job.'

Corbett shook his head. 'Nobody else could do what you're doing, in your place.'

'I know. But that's the man's job today – the only job. To see your people safe.'

Corbett rubbed his chin. 'That's very different to the ideas one's always had. I've always thought that in a war the right thing was to join the Army, or the Navy, or the Air Force, and fight for the country.'

The surgeon said: 'With a bloody great sword, I suppose.'

He shook his head. 'I know those were the old ideas,' he said. 'But a new war – and this war's very new – brings new conditions and the old ideas won't fit. Then you've got to hack out a new set of ideas for yourself, and do the best you can. Put away the red coat, and invent a khaki one.'

He got up from the desk. 'Good luck, and remember me to Joan. Remember what I said about getting them away.'

Corbett turned to go. 'Good luck to both of you.'

'We've got it,' said the surgeon quietly. Corbett glanced at him.

Gordon said: 'I've got no children to look after. And Margaret – she's working like I am. I've got my luck, and she's got hers. I'm working sixteen hours a day where I'm most needed, at work I can do damn well. I never worked better in my life. I don't get any money for it. I don't expect anyone will even remember that I've done it, when this thing is all over. But this is my peak, and I know it. This is what I came into the world for. Whatever I do after this will be – just spinning out my time.'

He picked up a raincoat from the chair. 'And now if you don't mind, old man – I must get back to the hospital.'

Corbett left him and drove back to his house. He found Littlejohn there. 'No inoculations for two days at least,' he said. He told him what the surgeon had said. 'But keep it under your hat, and don't go spreading it around. We don't want to start a panic, or anything like that.'

'That's right,' said Mr Littlejohn. 'Least said about things like that the better. I been round and about this morning. Most people don't know anything at all about the sickness. I didn't let on.'

Corbett nodded. 'Better not.'

The builder said: 'What do you say if we take a car, and find out if there really is this cordon that they talk about?'

'It's there all right,' said Corbett. 'Anyway, it was this morning. I heard about it at the Civic Centre.' He paused. 'Still, I'd like to take a run out on the Hamble road.'

'Aye,' said the builder. 'Mrs Corbett was telling me that you was thinking of moving to your boat. You're doing the right thing, if you ask me.'

They got into the car, and drove down to the Cobden bridge across the River Itchen. On the bridge all cars were being stopped by the police.

The constable said: 'Have you got a pass, sir?'

'No,' said Corbett. 'Do I need one?'

'Can't leave the borough boundary without a pass. Where are you going to?'

The builder said quickly: 'Sholing. That's inside the borough. I got property there. You know me – Littlejohn's the name.'

'Oh, aye,' said the constable. 'Sholing's inside the boundary – you don't want no pass for that. That's all right, Mr Littlejohn.' He moved back from the car.

Corbett said: 'I may want to go out to Hamble this afternoon. Will that be all right?'

The policeman shook his head. 'No, sir, it won't be all right. You'll not be able to go beyond the borough boundary, just this side of Netley Common. Not without you have a pass from the Chief Constable's office.'

'Why is that?'

'I couldn't say, sir,' said the man impassively. 'Them's the orders that we've got. You can pass along for Sholing now.'

They drove through. Corbett said: 'Let's go on and have a look at Netley Common.'

They went on down the road to Bursledon. Three hundred yards from the boundary they came upon a mass of cars parked by the roadside, all filled with bedding, trunks, and children. Corbett parked his car a little way behind the crowd; they got out and went forward on foot.

A rough barrier of planks and barrels had been set across the road. Soldiers were billeted in a house near by; three of them were on guard at the barricade, with bayonets fixed upon their rifles. There were two policemen dealing patiently with inquiries from the crowd. A tired, worried-looking subaltern of infantry appeared to be in charge.

'It's no good hanging about here, sir,' the constable was saying patiently. 'You want to go back to the Civic Centre and get a pass. We can't let nobody through without a pass. Now, keep the roadway clear, please.'

They stood and watched a couple of ambulances go through. There was nothing more to be seen or to be learnt; they turned back to the car and drove home.

The builder was very thoughtful. 'That crowd's all right now,' he said at last. 'But when they find that they can't get a pass, and that they've got to stay another night ... I don't know.'

Corbett had nothing to say to that.

They parted at the gate, and Corbett went into his house. Joan met him. 'You've not had any lunch,' she said; it was early afternoon. 'Come on and have something to eat. Then I thought we might all lie down and have a rest.'

He smiled. 'I've heard of worse ideas than that.' He looked at the barograph, still falling slowly. 'That doesn't look so good.'

It was not raining, but the day was grey and cold. As soon as he had had a meal he went and lay down on his bed; Joan and the children went up to the nursery. He fell asleep almost at once.

When next he opened his eyes, it was dark outside. Joan was with him, with a candle and a cup of tea.

'It's six o'clock,' she said. 'You've had a lovely sleep.'

He sat up on the edge of the bed, and rubbed his eyes. 'What's the weather like?'

'Cloudy,' she said. 'But it's not raining.'

He took the cup of tea from her, and sipped it. 'Did you get any sleep?'

She nodded. 'I slept for about an hour. The children are still sleeping – I didn't wake them. The more they sleep the better. Baby's awake. I've just given her her feed.'

'I must go and put that car over the trench.'

'I've done that,' she said.

'Thanks.' He got up and went over to the empty, broken window, and stood looking out into the night. 'We'll have to see it out here for a day or two,' he said. 'While that cordon's there we shan't get to the boat.'

She sighed. 'I wish we were there now.' She raised her eyes to his. 'Peter, I've got the wind up for tonight. I don't know why. I'm scared of what may happen if they come again.'

He put his arm around her shoulders. 'We'll be all right. Tomorrow we may be able to get away.'

He took the candle and went with her up into the attic to see how much water they had left. The main tank was about one-third full, the hot-water cistern seemed to be nearly full. 'It looks as if we'd used about half of what we had to start with,' he said. 'That means about three more days, using it as we are now.'

'What do we do after that, Peter?'

He shrugged his shoulders. 'Go and get it from the Corporation water-carts, I suppose.'

He went out into the garden, and stood looking at the water in the bottom of the trench, wondering what to do about it. He looked over the garden wall; Mr Littlejohn was standing in the middle of his lawn, listening intently.

'Did you hear any shots fired just now?' he inquired.

'No. Were there any?'

'Well, I don't know. I was out here, and I thought I heard shooting. Listen again.'

They listened, but heard nothing but the sighing of the wind and the passing of an occasional car.

The builder stirred. 'It's just nerves, I suppose,' he said apologetically. 'I keep on thinking about them barricades. Properly asking for trouble, I call it.'

Corbett said: 'There's trouble either way, whether you keep them in or let them out. If they get out, the cholera may go right through the country with things as they are.'

'I suppose that's so.'

They stood one on each side of the wall, staring up into the sky. 'Do you think they'll come tonight?' asked Corbett.

'It's all cloudy,' said the builder. 'They've come the two cloudy nights we've had, and kept away the clear one. I reckon they may do.'

'Sing out if you should want any help.'

'Thank you, Mr Corbett. I'll do the same by you. It's better to stick together, times like this.'

Corbett moved away and spent a little time improvising a grating for the bottom of the trench, to raise the floor above the water-level.

Presently he went into the house. He found Joan in the drawing-room, cavernous with the windows boarded up, sewing something for the baby in the flickering light of a candle.

He touched her on the shoulder. 'Give it up,' he said. 'You'll hurt your eyes. Come on – let's have a game of cards.'

She laid her work down gratefully. 'I've been thinking about things, Peter,' she said, shuffling the cards. 'We'll have to get away from here. I want to go to the boat now, however difficult it may be living on it with the children.' She stared around the room. 'I mean, just look at how we're living here! It's ... squalor.' She caught his hand. 'I was cooking up that gruel stuff for the baby, Peter, and I was making it a big batch because I wanted it to last. And you have to do it in a double saucepan, and that iron one *is* so heavy. I had to do it over the dining-room fire – there wasn't anywhere else to do it. And I spilt it, lifting it off the fire, all over the carpet. It made a terrible stain. I don't think it will ever come out.'

Her eyes filled with tears. 'I want to get away from here, and go and live on the boat. It'd be easier than this, and we wouldn't be spoiling things.'

He pressed her hand. 'I know. I think we would be better there. I think we should be able to get there tomorrow. Would you like a whisky and soda?'

'I'd love one, Peter.'

He fetched the drinks, and they sat down together to a simple card game in the light of the guttering church candle. They played for an hour, and then stopped. When they stopped moving the silence was intense.

Corbett stood up. 'Let's go and see what sort of night it is.'

Joan went with him to the front door. The wind had dropped. There were no lights anywhere to be seen, except a chink of candle-light from a house up the road. In the darkness the clouds seemed to hang low, ominously. There were no sounds at all.

The girl shivered. 'I've got the needle tonight,' she said, laughing tremulously. 'It feels as if something is waiting to happen.'

He linked his arm through hers. 'You're tired,' he said gently. 'We'd better go to bed and get some sleep.'

'The children ought to have something to eat. They've not had anything since lunch.'

He helped her to mix some tinned milk with warm water, and prepare a little meal for the children. They took this up with them to the nursery on a tray, and gave it to the children in bed.

Phyllis asked: 'Are we going to have bangs tonight, Daddy?'

'I don't think so,' he said. 'If there are, we'll go out to the trench.'

She thought about it for a minute. 'I don't like bangs, Daddy,' she said at last.

Joan said: 'If you're terribly good, Daddy's going to take you on the boat.'

74

'Like last summer?'

'That's right.'

'Will I be able to take my rubber ring, and bathe, Mummy?'

John said: 'Am I going on the boat, too, Mummy?'

'He can't can he, Mummy? John's too little to go on the boat, isn't he, Mummy?'

'Of course he's not,' said Corbett. 'John's coming on the boat, and Baby, too. But you've all got to be very good, or I won't take you. Now lie down and go to sleep again.'

It took a quarter of an hour to get them settled off to sleep; there was much chat about the boat. Then Joan and Corbett went down to the kitchen for their supper; they smoked a quick cigarette and went upstairs to bed, she in the nursery and he in his own room.

He woke about midnight with the first concussion, far off in some distant part of the town. He slipped from his bed practically fully dressed, put on his shoes and went to the nursery. He found Joan dressing the children.

There were further explosions in the distance. 'Take Baby down into the trench,' he said. 'I'll bring the other two.'

Joan said crossly: 'I must say, I'm getting a bit tired of this.'

She took the child and went downstairs. Corbett got the other children dressed as quickly as he could and followed her; the explosions did not come very near. He saw them safely settled down with gas-masks, food, and drink; then he stood for a moment on the lawn above them, looking around.

'Littlejohn,' he called quietly. 'Littlejohn! Are you all right?'

There was no reply. He called again: 'Littlejohn!'

In the distance bombs were falling irregularly, not very loud. Gun-fire began to sound away to the south-east and south of them; there seemed to be more guns than he had heard the night before. He waited for a few moments, irresolute, and called again. Then he went back to his own trench.

In the dim light he peered down at Joan. 'I don't know what to do about them.'

'What's the matter?' she inquired. 'Don't they answer?'

'No,' he said. 'They may still be asleep. Do you think I ought to go and see?'

'They'll be all right,' she said. 'Stay here. Don't go wandering about.'

Almost immediately the point was settled for him. A vivid sheet of flame sprang up across the garden walls, less than a hundred yards away. He dived for the trench with the explosion and landed in a heap on top of the screaming children. A few fragments hit the car above their heads with sharp, metallic sounds. He crouched down in the trench trying to calm the children; the bombs continued falling very near at hand. He heard a crash of falling masonry.

He let the children scream to relieve their feelings, and pressed Joan's hand. 'Don't worry,' he said. 'We'll be all right here.'

Presently there came a lull. It seemed to Corbett, dazed and confused, that a dozen bombs must have fallen in their immediate neighbourhood in less than three minutes. In the ensuing calm he stood up and looked out of the trench. He saw a gleam of candle-light in the next house.

He laughed, and called Joan's attention to it. 'That woke old Littlejohn up,' he said. 'He wouldn't sleep through that.'

She laughed with him, a little hysterically. He felt for the whisky flask and poured her out a little in the metal cup.

'Come on – let's have a drink,' he said. 'We need it after that.'

She took the cup from him in the darkness and drank. As she did so, they heard the sound of voices from the next house; the Littlejohns were coming out to their trench.

Immediately there came a violent concussion, nearer than any they had known. The earth of their trench rose bodily beneath them, and fell again with a strange, tinkling noise mixed with the blast. They clasped their ears in pain; the children redoubled their screams. Within a few yards of the trench they heard the rumble of a falling wall. Something hit the car above their heads a tearing blow, and fell heavily upon the grass.

Before they had recovered from that explosion there came another, and another, gradually receding into the distance. They lay propped against the sides of the trench, half blinded with the pain of their ears, stunned, and dazed.

Presently, and very cautiously, they took their hands from their ears. In the lull that followed, through the noises in their heads, they heard a voice calling to them: 'Mr Corbett! Are you there, Mr Corbett?'

Joan raised her head. 'It's Mrs Littlejohn,' she said. 'Peter, they may be hurt.'

'I'll go and see.' He groped in the bottom of the trench. 'Where's that basket with the first-aid stuff?' He called: 'All right, Mrs Littlejohn. I'm coming over to you.'

Joan laid her hand upon his arm. 'Peter – be careful.'

He nodded. 'I must go and see if they're all right. They'd do the same for us.'

He got out of the trench, basket in hand; his head was reeling, and he staggered as he walked. There was no wall separating the two gardens, only a heap of rubble on what had been flower-beds. He clambered over this and went up to the Littlejohns' car, straddling across the trench. There was no movement there.

'Littlejohn?' he called. 'Where are you?'

From the darkness beside the house the woman said: 'Over here, Mr Corbett. Do come and see to Ted.'

Guided by the voice, he found her sitting on the ground, propped up against the side of the house. He stooped down to her. 'Are you hurt?' he asked.

She said: 'I got something the matter with my leg, but that ain't nothing. It's Ted, Mr Corbett. I'm afraid he's hurt real bad – I can't make him hear me.'

'Where is he?'

'Over there, Mr Corbett.'

He bent over the body of the man, lying face downwards in a flower-bed. He was still breathing, but heavily and unevenly, with a snoring sound. Corbett rolled him over in the darkness, and began feeling him for broken bones. Presently he discovered a three-inch gash in his scalp. It did not seem to be bleeding to any extent; he felt the skull very delicately, but could not detect any movement.

He said: 'I think he's all right, Mrs Littlejohn. I believe he's just knocked out.'

She said very quietly: 'He's been ever such a good husband to me, Mr Corbett. You wouldn't think.'

Bombs were still falling in distant parts of the city. Corbett got up, re-crossed the rubble of the wall, and went back to Joan. 'Let's have that whisky,' he said. 'Littlejohn's had a knock on the head, but I think he'll be all right.'

He took the flask, and felt his way back through the darkness to the other garden. He knelt down beside the builder and lifted him to a sitting position, propped against his knee. He loosened the starched collar that the man was wearing, even in the middle of the night. Then he wet a handkerchief in whisky and water, and began to bathe his face.

In a few minutes he felt a stir of returning consciousness in the heavy body.

'All right, Mrs Littlejohn,' he said. 'I think he's coming round.'

She did not answer; the builder raised his head and seemed to moisten his lips. Corbett put the neck of the flask into his mouth and gave him a drink. 'Take it easy,' he said. 'You've had a knock on the head.'

In a slow minute the builder raised his hand and felt his head. 'Love us,' he said thickly. 'I should think I bloody well had.' He stirred in Corbett's arms. 'That's all right – I can manage.'

Corbett released his hold; the man leaned forward and sat alone. 'Can you feel if you're hurt anywhere else?'

'I'm all right,' said the builder heavily. 'I can manage. Is the missus all right?'

'She's hurt her leg,' said Corbett. 'If you think you can manage by yourself now, I'll go and have a look at her.'

He got up, and crossed over to where the woman was still sitting propped against the wall. He bent and spoke to her;

she did not answer. He touched her, and cried in alarm: 'Littlejohn! Come over here – quick, man!'

But she was already dead. The bomb had fallen on or near their greenhouse. A flying fragment of the glass had sheared through all her clothes and wounded her behind the knee. She had bled to death, quietly and unostentatiously, as in everything that she had done.

It was incredible to them; they worked for a long time before they would admit defeat, while the bombs continued falling, sometimes near, sometimes far away.

Presently the builder picked her up in his arms and, staggering a little, carried her into the house and upstairs to the bedroom, where the candle was still burning. He laid her on the ornate, gilded iron bed beneath a picture of the 'Stag at Bay' and a text in a wood Oxford frame that told them 'God is Love', and covered her with a counterpane.

Then they had done all that they could do.

Corbett touched the builder on the shoulder. 'Come down into our trench for the night,' he said gently. 'It's safer down there.'

The builder said: 'I'll stay here for a while, thanking you, all the same.'

Corbett hesitated. 'You're quite sure? It would be better in the trench, you know.'

The man shook his head. 'You go back to your family, M. Corbett. I'll be all right.' He said: 'I want to sit with her a bit.'

Corbett went down into the garden, and back to his own trench across the rubble. He told Joan what had happened. 'Leave him alone,' she said. 'It's best that way.'

They sat in the trench for about two hours after that, aching and wet, cold and sad. In the window of the house next door the candle burned on, flickering in the draughts. From time to time the bombs fell in their neighbourhood, none very near; the distant gun-fire was continuous, and apparently quite ineffective. At last came the long lull that they knew from experience meant the end.

'It's over now,' he said at the end of twenty minutes. 'We can go back to bed.'

They got the children up out of the trench, muddy and exhausted, took them back into the house, washed them in warm water, and put them to bed. Then they went down into the kitchen.

'Let's have something to eat,' said Corbett.

'All right.' She looked at him irresolutely. 'I just hate to think of him in there, alone,' she said. 'He wouldn't come and have a meal with us, would he?'

Corbett shook his head. 'He wouldn't want to do that.'

'Do you think I could take him in a tray?'

'You might do that. If so, have a look at his head. He's got a nasty flesh wound in his scalp. Had I better come too?'

She shook her head. 'I think I'll go alone. Start cooking something I can eat when I get back.'

She cut a few sandwiches and warmed up some coffee and some milk. Then she fetched bandages and lint, and went with the tray out of the front door and round to the next house. She entered the hall and stood for a moment in the dim, shadowy darkness, not knowing where to put the tray down. Then there was a movement on the floor above, a door opened upstairs with a gleam of light, and the builder came slowly down the stairs, carrying the candle.

Joan said: 'It's only me, Mr Littlejohn – Mrs Corbett. I brought you round some hot coffee. I want you to drink it.'

He came down and stood beside her. 'Eh, that's real kind, Mrs Corbett,' he said heavily.

She led him into the sitting-room. 'Sit down and drink it up,' she ordered. 'Then I want to have a look at your head.'

He obeyed her, silently. There was a spirit stove and a kettle in the grate; she lit it to warm the water. When he had finished eating she cut the straggling grey hair away and washed the wound with a little antiseptic; then she bandaged it.

'I'll do it again tomorrow,' she said.

'You don't want to be here tomorrow,' he said heavily. 'You want to get away to Hamble, to that boat.'

She caught her breath. 'If only we could . . .'

He stood ponderously erect, the bandaging finished. 'I been thinking it out, sitting up there with her. I got to help you get away now, you and the kiddies and Mr Corbett. That's what I got to do.'

He laid a heavy hand upon her shoulder. 'Go in and have a sleep now. I'll be along and have a talk with Mr Corbett in the morning.' He turned away. 'I want to thank you for what you done for me, and for her,' he said, with his back towards her.

Joan said: 'Please don't, Mr Littlejohn,' and went away.

In her own house Corbett had prepared a little meal for her in the kitchen. 'We've got to get away from here today, Peter,' she said. 'It's no good staying on here and waiting for it.'

He nodded. 'You're quite right. We'll go today.'

She stared around. 'We shan't be able to take much with us.'

'It'll only be for a short time, and Hamble's only seven miles away. We can come back here every day if we want to – to see that everything is still all right.'

She laughed bitterly. 'Leave the house empty with no glass in any of the windows. Anyone will be able to walk in and pinch anything. But I suppose we can't help that.'

He shook his head. 'I'll take the silver to the bank. Perhaps Littlejohn will be able to help us get the windows boarded up a bit more.'

They went to bed.

Corbett slept only for a short time; he got up with the first light, at about six o'clock. Joan was sleeping, and he did not wake her. He dressed and went out into the streets. There was a great deal more damage in his neighbourhood than there had been before. Ambulances were still about the streets collecting the wounded from the houses and the gardens; the cars were much hampered in their work by the unrepaired bomb-holes in the streets. In places it was impossible for the ambulance to approach the house. Over by the University there seemed to be a considerable fire;

dense volumes of smoke were wreathing up into a grey sky.

He met and talked to one or two people that he knew. All were now resolute to get out of the city. It seemed to Corbett that the ambulance crews alone of all the services were now working for the city as a whole. Everyone seemed to be concentrating on his individual needs, to the exclusion of his public duty. 'I've been with the Fire Service these last two nights,' one man told him, tired and worn. 'We haven't half had some work to do. But they'll have to get along without me, from now on. I'm taking the wife to Romsey.'

When he got back to his house, Littlejohn was there, his car drawn up outside his door. He was bare-headed but for the white bandage that Joan had put on; his clothes were dirty and there were streaks of blood on his grey face.

He said: 'There's no cordon on the roads now, Mr Corbett. You can get through to Hamble.' He hesitated, and then said: 'You want to get there quick, while the going's good.'

Corbett asked: 'When did they take the cordon off?'

'Last night. When I said I heard that shooting.'

'Was that there?'

The builder nodded. 'I said they'd have trouble at them barriers, didn't I? Never heard of such a daft thing to do.'

Corbett was appalled. 'You mean, the troops fired on the crowd?'

The builder shook his head. 'From what I could make out, the crowd fired on the troops. Then they gave way, and let them through.'

They stood in silence for a minute. 'It's just another thing,' said the builder. 'You don't want to think too much of it.'

He glanced up at the house. 'I took a run out there this morning, just to see,' he said. 'I got something I been meaning to give you, but I didn't want to in front of Mrs Corbett.' He fumbled in the pocket of his raincoat and pulled out a very large, black automatic pistol, with four clips of cartridges. 'There.'

Corbett took it from him and examined it diffidently. 'It's awfully kind of you. Don't you want it for yourself?'

The builder shook his head. 'I shan't want nothing of that. But when I saw it I thought – well, you never know. Times is different now to what they was a week ago, and you've got your family to think of. I brought it home for you.'

'Where did you get it?'

The builder said evasively: 'I found it. I've been looking around for a bit of stuff to give it a pull through – you can see, the barrel's dirty.' He took it from Corbett, pulled the block, and squinted down it. 'See? It was fired last night. But you don't want to worry about that. Just get a bit of stuff and give it a pull through.' He gave it back to the solicitor.

Corbett persuaded him to come in and have breakfast before Joan came down with the children. They cooked a meal of bacon and fried bread and coffee over the Primus stove. The builder said very little till the meal was over.

Then he said: 'You want to hurry up and get away, Mr Corbett.'

The solicitor nodded. 'I'm going this morning.' He paused, and then asked gently: 'What will you do?'

'I got to . . . make arrangements for her.' There was a short pause. 'And after that I'm going back into the Army. I'm not that old, and I was a company sergeant-major in the Machine-Gun Corps last time. They got new guns now, I hear, but I could soon learn them.' He paused. 'I figured it out when I was sitting up there with her last night, and the bombs going and all. And I thought she'd want me to go back into the Army, like I was before we met.' He was silent for a moment.

'So I'll be all fixed up, Mr Corbett. But you want to think of your family, and get them away out of this.'

Joan appeared then, with the children. Littlejohn went away and Corbett, cooking a second breakfast for his family, discussed the position with Joan. 'I'll take the silver and your jewel-box down to the bank first of all,' he said, 'and get them to store that for us. Then I'll come back with the car, and we'll get off to Hamble as soon as we can. You'd better get your packing done while I'm away.'

She nodded. 'But we must have some more milk to take with us. I've only got two tins left. See if you can get any in the town. And we'll want some meat.'

He laughed. 'What about a bottle of fizzy lemonade?'

She laid the dish down, and laughed with him. 'I can't believe it. Like a sort of picnic!' She went on laughing, and he laid his hand upon her arm.

'Stop that,' he said.

She pulled herself together. 'I'm sorry, Peter.'

He smiled. 'Would you like to see what Littlejohn gave me this morning?'

'What was that?'

He pulled the automatic from his pocket and showed it to her; the light shone on the blued steel. She turned it over curiously. 'Is it loaded?'

'No. I do know that much about it.'

She glanced at him, smiling. 'Peter, do you know how it works?'

'I'm not quite sure,' he admitted. 'I've seen Humphrey Bogart with one often enough....' They examined it together. 'I believe the empty cartridges come popping out of here.'

He paused. 'He was so – so genuine. I couldn't possibly refuse to have it. What shall we do with it?'

'Keep it,' she said. 'I like to know it's there.'

He washed and shaved, packed the silver and Joan's jewellery in a wooden box, locked it, carried it out to the car, and drove down to the bank. In the city he noticed listlessness for the first time. The new damage was extensive, but the repair squads were few in number, and weakly manned. They were mostly soldiers of the Royal Engineers; civilian labourers were in the minority. He saw a good many shops damaged and open to the street, with nobody to guard the goods.

He found the bank manager exactly in his normal guise, spotlessly dressed, pink-cheeked, and with a flower in his button-hole. 'Just room for one more in the strong room,' he said pleasantly. 'Of course, you understand that we take no responsibility for risks directly or indirectly attributable to the war. You see, that is quite clear on this form of receipt. Would you mind signing here?'

Corbett signed. 'What's my balance today?' he asked.

A clerk looked up the figure. 'A hundred and nine pounds, fifteen shillings and fourpence, Mr Corbett.'

He nodded. 'I'll take the hundred and nine pounds in notes. As many ones as you can give me.'

He pocketed the money, and then turned to consider his stocks. He had a few small English securities, and about fifteen hundred pounds in the Canadian Pacific Railway. He sorted out the share certificates of that, put them in a separate envelope, and took them away with him.

In the street near the bank there was a lorry selling milk, without bottles or cartons. He went into an ironmonger's shop and bought an enamel hot-water jug holding about a gallon, had it filled, and took it to the car. His search for food was not very productive, but he got a piece of bacon about seven pounds in weight, a few more tins, some baking-powder, and some more flour. Bread seemed to be unobtainable.

'The men won't work,' they told him at one baker's shop, a little ruefully. 'All they think about is getting out into the country with their families.'

Corbett laughed. 'You surprise me.'

The girl was nettled. 'Well, I mean to say, somebody's got to make the bread, haven't they?'

He did not attempt to answer that.

He went to his office, and let himself in with his key. The building was still intact, though every window had been smashed; papers and carpets in the rooms were wet and sodden. A few, a very few, letters had been thrust in at the letter-box; he could not wait to attend to them, and laid them unopened on a table. There was no sign that anybody else had been there since he had left. He tried the telephone; it was dead. He locked the office door and went away.

He drove back to the house. Joan had packed two suit-cases and put them in the hall; Corbett went up to his room and packed a few clothes for himself. Then they took the luggage out to the car with all the food that they had in the house, and a large quantity of blankets and pillows.

Mr Littlejohn arrived in his car and drew Corbett on one side. 'I got seven cans of petrol,' he said quietly. 'Fourteen gallons. You want to take them with you – I got them for you. But put them somewhere where they won't be seen. Petrol's not to be had for love or money in the town today, and if some of the rough chaps saw you with all that . . . well, they might make trouble, and you don't want that. But you'll need petrol.'

'That's terribly good of you. How did you get hold of them?'

'Never you mind where they come from, Mr Corbett. Same place as the pistol. You got that all right?'

Corbett nodded.

'Better keep that with you, Mr Corbett. Not that you'll ever need it, or anything of that. But there's a lot of the rough lads out and about what don't care nothing for nobody, if you take my meaning. But they'd keep right away from anyone they knew carried a gun. See?'

Corbett said: 'What about you, Littlejohn? Can we help at all?' He glanced towards the house.

The builder shook his head. 'I got the undertaker coming this morning,' he said. 'Don't seem like it was her at all, somehow. . . . And her sister Aggie, from Millbrook, she said she'd look round.' He shook his head. 'You can't do nothing, Mr Corbett, thanking you all the same. You want to get away. Soon as I've seen her put away I'll be going down to join up.'

Corbett went back into the house. Joan had packed the children's clothes; he carried them out to the car, now stuffed as full as a removal van. Then he went back into the house.

'How much can the children take in the way of toys, Peter?' she asked.

He hesitated. 'Nothing very big.'

They went up with the children to the nursery. He asked Phyllis: 'Which of the dollies are you taking on the boat with you?'

'Mary and Teddy. And we'll take the dolls' house, Daddy?'

'Not the dolls' house. Big girls don't take dolls' houses on boats with them. Take Mary and Teddy.'

'May I take my engine, Daddy?'

'Yes, you can take that.'

'And my tricycle?'

Joan said: 'We'll come back and get the tricycle another day. That's enough toys for you. Now a few books.'

They took *Peter Rabbit*, and *Jemima Puddle-Duck*, and *When Jesus Was a Little Boy*, and *Nicodemus and his Gran'-pappy*, and, by special request, *Ameliaranne at the Circus*. And they took a disreputable wooden horse for John, and the wooden bricks with letters on them, and a vehicle consisting of a pair of wheels and a bell that tinkled when you pulled it along. They took a couple of woolly animals for the baby. And they took the hot-water bottles, the one that looked like a rabbit for Phyllis and the one that looked like Donald Duck for John.

Then they went downstairs.

They took the children and the baby out to the car, left them there, and went back into the house for a last look round. 'It's hateful to be leaving it,' said Joan, a little sadly. 'We've had a good time here.'

She went into the drawing-room, cavernous and dark behind the boarded windows, and picked up a little ebony elephant from the dusty, littered mantelpiece.

'I want to take this with me, for remembering,' she said.

Corbett laid his hand upon her arm. 'Don't worry,' he said gently. 'It's rotten having to leave home like this. But we'll be back before long.'

She gazed around the room and shook her head. 'I'm not so sure of that,' she said quietly. 'I think we're going for good. I don't think we shall ever come back here again.'

4

THE VILLAGE of Hamble lies upon the Hamble River, a tidal tributary of Southampton Water, about six miles as the crow flies from Southampton. In the last century Hamble was a fishing village; by 1914 it had become a prosperous centre for the building, fitting out, and laying up of yachts. In later years an aerodrome, a seaplane station, and three small aircraft factories came into being near the village, while the yachting industry increased enormously. In consequence the village spread out in a rash of villas, clubs, and week-end cottages.

Peter Corbett kept his yacht, the *Sonia*, at Hamble. She was not the sort of yacht worn with white duck trousers. She was nearly forty years old, a gaff-rigged cutter with a straight stem and a long old-fashioned bowsprit, based upon the style of the fishing-smacks belonging to the east coast village where she had been built. Her hull was low in the water and painted a dull black, her sails were tanned, her decks painted with buff paint which made them tolerably water-tight when the paint was new and unbroken in the spring.

He used her in the summer for week-ends in the Solent, and for an annual short summer cruise westwards down the coast. Joan and Peter sailed her normally alone, sometimes with a friend or two. On very fine, hot, calm week-ends they would take the children on board and drive her to Seaview for a bathe, under the power of her ancient engine, noisy and difficult to start, converted from a Model T Ford of a bygone age. She was an aged, dirty little boat, not very sound, but Joan and Peter thought the world of her. She was their hobby and their holiday, deep-laden with sweet memories of escape from their routine.

As a permanent residence for two adults, two children,

and an infant, her accommodation was not impressive. From the bows, she had a forecastle where a water-closet stood starkly between the chain locker and the cooking galley. The galley was served by two Primus stoves, one of which carried a rusty tin cooking oven. A water-tank of about fifteen gallons' capacity was clamped to a bulkhead; a little crockery was stored with the frying-pans and saucepans in a cupboard. Aft of the forecastle the saloon was furnished with a settee berth on either side and a swinging table in the middle, with one or two small lockers beside the settees. A paraffin lamp in gimbals swung from the bulkhead. Aft again, one passed up on deck into the cockpit by means of a couple of steps forming the fore end of the engine-cover, removable to permit the flywheel to be cranked, knuckles to be damaged, or, occasionally, arms to be broken. On either side of this contraption were the head ends of two very narrow berths, the feet of which extended aft under the cockpit seats. In summer-time these berths were filled with odd lengths of old rope, sails, damp towels and bathing-dresses, solitary canvas shoes bereft of their laces, mildewing straw sun-hats.

Corbett had paid two hundred pounds for her six years before. It was a lasting wonder to him that two hundred pounds could have bought so much happiness.

For the winter he had laid her up in a mud berth in the salt marshes of the estuary, where he could come and potter about on her in the short daylight hours of Sunday afternoon, and where an aged fisherman kept an eye on her in stormy weather. He had stored her sails and gear with a local yard; her mast and standing rigging he had left in place. Her dinghy was stored in the yard. At high tide he could get at her with a boat, but at low water the depth of mud made access to her difficult, if not impossible.

As he drove his overloaded car through the streets of the malodorous, stricken city that morning in March, Corbett was not depressed. It takes a very little thing to lift the spirits of a man. He was leaving his home for an indefinite time, leaving his house, his business and his office ruined and abandoned, flying with his family from death by high explosive or disease, journeying towards a future all un-known. And yet, his heart was light. Routine was broken; there would be no more drafting of conveyances for a time, anyway. The sun was shining after the rain of the night. He had a hundred pounds in his pocket. And, above all, he was going to his boat.

He began to hum a little tune as he drove the heavy car. Joan looked up at him in surprise, troubled and still cling-ing to her elephant. Then she smiled a little, and relaxed. If he was happy, things would be all right.

She touched him on the arm. 'We'd better have some sweets for the children. If you see a shop open, let's stop and get something.'

He nodded, shifting in his seat; the automatic in his coat pocket was hard to sit upon. 'All right. We'll make a picnic of it.'

She laughed. 'I must say, it's a relief to get away. I was getting to hate it – and that awful trench, every night. It'll be fun, being on the boat.'

He nodded. 'We ought to have come before.'

He turned off the main road down a lane towards Hamble village. The lane was choked with Royal Air Force lorries; driving behind one and meeting many others they made slow progress. As they approached the aerodrome they saw that there was much activity. The road ran along one boun-dary for a short distance; Corbett ran the car off the road on to the grass verge and stopped to watch.

He knew that the aerodrome was the home of a training school of some sort. He did not take much interest in aero-planes, but the score of small machines with yellow wings which infested the air round Hamble made the function of this place unmistakable. But now the aerodrome seemed to have been turned into a base for a fighter squadron, or several squadrons. Nearby a breach had been made in the hedge that separated the aerodrome from the road, and through this breach the lorries ground and swung, to lurch across the grass to where a city of tents was growing up in an adjacent field. Along the hedge the low-wing monoplanes were parked, grey-green in colour, single-seaters with retractable undercarriages and cellon hoods over the cockpits. There were a great many of them. From where he sat Corbett counted over fifty picketed down along the edges of the aerodrome; there were several in the air. In the adjacent field, and round the aeroplanes, men were swarming in an orderly bustle of improvisation. Engines were running up; a singing grind came from a workshop lorry. An empty petrol-tank lorry came lurching out of the aerodrome and joined the traffic of the lane.

Joan touched him on the arm. 'Let's get along,' she said. 'You can come back and look at this afterwards.'

Corbett nodded and moved the car back into the traffic stream. He drove round the aerodrome and down the hill through the village to the water's edge, parking the car above high-water mark. The tide was nearly full.

He got out of the car and looked about. 'I'll go and see if I can find a dinghy,' he said. 'If not, I'll have to get our own out of the yard.'

Joan nodded. 'I'll stay here and give Baby her bottle.'

'All right.'

Phyllis said: 'May I go with Daddy?'

John said: 'May I go with Daddy, Mummy?'

Corbett said: 'You can come, Phyllis. You'd better stay with Mummy, John. You can come when you're a big man.'

'May I take Teddy with me, Daddy?' asked Phyllis.

'Yes, you can bring Teddy.'

John said: 'May I give Baby her bottle?'

Corbett left Joan to deal with that, and taking his daughter by the hand, went off to the yard.

He found a good deal of activity. Practically all the boats laid up in the yard seemed to be being lived in; evidently the owners of boats had come to the conclusion that their boats were safer residences than their houses in the towns. There was much coming and going by well-dressed, well-educated people in the yard. But there were no dinghies to spare. After a good deal of delay Corbett located his at the back of a far shed; he got a young man in a pullover and plus-fours to help him get it down to the water.

'Lammermoor's the name,' said the young man. 'My dad, he's the Lammermoor of Pearson and Lammermoor, in Commercial Road, Portsmouth. Drapery, toys, and all sorts. Maybe you know it?'

Corbett nodded. 'I've passed it. How are things in Portsmouth?'

'It's been terrible. They say that London's had it bad, and Bristol, but they couldn't possibly have had it worse than we did. Bombs every night, hours on end.' The young man's lips twitched like a rabbit. 'Dad, he stayed on to see the business right, and he made me bring Mummer and Sissie and Ted here. We've got a motor-cruiser just up there, the *Happy Days*. Come up and have a cup o' tea if you have a minute.'

Phyllis, clutching her teddy-bear, stared at him wide-eyed. Corbett excused himself, took the dinghy, and rowed round to the hard where Joan was waiting in the car.

She got out and came to meet him, the baby in her arms. 'You'd better put me on board with the children first,' she said. 'We'll take this basket and the paraffin, and then I can get the children something to eat. Is there any water on board, do you think?'

He nodded. 'About half a tank. But it's been there since last summer.'

She forced a laugh. 'I'll have to boil that before we give it to the children.'

He smiled. 'You'd better boil it before you give it to me – let alone the children. But don't waste any of it, not until I can find out how water is round here.'

He helped Joan and the two children into the dinghy and pushed off. The mud berth where his vessel lay was half a mile down river. He rowed down to her and drew the dinghy up by her counter, and held the boat while Joan got on board with the baby; then he passed the other children up to her. She unlocked the cabin hatch and went below. Corbett rowed back upstream to his car.

He made the seven cans of petrol the foundation of his next load; he was sensitive about them and glad to get them on board out of sight. Two more trips emptied the car; after the last load he climbed on board himself and surveyed the mass of gear accumulated in the cockpit.

'Better get some of this stuff stowed away,' he said to Joan.

She looked up at him appealingly from the cabin, feeding the children with milk and bread and jam, tired and hot. The baby was yelling furiously on the bare foundation of a settee bunk.

'Get the mattresses next, if you can,' she said. 'Then we can get the children into bed and turn around a bit ourselves.'

He nodded, glancing at the sky. It was not going to rain; there was no harm in leaving the stuff out on deck. He rowed back up the river to the hard, went to the store, and carried down the mattresses one by one to the dinghy.

He took them back to the yacht, passed them below to Joan, and helped her to lay them down. He was tired then; while she began putting the children to bed in their novel surroundings he sat down on the heap of dunnage in the cockpit and lit a cigarette. But she would not let him finish it.

'There's very little water in the tank,' she said. 'You wouldn't like to go on shore and get some more?'

'I'd hate it,' he said. He got up wearily, fetched the canvas water-bag from the sail-locker, and, in the falling dusk, rowed to the hard again. He landed, pulled the dinghy up a little, and walked with his water-bag towards the houses. Suddenly he brightened. It was after six o'clock, and the pubs were open. Light streamed from the wide-open door of the 'Hamble Arms'; he heard a buzz of conversation and the clinking of tankards.

He made his way into the saloon bar. The room was thronged with people from the yachts, all listening to the news broadcast from a wireless set. He stood there a time quietly in a corner and listened with them; in a quarter of an hour he learned a great deal about the progress of the war. Queerly enough, it did not seem to touch him personally; it was as if he had been reading of the war in Spain. It was a restricted and censored broadcast. A few sporadic air-raids on a few towns in the country were admitted, but no details were given and the topic was passed over quickly. A full account was given of the raids carried out by our own Air Force 'as measures of reprisal'. There was no mention of any action by the Army or the Navy, though the broadcast ended with a stirring call to enlistment in all Services.

The news ended, the set was switched off to conserve the batteries, and a subdued hum of conversation broke out in the crowded room. The reception of the news was mixed. There was little enthusiasm, no keen discussion of the war. Most of the men in the saloon seemed to be of military age, some of them with their wives, many of them evidently in good circumstances. To Corbett, there seemed to be an atmosphere of uncertainty, of bewilderment, among them. They were all men of the officer type, who might have been expected to be serving in a war that was now nearly a week old. It appeared to Corbett that they were all in the same boat as he was himself. They were delaying and procrastinating, waiting to see their families established in safety before they went to serve. And each of them, secretly and individually, was unhappy and ashamed of the line that he was taking.

They did not stay and gossip much. The news broadcast ended, they finished their drinks and went quietly back on to their boats.

Corbett ordered a pint of ale. The barman recognized him and wished him good evening. 'Come down to stay on your yacht, Mr Corbett?'

'That's right.'

'Mrs Corbett with you?'

He nodded. 'She's on board with the children.'

The barman nodded. 'Most people seem to have come to their boats,' he said. 'Boats, cottages, or tents. Cold comfort in a tent this weather, if you ask me. But there's a regular camp by the old reservoir. People living in their cars, and all sorts.' He laughed shortly.

Corbett said: 'I want some water. Can I fill a water-bag?'

'Surely, Mr Corbett. You know where the tap is – out in the yard. It's running all right now.'

Corbett looked up, startled. 'Have you had a water shortage here?'

The man nodded carelessly. 'Thursday, it was off. Or was it Wednesday? One or other of them. After one of them raids you had in Southampton. One of the mains was bust, but they seem to have got it mended now.'

'Do you get your water from Southampton, then?'

'Oh, aye. All our water comes from Southampton, saving one or two of the cottages that have wells. That's why the people went up to the old reservoir to camp, because the water was off. Still, can't say I'd like to drink that water from the reservoir myself, nor out of them old wells either. Rather drink beer.' He laughed comfortably.

'Have a pint with me.'

'Thank you, sir. I don't mind if I do.'

A man standing near the bar and listening to the conversation, said: 'Most country districts get their water from the towns, these days.' He paused. 'When they're near enough, I mean to say.'

'I suppose they do,' said Corbett.

He stood thoughtfully for a few minutes, drinking his beer. Presently he said to the barman: 'I shall want some milk in the morning. Where had I better go for that?'

The other man laughed. The barman said: 'I really couldn't tell you, Mr Corbett. Everybody's after milk.'

'You won't get any milk in Hamble,' said the other man. 'Better stick to beer.'

'I can't give the baby beer. Isn't there any milk at all?'

The barman shook his head. 'There was a cart come in the day before yesterday. Regular scramble for it, there was. I don't know where you'd go for milk, Mr Corbett – really and truly I don't. You might try one of the farms on the Warsash side, over Titchfield way.'

The other nodded. 'That's your best chance to get milk, if you've got young children. It's no good going to the farms between here and Southampton. There's a milk queue half a mile long at each one of them.'

Corbett finished his beer, stood up, and stretched. His fatigue had left him. 'I'll get the water, anyway,' he said, 'while the going's good.'

He went out into the yard, filled his water-bag, and carried it with difficulty and with many pauses down to the dinghy. The tide had fallen quickly while he had been on shore. He dragged the boat down till she floated and rowed back to his yacht. The dinghy grounded on the mud fifty yards from the vessel.

Joan was sitting in the hatchway, smoking a cigarette and watching him. 'I say,' he said, 'I'm stuck. What do we do now?'

'Get out and walk,' she said.

'I can't. I'd go in up to the waist.'

'Well, you'll just have to sit there, then. Why did you stay so long on shore?'

'I was drinking in the pub.'

'Pig,' she said, without animosity. 'Did you get any water?'

'I got that. What about the children?'

'They're in bed and asleep. You'd better go back on shore and get yourself something to eat there.'

'Are you all right? If you chuck me my gum-boots I'll have a crack at getting on board.'

'I couldn't chuck them that far.' She blew a long cloud of smoke. 'Don't worry – there's nothing for you to do here. I'll make myself some cocoa and go to bed. You go on shore, and come back when the tide comes in. When will that be?'

He thought for a minute. 'I should be able to get on board about eleven.'

She nodded. 'I shall be asleep. Don't make a row when you come back.'

He pushed the dinghy off the mud and rowed towards the hard. On the way she hailed him.

'Oh, Peter. Get some more cigarettes, if you can!'

He went back to the inn and had a cold meal in the snack bar. There was evidently a food scarcity, but he got a small plate of cold beef and some bread and cheese after a time. There were several others in the snack bar, like him, dining on shore. There was no conversation; everybody seemed to be uneasy and depressed. As he finished his meal it began to rain.

He paid his bill and went to the door of the inn. The night was wet and windy, but the rain was light. As he stood there looking out, an aeroplane roared overhead in the pitch darkness, then another, and a third. The barman collecting dirty glasses in the saloon, came to the door and stood beside him, looking up into the dark night.

'Going off again,' he said. 'They get the hell of a time, them chaps.'

'Are they from the aerodrome here?' asked Corbett.

The man nodded. 'Every night they goes up, just the same, wet or fine. Mostly wet. And they don't do no bloody good, either.'

'They don't seem to be able to get at the bombers.'

The man shook his head. 'You should hear them talk. . . . Proper fed up with themselves, they are.'

'Do they get any accidents?'

'Plenty, nights like this. There was one fine, starry night – Wednesday, was it? They didn't have none at all that night. But wet, dark nights like this, in them fast single-seaters – they goes piling 'em up right and left. 'Tisn't reasonable to expect otherwise.'

'When do they come back to land?'

'They'll be at it all night, in shifts, like. Up and down, all night long. You want to go up there and see. It's quite a sight.'

He went back to the bar. Overhead the aircraft roared up into the darkness at half-minute intervals, interminably. Corbett stood for a time in the doorway finishing his cigarette, then buttoned his coat round him and walked up towards the aerodrome.

The entrances were unguarded. He had no difficulty in walking up between the buildings to the edge of the flying field. The place was thronged with men, lorries, and cars, moving and crowding in an orderly, disciplined confusion, each intent on his own job. The lights shone shimmering on wet raincoats and on dripping lorry tarpaulins; beneath each tail-board the exhaust roared out in a great cloud of steam in the wet night. Corbett made his way forward to the edge of the tarmac, near the control, and stood for a time in a sheltering doorway to see what was happening.

The flare-path was laid out into the wind. Five open buckets filled with blazing rags and paraffin stretched in a line down the grass, with one placed transversely at the windward end. The machines, greenish-black in the yellow, flaring light, were taxi-ing one by one to the far end for the take off, as each was ready a light flashed at the control. The pilot opened his throttle with a high-pitched scream from engine, supercharger, and propeller, accelerated down the line of flames, slowly at first and then more quickly, rolled into the air, retracted his undercarriage at once, and vanished into the dark rainy night, over the trees. Then the next was ready.

A squadron of eleven machines went off as Corbett watched; there was a pause after that. It seemed that no more was to happen for a little time. The crowd of officers round the control thinned out; one or two of them walked away past Corbett.

He saw a well-known face half-buried in a turned-up raincoat collar, beneath a forage cap. He swung round and called impulsively after the retreating figure: 'Collins!'

The man came back and peered at him; on his shoulders he wore the stripes of a flight-lieutenant. 'Who's that?'

'It's Peter Corbett.'

'Corbett? What on earth are you doing here?'

'Looking around. I'm living on my boat in the river.'

'Good stuff. I thought about you, in Southampton. I hoped you'd had the sense to get out of it. Is Joan with you?'

'She's on board, with the kids.'

'Fine. I say, I'd like to come down tomorrow, if I may. Where's the boat lying?'

Corbett told him. 'Come and have lunch,' he said. 'God knows what you'll get to eat, but come along.'

The other laughed. 'I'm not going to eat your food. I'll drop in some time in the morning. Look – I must get along, but that's a date. I'm terribly sorry that I can't stop now, but I'm on duty in a few minutes.'

'That's all right. Are you flying tonight?'

The other nodded. 'There's a squadron coming in pretty soon. I'm taking one of those machines as soon as it's re-fuelled.' He laughed shortly. 'We've got more pilots than machines these days. Playing Box and Cox. I tell you, Corbett, it's a ruddy picnic, this.'

He turned away. 'Tomorrow morning, then.'

He vanished into the darkness. Corbett stayed for an hour longer. The squadron landed in the wind and rain, coming in one by one out of the darkness into the flickering light of the flares, to touch down gently on the grass, run along, then swing round and taxi in towards the hangars. The fifth machine to land overshot, landed nearly at the far end of the flare-path, and ran forwards into the hedge, coming to rest abruptly with a cracking noise. An ambulance and a fire-car ran quickly over the grass towards it, but there did not seem to be a need for either.

The machines were refuelled and ammunition checked in about half an hour, the pilots standing round them, clumsy in their flying kit and parachutes. Another squadron landed without incident; then the machines of the first squadron were ready to take off. Corbett tried to identify Collins in his flying suit and helmet, but could not pick him out. One by one the machines taxied to the end of the flare-path, took off uneventfully, and were lost to sight in the dark racing clouds.

There was another pause. Corbett left the aerodrome and walked back towards the river.

He launched the dinghy. The tide was on the flood and

he had no difficulty in getting back on board. There was a light in the saloon; Joan was reading in bed. He made the dinghy fast and went below.

'I must say, you're a nice one,' she said. 'I believe you did it on purpose, so that you could get a decent meal at the pub.'

He smiled, taking off his sodden coat. 'I didn't have a decent meal – or not very. I could eat another now.'

'There's some cocoa in the saucepan if you like to hot it up.'

He told her, as he heated the cocoa, the substance of what he had learned while he was on shore. Over some of it she wrinkled her brows.

'It's not so good about the milk, Peter,' she said. 'We've not got very many tins, and they get through an awful lot. I did think that we'd be able to get milk here, out in the country.'

He nodded. 'So did I. I suppose we can't sort of wean them – give them soup and stuff instead?'

'We might with John and Phyllis. But the baby must have milk.'

He bent and kissed her. 'Don't worry about it tonight. We'll get some milk, somehow.'

He eyed her for a minute. 'Have you had the hell of a time with them?'

She shook her head. 'Baby was troublesome, but the other two were good as gold. They're simply loving every minute of it.'

'Next thing, they'll be falling overboard into the mud.'

'I know. I thought John was over once or twice this afternoon. I'd hate to have to go over and fish him out. Peter, couldn't you rig a sort of life-line round the bulwarks for them?'

He nodded. 'I'll fix up something in the morning.'

He undressed and got into the blankets on the other berth. He stretched his head upon the pillow and relaxed. 'It's better to be here than in the house,' he said. 'At least we won't have to get up and go out to the trench.' He rolled over and looked at her. 'You'd rather be here, wouldn't you?'

She nodded. 'I believe something terrible might have happened if we'd stayed at home,' she said soberly. 'I'm glad we came away.'

'So am I.' He reached up and put out the lamp. 'Goodnight, Joan.'

'Goodnight, Peter dear.'

Silence closed down upon the little yacht. The rising tide made lapping noises on the hull; as it came up the vessel stirred in the mud. The two children slept quietly, the baby made snuffling noises in her sleep, like a puppy. The wind sighed through the bare rigging of the mast; away in the distance was the sound of aeroplanes. Corbett lay listening to these little noises for a time, tired and content. It was better to be here. Here he felt master of his fate, able to sway their destiny by his own work and his own efforts. At home he had felt powerless, a pawn.

He must rig that life-line for the children in the morning. His big job tomorrow would be to get milk.

He slept.

In the middle of the night he woke up suddenly. Joan was standing by his side in her pyjamas, shaking him by the shoulder. 'Peter,' she said. 'Peter, wake up!'

He sat up suddenly. 'What is it?'

'It's another raid. Listen.'

They were silent. In the distance he heard the sharp crack of gun-fire. Then there was a heavy concussion, and another, and a third. 'That's right,' he said soberly. 'They're at it again.'

They went together to the hatch, slid it back quietly for fear of waking the children, and stood with their heads out on deck, listening. Intermittently they heard the concussions in the city; occasionally an aeroplane passed over their heads, landing upon the aerodrome. The rain had stopped, but it was still heavily overcast.

'We can't do anything about it,' Corbett said at last. 'Better get back to bed before you catch a cold.'

Joan did not stir. 'It's terrible,' she said. 'I believe one feels worse about it listening to it from outside than when you're right in it. Peter, I do hope Mr Littlejohn's all right.'

He put his arm around her shoulders. 'I expect he is. He knows how to look after himself.' He thought of Gordon operating in the hospital, of his wife nursing cholera, of all the people in the city who were still carrying on with the essential jobs, and he was bitter with himself that he was out of it.

The girl stirred beside him. 'Don't think me awfully soppy, Peter,' she said tremulously, 'but I'm going to say my prayers.'

He nodded. 'That's not a bad idea. I believe I'll say mine.'

They turned back into the dark, narrow little cabin and knelt for a time against their settee-beds, repeating to themselves what they could remember of the prayers they had learned as children. Then they got back to bed and lay for a long time listening to the aeroplanes and the concussions, till presently they fell asleep.

Dawn came next morning, sunny and bright after the rain. Corbett got up at about seven o'clock and put the kettle on. Then for a couple of hours there was the turmoil of getting the children up, washing, shaving, changing the baby, getting the breakfast, getting the baby's breakfast, eating breakfast, washing up breakfast, till at the end Joan and Peter, exhausted, had time to sit down for a cigarette.

Corbett blew a long cloud of smoke. 'This is a bit too much like work,' he said.

Joan laughed shortly. 'You're telling *me*!'

He eyed her sympathetically. 'If you like to go off and look for milk, I'll stay on board this morning and look after the kids. I had a walk yesterday.'

She brightened. 'I'd love a run on shore. It's too bad we can't go together.'

'Never mind. Besides, I'd just as soon stay here this morning. I've got a lot to do on board, and Collins may be coming off.'

He helped her with the dinghy, and watched her as she

rowed on shore. She landed, pulled up the dinghy on the hard a little way, and tied it to a post. Then she took her shopping basket and went up into the village.

It did not take her very long to confirm that there was no milk to be had. At the general shop where she had bought milk before she asked what had happened to all the milk.

'I don't know, I'm sure,' said the woman. 'The car hasn't brought it from the depot, not for three days. But Mr Child, what drives the car, he lives in Woolston, in Southampton. Maybe he's gone away with his family, evacuating like. Anyway, there's no milk.'

Joan bought one or two other stores and came away. It was no good trying the farms on the Southampton side of the river for milk; she took the dinghy and rowed across the Hamble, and landed on the Warsash side.

She spent all morning wandering from farm to farm. She was not alone in her quest. Other people from the swollen population of the village had been before her. Most of the farms were genuinely sold out of milk. She felt convinced that others had milk, but they would not sell it to her. At last, tired and depressed, she got a pint in an old lime-juice bottle.

'It won't go far,' she thought ruefully. 'Still, it's better than nothing.' She began to revolve schemes in her mind for getting the two older children off milk altogether, in order that the baby might have what there was.

On her way back towards the dinghy she passed a village general shop at a cross roads, and went in and inquired for milk.

The slatternly woman who came to the counter said: 'We haven't got no milk. Got plenty of tinned salmon.'

Joan shook her head. 'I don't want that.' She looked around the shelves a little absently. Her eye was caught by an open packing-case standing behind the counter in a corner, half-full of familiar grey paper-covered tins. 'Look,' she said. 'That's milk down there, isn't it?'

The woman moved in front of the case. 'We haven't got no milk to sell,' she said obstinately.

'But that's milk down there.'

The woman repeated: 'We haven't got no milk to sell. The shop ain't open, really, only to oblige.'

Joan said: 'Look here, I've got a little baby. My other two children can get on without milk, but I must have milk for the baby. Let me have a few tins.'

The woman tightened her lips. Then she called: 'Joe!' and a man came from the inner room.

'Tell the lady we ain't got no milk to sell, Joe,' she commanded.

The man said: 'Sorry, lady, but the shop ain't open. The girl must have left the door on the latch. We ain't open today.' He pushed her towards the door.

In the doorway Joan turned on them. 'All right,' she said, 'I'll go away. But I know this – you've got all the milk in the world there, in that case. And I hope it bally well chokes you.' She walked away, half in tears.

On the yacht, Corbett put in a domestic morning. He rigged a warp twice round the vessel to keep the children from falling overboard, stopping it to the rigging, forestays, and backstays. He cleaned and filled the lamps and Primus stoves. He made the beds, and kept the children playing with their toys between his feet upon the narrow, cluttered floor of the saloon.

In the middle of the morning a small motor-launch came alongside, flying the flag of the Royal Air Force. It was Collins. He came on board; the launch backed away and went off upstream.

'It's good seeing you again,' said Corbett. 'Come on down and have a whisky. I haven't got any soda, I'm afraid.'

They went below, stepping over the children. 'These your kids?' asked Collins.

'That's right,' said Corbett. 'There's another in the fore-castle, asleep.'

'Over the lavvy,' explained Phyllis.

For a few moments Corbett showed his guest the layout of the ship. Phyllis stood erect and looked at the newcomer. 'This is Teddy,' she said helpfully.

John said: 'This is Horsey, but his tail came off.'

'All right,' said Corbett. 'Go on playing with them on the floor.' Pouring out the whisky, he turned to his friend. 'Joan's on shore, looking for milk – she'll be back before long. Is Felicity down here with you?'

The flight-lieutenant shook his head. 'I left her up at Abingdon – we've got a house there. We came down here in such a hurry, too.'

'You've been here long?'

'We came down here after the first raid, the day war was declared. Tuesday, was it? I forget.'

He raised his glass. 'Here's luck.'

Corbett nodded, and drank. 'We could do with a bit of that.'

Collins said: 'By God, you're right.'

He glanced at Corbett. 'You didn't come to any harm in Southampton? I see you didn't. I went in there yesterday. It's in a terrible mess.'

Corbett nodded. 'We stuck it out till yesterday. I had a trench in the back garden. But then – well, we came here.'

He turned to the officer. 'How long is this going on for?'

'God knows. For ever, as far as I can see. Or until we can somehow get and bomb their aerodromes. The barrage is no bloody good when we don't know the height. You know how they're doing it?'

Corbett shook his head. 'I'd like to know.'

'They're getting a star fix, and bombing through the clouds.'

There was a momentary silence in the yacht.

Corbett said: 'You mean, they're taking sextant observations of the stars and fixing their position above the clouds?'

'That's right. They've got a sextant – boy, what a sextant! But they're wizard instrument makers, of course. This one that I saw came out of one of their bombers that crashed at Sevenoaks.' He laughed, a little cynically. 'Oh, we didn't shoot it down, or anything like that. It collided with one of our own fighters in the middle of a cloud, and they both crashed.'

He said soberly: 'That sextant's going to win the war for them, if we don't look out.'

'How do you mean?'

The flight-lieutenant blew a long cloud of smoke. 'This way. I don't know if you know – with a marine sextant, bringing the sun down to a good horizon, you can fix your position within half a mile or so – less, perhaps. In the air, you haven't got a horizon level with you, so you use a bubble sextant. You bring the sun or star down on to a sort of spirit-level bubble.'

Corbett nodded. 'I know that.'

'Well, that's not so accurate. We use them in the Service, of course, but if you get within four or five miles of the true position it's all you can do. You've got to hold the bubble in your hands, you see, and you can't hold it still enough. You can't get greater accuracy than that. But that's good enough for ordinary navigating by.'

'I understand that. What's their sextant like?'

'It's like a dumb-bell. You hold it vertically in both hands. The top knob is the sextant – fairly normal, just a very good averaging bubble sextant. The middle, the part that you hold, is a sort of composite rubber vibration damper. And the bottom knob has two little electrically driven gyroscopes tucked away in it, simply to help you hold the sextant still. Our people tried it out in the air. You can get your position within half a mile, every time.'

Corbett said: 'I see what you mean. Southampton's about four miles long and three miles wide – roughly. With the old type sextant they couldn't fix their position accurately enough to bomb through the clouds and be sure of hitting the town. Now they can.'

'That's right.'

There was a silence, broken only by the subdued chatter of the children playing on the floor.

'I should have thought you could have got at them while they were bombing, with your single-seaters,' Corbett said at last. 'I suppose they're up above the clouds taking their star-sights, circling round in the clear air?'

The other shook his head. 'They're never there. They're actually *in* the clouds while they're bombing.'

He turned to Corbett. 'I tell you,' he said, 'we're worried sick about this thing. We're up against an air force that's magnificently trained – well, that's no news, of course. What we think they do is this. First, they don't come in squadrons. They come one by one, at intervals of a minute or so. I'll tell you why presently. They always choose a rotten, cloudy, rainy night for it – they don't come on a fine night. They carry a crew of either three or four, two of them navigators, with two of these sextants I was telling you about. They come along just over the top layer of cloud, half in it, and half out of it, fixing their position by star-sights as they come. They get it so that they know where they are to within half a mile, at any point of the journey.'

He paused. 'All the time, they're only just out of the cloud. When they get within fifteen or twenty miles of the town they take their last sight and go down into the cloud a couple of hundred feet or so, flying blind. In the cloud they go by dead reckoning from their last known position. When they get over the target they just dump their bombs.'

'They've got an integrator on the airspeed indicator,' he said. 'An air log, that gives them distance run. That's what they must use for their dead reckoning.'

'How do they get away?'

'They just turn round and go home in the cloud, flying blind, as far as they like. That's why they come singly and not in squadrons. There's less risk of collision in the cloud.'

There was a long pause.

Collins said quietly: 'It's the very devil, Corbett. Search-lights are no good, of course, nor anti-aircraft guns. The barrage is about as much use as a sick headache. The only thing that has a chance of getting them at all is the single-seaters – us.' He blew a long, nervous cloud of smoke. 'We've had three raids since the Squadron moved down here, and I've been up four times – twice the night before last. I've seen them twice, once the first night and once last night. The first time I got in a very long-range burst at him with my forward guns, but he was down into the cloud before I could do any good. Last night I only just got a quick glimpse as he was going in. I didn't get a shot at all.'

'What's going to be done about it?'

'God knows. As things are, we're losing more machines than they are every night, just by the normal risks of flying in this filthy weather. We wrote off two machines last night, and three the night before, on this aerodrome alone. Still,' he said, 'they were less accurate last night. A good many bombs fell right outside the city. That's because we're pushing them back.'

'What do you mean?'

'Well, they know we're up there waiting for them, now. Soon as they see us they have to duck down into the cloud. We're intercepting them farther out each night. That means they have farther to go in the cloud, you see, and then the errors of their dead reckoning come in and spoil the show for them. The one I saw going into the cloud last night must have been nearly over to the far side of the Channel, fifty miles away.'

He was silent for a minute. 'But this bloody weather! It's simply suicidal. When I think of the night exercises we used to do! Beautiful, fine, clear, starry nights. I never thought we'd have to do our stuff in muck like this.'

Corbett thought about it for a minute. 'This method of attack is only good for towns, I suppose? I mean, you couldn't hit an isolated building in this way?'

The flight-lieutenant shook his head. 'Lord, no! Nor ships, either. You heard what happened at Chatham?'

'No. What was that?'

'Last Wednesday. They had a good crack at the ships in the dockyard there, and lost sixteen of their machines. And they didn't do any good with their bombs either. They won't try that again in a hurry.'

'I don't understand. They didn't come at night, then?'

'Just after dawn. It was full daylight. The Archies made a proper mess of them.'

He ground his cigarette out on the ashtray. 'Accurate bombing on a properly defended target is a back number,' he said. 'I believe we've got that pretty well taped. But this blind bombing upon towns – it's merry hell.'

Corbett laughed shortly. 'You're telling *me*!'

He thought about it for a minute. 'How many of them come each night?'

'To Southampton? About forty or fifty machines.'

'Is that all?'

'I think so. They drop about a thousand bombs each night, and they're using hundred-pound bombs. That means forty or fifty machines. But I'm afraid I can't say that I've counted them, old boy.'

'How many towns do they bomb each night?'

The other shrugged his shoulders. 'Twenty?'

'Then they must be using about a thousand machines, all told?'

'I suppose that's about it. They must have a lot in reserve. That's nothing like the full strength of their Air Force.'

'It's enough to be going on with,' said Corbett dryly.

The flight-lieutenant nodded. 'Plenty.' He was silent for a minute. 'We've known for years that if ever a war came, they might try this sort of thing,' he said quietly. 'It's trying to break the morale of the people. They won't do it, of course. The raids don't do any military good. We go on functioning just as if they weren't happening – so do the Army and the Navy. In a month or two I believe the country will adjust itself to them.'

'That may be,' said Corbett. 'It's going to take a bit of doing, though.'

'It always happens.'

The officer considered for a minute. 'This new way of bombing – it's like every new thing that's been tried out in war – aircraft, gas, tanks – everything. They're none of them decisive factors, and this won't be, either. Their only real asset is surprise. All they do is to make war more unpleasant for everybody.'

'They do that all right.'

'Yes. But wars are won by men walking on their own flat feet, with a rifle and a bayonet. Not this way.'

'Maybe.'

There was a little silence. 'Felicity's staying up at Abingdon, then?'

'For the present. Our house there is out in the country, and I don't feel much like bringing her down here. All this disease about, you know – it makes one think.'

Corbett nodded. 'Have you heard how things are in Southampton today?'

'You mean the cholera? It's pretty bad. I was in there yesterday, but last night it was put out of bounds for the troops. Still, that's a fat lot of good. Half Southampton's camping out alongside the aerodrome.'

'You haven't heard of any cases here?'

'Not yet. It's the bloody water that does it, and that's been all right here so far, touching wood.'

'It was off one day. What would you do for the troops if it went off altogether?'

'Start carting water for them in lorries, I suppose.'

'And what about the people camping out beside the aerodrome? Would you start carting water for them, too?'

There was a silence.

The flight-lieutenant shrugged his shoulders. 'I don't know. We'll cross that ditch when we come to it.'

5

THAT EVENING Joan and Peter discussed the tides.
They had spent the afternoon alternately on shore; Joan had
taken the children on shore for a walk. By the time the
children were in bed, however, the tide had fallen and a
wide expanse of mud separated them from the shore, to their
annoyance.

'What we want,' said Joan, 'is a nice quay that we could
tie up against, so that we could walk on shore.'

Corbett rubbed his chin. 'You won't find that here,' he
said. 'We might move the boat out on to a mooring in the
middle of the river tomorrow, if you like.'

She considered this seriously. 'I believe that would be
better. We'd be able to get on shore at any time, then.'

They eyed the entrance to the inn across the wide expanse
of mud a little wistfully. 'It would be nice to be able to get
on shore at any time,' said Joan.

'Gin and Italian,' said Peter. 'I know.'

The evening was clear and fine. All night the aircraft
roared over their heads beneath the stars, protecting them;
there was no raid. Joan and Peter slept soundly, and awoke
refreshed.

It took Corbett, single-handed, the greater part of the
next day to move his vessel out on to a mooring in the
middle of the river. First the engine, unused since the previous summer, had to be induced to function. Then anchors
had to be laid out to warp her out of the mud berth, with
a great deal of going backwards and forwards in the dinghy,
and laying out and taking in of warps. It was not till four
o'clock in the afternoon that she was lying on the mooring, clean and washed down, and with everything stowed
away.

Corbett rested on the cabin-top and smoked a cigarette.

The glass was falling again and the weather was clouding up for rain.

Joan had been on shore early in the morning, and had got a couple of pints of milk from a farm. In spite of these occasional replenishments, and in spite of having cut the older children off milk altogether, they had made heavy inroads into their stock; only two tins now remained of what they had brought with them from Southampton.

'We'll have to do something about this milk business,' said Joan. 'It's getting worse and worse.'

Corbett nodded. 'There are a lot more people here than when we came. Those two boats over there – they've got people in them now. They hadn't when we came.'

Joan said: 'I know. The farms just round about here can't possibly supply all these people. Do you think it would be worth trying for milk in Southampton?'

'We might get some tins. I've been thinking about going in to Southampton one day. I ought to see what's going on at the office. And there's the house, too. . . .'

Joan nodded. 'I want some things from the house. I left my powder-compact on the dressing-table, like a fool. And there's a little thing of lipstick there that you might bring along if you're going.'

That night there was another raid. Again they woke up in the middle of the night to the concussion of the bombs, draped themselves in blankets, and huddled together in the hatchway looking out into the windy darkness. They stayed there for a long time, listening to the explosions and to the fighters taking off and landing on the aerodrome.

It seemed to them that the falling bombs were very much more dispersed. Two salvoes were definitely closer to them than to the city. One set of concussions seemed to come more from the direction of Bursledon than from Southampton, and there seemed to be bombs bursting on the far side of Southampton Water, in the New Forest. 'They're getting wilder, I believe,' said Corbett. 'That's a good sign. It fits in with what Collins said.'

Joan shivered. 'It won't be worth their while bombing

Southampton much longer,' she said. 'There won't be anything left there to bomb.'

Corbett rubbed his chin thoughtfully. 'There's this about it. We don't want to see them getting too dispersed. I'd rather see them getting a bit nearer the bull than they are tonight. We don't want to cop an outer, here.'

They stood there staring out over the dark water to the shore, the aircraft passing and re-passing over their heads. Once there was a thudding noise from the direction of the aerodrome and a red glow appeared above the trees, that quickly grew.

'Peter!' cried Joan. 'What's that?'

They watched it, tense and motionless. It grew to a great ruddy blaze in a few seconds, with showers of red sparks whirling up above the trees. Then it began to die away as quickly as it had appeared; within a very short time it was black night again.

They relaxed. 'It was a fire of some sort,' Corbett said. He hesitated.

'Peter. Do you think it was an aeroplane?'

'It looked very like it.' He passed his arm around her shoulders. 'Come back to bed. We can't do anything to help.'

Her lips were trembling. 'This beastly war ...'

He helped her back to bed and tucked her up. They lay awake for a long time, listening to the bursting of the bombs in the dark night. Presently the raid came to an end, and they slept.

Next morning it was raining heavily. Corbett had breakfast; then Joan rowed him on shore to the car to go into Southampton.

He had left the car parked in the open. Trying to start it, he discovered that the tank was empty; the drain-plug and the washer were placed neatly on the running-board. Petrol in Hamble was at a premium. He replaced the drain-plug angrily and went back on board to fetch a can out of his store, returned to the car, filled it into his tank, and got going on the road to Southampton.

The road past the aerodrome was choked with Air Force

lorries and tank wagons. The continual forced stops in the traffic gave him a measure of time to look about him; the whole countryside seemed to be littered with people camping out. Wherever a hedge-corner made a shelter from the wind among the fields, a car had been parked as the basis of a settlement; in some instances a tent had been put up as well. Most of these temporary camps were littered and amateurish, with a touch of squalor. The people looked pinched and unhealthy in the streaming rain. Over the fields towards the disused reservoir the cars were thick; there seemed to be a great number of people camping out among the trees around the water.

He drove on into the town. At Northam Bridge, before entering the city proper, there was a barricade guarded by police. He was stopped and asked where he was going to.

He told the constable his house and his office. 'You'll have to go round by the other bridge, sir,' said the man. 'You know it, of course?'

Corbett nodded. 'Why is that?'

The man hesitated. 'It's Mr Corbett, isn't it? The solicitor?'

'That's right.'

The constable said: 'We've got our orders not to allow any traffic in the Northam district. On account of the sickness, and that.'

'Is it the cholera?'

The man hesitated for a little. 'Well – we've got orders not to talk about it, sir. Spreading alarm, if you take my meaning.'

'I understand. It's pretty bad, is it?'

'I did hear it was better this morning, getting under control, like. It's typhoid now that they're most upset about.'

Corbett nodded. 'That's bad.'

'It is, sir. Seems to me there's not much to choose between them. Round by the Cobden bridge, if you don't mind. I wouldn't loiter in the city, sir, if I was you.'

Corbett swung his car round and drove on. As he went he noticed that the streets were smelling very bad; stagnant water stood about in pools, spotted with rain-drops, in the road and gutters. In one place he had to make a detour through side streets to avoid the debris that had been a house, now hurled into the road; in many places he had to edge his way around great cavities, roughly filled in or laid across with boards. There were no trams running. In places the overhead wires were down, roughly tied back to keep the roadway clear.

He reached his house with difficulty. It was untouched, as were the houses on each side of it. The house beyond Littlejohn's, however, had suffered a direct hit; it stood a ruined, roofless shell. The explosion had brought down a small part of the side wall of Littlejohn's house, but had not seriously damaged it.

There was a notice stuck on Littlejohn's front door. He went to read it. It said:

GONE AWAY
Address, care of Southern Counties Bank,
Southampton.

E. D. Littlejohn.

The notice, and the desolate, neglected appearance of the house, wrung his heart. It seemed to point an ending to the happiness that had existed in that house, a quiet, humdrum and plebeian happiness that had better have been allowed to fade into oblivion, that did not require to have been underlined. At the same time, the notice seemed to him to be a sensible and practical idea; he would put one like it on his own front door. But where should he give as his new address? Where should he say that he had gone to?

Better to give his bank address, as Littlejohn had done.

He turned away and went to his own house. The windows and the back door had been carefully boarded up; Littlejohn must have done that for them before he had gone away. He unlocked the front door and went in. Inside, the house smelt stale and damp. Wet drove in at the board-cracks over the windows, but little light or air came in; the house was cavernous and depressing. Materially, everything was quite all right; there had been no burglary nor, so far as he could see, had anybody been into the house.

He went upstairs. Joan's powder compact was still lying on the dressing-table, and her lipstick; he picked them up and dropped them in his pocket. The room was full of her things, redolent of her personality. He knew that if she had been with him she would have wanted other things; he was at a loss what to take with him. Finally he took her bedroom slippers and a little bottle of scent, and went about his business.

For some time he went from room to room, a pencilled list in hand, collecting the various articles and clothing which they had decided he should bring away. He took them all out to the car. Finally he went into the house again and up to the nursery. He selected a few more books for the children: *Little Black Sambo,* the *Story of a Fierce, Bad Rabbit,* and one or two others, and he took a battered kaleidoscope for Phyllis, and a little truck for John, and a much-sucked woolly animal for the baby. Then he was ready to go.

He went gladly. It did not seem as if it was his own home at all, that house. It was strange and rather unpleasant, a desolate shell where people once had lived a quiet, peaceful life and had been happy. His home, his real home, was on his battered, leaky little yacht.

'Home's where your people are,' he muttered, to himself. 'That's about it.'

He wrote out a notice similar to Littlejohn's, found a packet of drawing-pins, and pinned it securely to the front door. It would not last for long in that wet weather; perhaps when he came again he could do something more permanent for both houses.

In the road outside he paused and looked about him. Only about one house in three was still inhabited; the rest were empty, damaged and deserted. There was no drainage for the surface water in the road; it stood about in pools at the lower levels. One or two houses in the road had basements; it seemed to Corbett that they must be flooded.

He turned back to his car and drove away. As he drove through the shopping district towards his office he noticed that the small shops were shut up, practically without exception. The larger shops were open in a desultory sort of way; all windows had been smashed and boarded up, and there seemed to be very little business being done. He drove on to his office, parked the car outside it, and let himself in with his key.

There was nobody there. Someone had been there since his last visit; the windows were blocked with shelves roughly nailed across, taken from cupboards and presses whose contents had been neatly laid out on the floor of the various rooms. On his desk Corbett found a note addressed to himself, and dated two days earlier.

It was from his partner. It told him briefly that Bellinger was taking his family to stay with his sister in Ireland. He was motoring them up to Holyhead; he hoped to be back in Southampton in about a week.

'Ireland,' Corbett muttered to himself. 'That should be safe enough. There's nothing there to bomb.'

He pottered round in the office for a little while. There was a full bottle of milk by Miss Mortimer's desk; he picked it up gladly, but it was a week old and very sour. He wrote a note and left it on Bellinger's desk, telling him that he was living on his yacht. Then he left the office, shutting the front door carefully behind him, and went out into the town.

He was unable to get any milk at all. At one or two shops he was told that they might have some in the morning, but they did not seem sure about it. He visited an empty and deserted dairy. Nor was he any more successful with tinned milk. Finally he was advised to go to the hospital.

'There's ever so much milk at the hospital,' the girl said. 'They're selling it up there, I heard. You see, they got their own supply, or something.'

He managed to buy a good quantity of provisions, sufficient to last them a fortnight or so. Fresh meat was scarce, owing to the breakdown of refrigeration caused by the failure of the electric current. Rather unwisely, he bought a large lump of dubious beef, about ten pounds in weight, which the butcher assured him would be quite all right if it were cooked that day, and he had the foresight to get a pan big enough to cook it in. That would make soup for the children, anyway. Fresh vegetables were scarce, but he was able to get some more potatoes and a good supply of tins.

There seemed to be no petrol in the town at all.

He drove up to the hospital to try for milk. The short approach was thronged with ambulances evacuating the cases to some unknown destination, the entrance thronged with people. The building itself was damaged at one side. Baulks of timber had been placed to shore up a doubtful wall, and there were tarpaulins stretched across one portion of the roof.

He made some inquiries and was directed to a basement room, entered from the back of the building. A ward maid here sold him a pint of milk.

'Matron says we haven't got to let nobody have more than a pint, and then only for a baby,' she said. 'I'm sorry.'

He watched her while she poured it into his jug.

'You're having a bad time here, I'm afraid,' he said.

'They're getting all the patients that can be moved away today,' she said dully. 'After last night.'

'What happened last night?'

'Didn't you hear?'

He shook his head. 'I've been out in the country. They didn't hit the hospital, did they?'

She nodded dumbly. 'It's the second time.'

'I'm terribly sorry. Was it bad?'

She nodded again, without saying anything.

'Any of the staff hurt?'

She nodded for a third time. 'It was right on the theatre. Sister Morgan and Sister Burke – they were killed.' Her lips trembled. 'And Nurse Harrison – she died this morning. And Mr Endersleigh, and Mr Gordon, and Dr Sitwell, they were killed. It's been a terrible blow to the hospital, really and truly.'

There was a momentary pause. Corbett rallied himself. 'You say that Mr Gordon was killed?'

She nodded. 'Did you know him?'

'Yes,' said Corbett. 'I knew him very well.'

There was a pause.

'Do you know how it happened?' he asked. 'Did he – was he killed at once?'

'I think he was. He and Mr Endersleigh were operating at the time. They had two tables going, each of them. And they say the bomb fell right into the theatre. Nurse Harrison, she was in the next room . . .'

There was no more to be said. Mechanically Corbett picked up his jug and moved away.

'That'll be fourpence for the milk,' the ward maid said.

He turned back and paid her, and went out to his car, got into the car and sat motionless at the wheel for a long time, lost in thought. Gordon was dead. He sat there while the traffic to the hospital passed beside him, trying to realize it, to accept it as a new fact of his life. Gordon was dead. There would be no more Sunday trips in summer to Seaview to bathe with Gordon; there would be no repetition of the Whitsun holiday with Gordon to St Malo. Gordon was dead.

He wondered what would happen now to Margaret. Gordon had told him she was nursing cholera. He could at least go to the house, to see if she was there, to see if he could help at all.

He drove towards the surgeon's house. As he got near, the road was blocked with unrepaired bomb-holes. Rather than waste time in searching for a way round to the other end, he left the car and walked down to the house on foot. The front door stood open. He went up diffidently and rang the bell. There was no sound; he remembered the electrical supply and tapped with the knocker.

In the hall a door opened. Margaret was there, bare-headed, in a stained nurse's uniform. She said very quietly:

'Peter. Come in. Come in and have a cup of tea.'

He said a little awkwardly: 'I've just been to the hospital,

Margaret. They told me what had happened there. I came to see if there was anything that I could do to help.'

She shook her head. 'Come in and have a cup of tea,' she repeated. 'I was just making one for myself.'

He said: 'We were great friends, you know. I want to do anything I can.'

'It's good of you, Peter,' she said quietly, 'but there's nothing you can do.'

He followed her into a littered, windy drawing-room. Nothing had been done about the windows; the glass lay shattered on the carpet in the wet patches. In the grate a Primus was roaring under a tin kettle. 'It won't be long,' she said. 'What have you done with Joan?'

He told her how they were living, as she prepared the tea-pot. As he spoke he studied her furtively. She was dry-eyed and very calm; he was a little afraid of her, and did not dare to offer her any further sympathy.

She poured a little hot water into the teapot and set it down to warm. 'You did right to go away,' she said evenly. 'Everybody ought to get out of this town. It's got a curse on it.' She was silent for a moment, and then she said: 'It makes it terribly difficult when they won't go.'

He recognized in that the detached attitude of a nurse; in one way he was glad of it. 'I know you've got your work to do,' he said gently. 'But you must need a rest. Would you come back with me to Hamble for a night or two?'

She raised her head and smiled faintly. 'You haven't got room in your little boat. I don't know how you've all got into it as it is.'

'We could manage somehow. We'd like to have you, and you'd help Joan a lot.'

She shook her head. 'I've got my work to do here. It's sweet of you to offer, Mr Corbett. But the best thing I can do is to go straight on working. I don't want to stop and think about things – yet.'

He nodded. 'I'll be coming in again in a few days. Perhaps you might like to come then.'

She shook her head. 'There's too much for me to do here.'

'Is it the cholera?'

She nodded. 'Now that we've got the serum, that's not quite so bad. Typhoid is worse. And the difficulty now is that it's got out into the country. People evacuating, you know – and you can't stop them, well or ill. We've got cases of both cholera and typhoid at Botley, and round about there. And every day we hear of new ones that we can't isolate, or even treat....'

She turned to him. 'And it's so difficult to make a hospital. Even the barns and cow-sheds are crammed full of people camping out. We're getting near the stage when we may have to bring patients back into the city for sheer lack of room, and chance the bombing.'

She laid her hand upon his arm. 'Get away from it, Mr Corbett,' she said earnestly. 'You've got a boat. Take Joan and the children over to the Isle of Wight, or somewhere. This bit of Hampshire's got a curse on it. Allan...' Her voice faded, and she stopped. Then she spoke again. 'He was John's godfather, and I know he'd have said the same. Get them away to the Isle of Wight, or farther still.'

He eyed her for a moment. 'You think it's going to be really bad?'

She nodded. 'I know it is. While this bombing keeps on every night – we're not even holding our own. Disease is bound to spread, and it is spreading. We're getting used to it a bit now, and we can see what we're up against. But things will be much worse before they're better.'

He said: 'Thanks for telling me, Margaret. It's decent of you. We could go over to the Isle of Wight at any time.'

'Go now, before it gets too late.'

He rose and helped her clear away the tea-things. 'Is there nothing I can do for you?' he asked. 'You know how much I want to help.'

She shook her head. 'I'll go on working. That's all I need.' She stared around the littered room, the window gaping open to the wind. 'I don't know what to do with this house and everything. What have you done with yours?'

'Shut it up and left it. You'll have to do the same. Just lock the door. It will be quite all right.'

She laughed, a little bitterly. 'What's the good of locking the door, with all the windows in this state?'

She did not need him; there was nothing he could do for her. He left her there, dry eyed, gathering up a few clothes before she went back to her work, and walked back to his car.

He drove back to Hamble in the middle of the afternoon, parked the car, and hailed Joan on the yacht. She came off in the dinghy to fetch him with his purchases. The first thing she asked was:

'Did you find my powder-compact, Peter?'

He gave it to her, with the lipstick; she took them gratefully. He smiled. 'Go on – laugh,' she said. 'But it does help to know you're looking decent.' She opened the compact and peered at the little mirror.

The next thing she asked about was the milk. He told her he had only got a pint.

'But, Peter,' she said, 'that's only two feeds! What are we going to do?'

There was an urgency about her manner that was new to him. He said: 'Can she go on soup for a bit?'

She shook her head. 'I've been trying that, and it's awful. I gave her some of the tinned soup this morning. She was sick at once. Then I opened a tin of milk and gave her that, and she had that up, too. The little brat's been crying steadily since ten o'clock.' He noticed that Joan was looking tired and worn.

He took her arm, resolving not to tell her about Gordon for the time. 'Never mind,' he said gently. 'We'll give her this lot when we get on board. And then you come on shore and take the car, and see if you can get any at a farm.'

She nodded. 'I'll do that. It'll be a relief to get away from the baby for a bit.'

They went on board. In the steady roar that came from the baby he helped her to prepare a bottle of the fresh milk, watched her offer it. The noise stopped, and the silence could be felt. Phyllis looked up from playing with the little musical truck upon the cabin floor, and said:

'I've got a piece of soap, Daddy.'

He expressed interest and went and fetched the kaleidoscope. 'I got this for you from home,' he said. 'I thought you'd like to have it.'

She took it without much enthusiasm. 'You didn't bring my dolls' house, did you, Daddy.'

'No. Big girls don't take dolls' houses on boats with them. Only little girls do that.'

She was satisfied. John said: 'Did you bring anything for me, Daddy?'

He gave him the little truck that he had brought, and set him playing with it on the cabin floor. Then he turned to Joan. She motioned him to be quiet.

'She's taken nearly the whole of this,' she said very softly. 'She must have been terribly hungry. Look, she's practically asleep.'

He smiled. 'Don't shake her, or she'll have it all up again.'

He watched his wife as she laid the baby gently in the cot, sound asleep. Then she came through into the saloon. 'I'll get on shore now,' she said. 'I'll take the children with me.'

'Aren't you fed up with them?'

She smiled. 'I'll take them. They aren't any bother, and they ought to have a run on shore.'

He helped her with the dinghy. 'Where would you go for milk?' she asked.

He rubbed his chin. 'I should try Swanwick, or go on towards Wickham. Don't go by Botley – there's sickness there. I'll tell you all about it when you come back. And I say, go easy with the petrol. Get some more if you can find any.'

He watched her row on shore, then went below. He looked to see that the baby was sleeping quietly, and then put on the meat to boil. Then he turned to the consideration of his yacht.

He had not talked to Joan about it, but the idea of leaving Hamble was in his mind. Everything seemed to point that way, now. But if he were to do that, he would have to finish fitting out the boat. Most of the spars and sails and gear were stored on shore; he went aft to the sail-locker and dragged out various coils of rope, with their blocks and sheaves, looked them over dubiously, and put them back again. Then he sat down on a settee with an old envelope and made a list of what would have to be done before the vessel would be fit to go to sea. Presently he relaxed, lay back in meditation on the couch, and slept.

He was still sleeping when the dinghy bumped against the side and woke him up. He went on deck, helped the children on board, and took the milk from Joan. They made the painter fast.

'I only got a quart,' she said. 'I had to go nearly to Wickham to get that. Swanwick was hopeless. It's chock full of people camping out upon the green, and in the fields, and everywhere. And not a drop of milk in the place. I tried three farms after that, and then at the fourth they were actually milking in the cow-shed. So they couldn't say they hadn't got any. But I had to pay half a crown for that quart.'

'How long will that keep us going for?'

'About a day.'

'Did you get any petrol?'

'There wasn't a drop to be had, anywhere.'

He smiled ruefully. 'You must have used about a gallon. A gallon of petrol for a quart of milk. We can't go on for long like that.'

'I know. But what are we going to do?'

He shook his head.

She took the children down below and gave them for their supper a plate of soup and a little loaf of bread that she had made in the Primus oven. John said:

'Can I have some milk, Mummy?'

'You don't want milk,' said Corbett, a little hurriedly. 'Only babies have milk. When you're big enough to go on a boat you eat soup and bread and jam, like real sailors. Makes the hair grow on your chest.'

'Will it make hair grow on my chest, Daddy?' asked Phyllis.

'Girls are different. It'll make hair grow all over you, till you're like a little dog.'

They thought this was a great joke, and forgot about the milk.

He helped Joan to put them to bed. When that was done they went up together into the cockpit; it was windy and fresh up there; they sat for a little looking out over the river. Joan said: 'You haven't told me about Southampton yet. What did you do?'

He was silent. She looked at him curiously. 'What did you do?' she asked again.

'I heard about Gordon,' he said unevenly. 'Joan, he – he's dead.'

'Oh, Peter . . .'

He told her of his visit to the hospital, of his talk with Margaret. She heard him to the end. Then she asked him for a cigarette; he lit it for her.

She blew a long cloud of smoke. 'She was quite right, Peter,' she said at last. 'We shan't be able to stay here much longer. I thought we'd be all right here, but after seeing Swanwick – well, I'm not so sure. It was awful. Cars just parked about, higgledy-piggledy, everywhere. And people sort of living in them like gipsies, only not so well able to do it. Cooking on frying-pans in the rain over a methylated spirit stove like you use for curling-irons – that sort of thing. And no proper lavatories, of course. Pits dug about here and there – not nearly big enough. I wouldn't be a bit surprised if there were epidemics. It looked sort of – squalid.'

He nodded. 'Well, that's what she said. They've got both cholera and typhoid at Botley now.'

They sat in silence for a time, watching the grey clouds rolling past.

'Where could we go to, Peter?'

'Bellinger's taken his family to Ireland.' He told her of the note that he had found in his office.

'That's an awfully long way away,' she said. 'I think that's overdoing it a bit.'

He said: 'I should have thought Scotland would be all right.'

'We ought to know where it's all right and where it's not. But I haven't heard any news for days.'

'Nor have I. I've been too busy to bother much about it.'

'You might have got a paper in Southampton.'

'I don't think there were any. I didn't see any about.'

They came back to the matter in hand.

'I should think it would be all right in the Isle of Wight,' he said. 'We might try Wootton Creek.' He paused. 'But if we're going to do that, I'd better get the sails and boom on board and fit her out properly.'

'How long would that take us to do?'

'A couple of days, perhaps.'

They went below and cooked their supper. They ate it and washed up; it was then about nine o'clock. Across the black water the light streamed from the windows of the inn, invitingly.

Peter turned to Joan. 'Go on shore and see if you can pick up any news.'

She smiled. 'You go. I'd just as soon go to bed. Besides, you'll pick up more than I should.'

He took the dinghy and rowed off to the hard. The inn was full of men, but they were sitting dour and glum; there was little talk. Corbett made his way up to the bar and ordered a pint.

He asked the barman if he had a paper. The man produced one that was two days old, a single printed sheet. Corbett retired with it to a corner of the room. In a quarter of an hour he came to the conclusion that in the game of bombing cities we were more or less holding our own. Our raids, however, were referred to as reprisals, which seemed to put them on a higher plane. There was very little other news, but there were columns of enlisting propaganda. He sheered hastily from that, with averted eyes.

He rose, and gave the paper back to the barman. 'There's not much in that,' he said.

'That's right,' said the man. 'Difficult to know what really is going on, these days.' He laughed shortly. 'Not that we want to hear any more bad news than what we've got round about here. Still, it would be nice to hear something good for a change.'

There was a short pause.

Corbett asked: 'What do you mean by that? Is anything wrong – specially, I mean?'

The man dropped his voice. 'You know up by the old reservoir, where all them campers are? Up past the aerodrome, Netley way. There was a woman took sick up there, Sunday night – and there's several more of them sick now, so they say.'

There was a momentary silence.

'I don't like it,' said the man in a low tone. 'Straight, I don't. If it gets any worse, I'm hopping it. I don't want any of that cholera.'

Corbett asked, equally furtively: 'Where would you go?'

'Gawd knows. That's the only reason that I haven't gone.'

He turned away to serve a customer.

Corbett left the inn and went back on board his yacht. As he was tying up the dinghy Joan put her head out of the hatch and asked if he had any news. He told her shortly what he had seen in the paper. And then, a little diffidently, he repeated to her what the barman had said. She listened to the end.

'I don't much like the sound of that, Peter,' she said at last. 'Getting a bit near home, isn't it?'

He sighed. 'There's nothing to be done about it. But I do think this – we'll start to fit out properly in the morning. Then if we don't like the look of things we can slip across to the Isle of Wight.'

'Do you think we'd be able to get any milk over there?'

'I don't know. I should think we ought to be able to.'

That night there was another raid. Corbett was awake

and reading in his bunk, waiting for it; he knew from experience by now the sort of night that brought a raid, and the time when it might be expected to begin. Presently it came; he lay quietly in his bunk listening to the distant concussions and the gunfire. In the end Joan woke up.

'It's all right,' he said. 'They're at it again. I don't think there's any point in getting up.'

They lay and listened for an hour or more, reading a little, talking now and again. Then that happened which brought them leaping from their bunks up to the cabin hatch, in time to see the last spurts of flame from a salvo that fell in a field half a mile away upon the Warsash side.

They stared at each other speechless, in consternation. 'Peter,' said Joan at last in a very small voice, 'that was the wrong side of the river. Right away from Southampton. Do you think they're bombing us?'

He dropped an arm around her shoulders. 'I don't think so. It's a very bad shot. It's what Collins said – our fighters are up there, harrying them. They're getting very wild.'

She shivered. 'It was awfully close.'

'I know,' he said. 'This puts the lid on it. We'll get away from here now, soon as we can.'

Neither of them felt inclined to go back to bed again while the danger lasted. They put on coats and huddled up together in the hatchway, listening to the falling of the bombs. None fell again so close, but they heard bursts in the direction of Bursledon and a series of deep, watery explosions near the junction of the Hamble River with Southampton Water. Presently there came the long lull that they knew must be the end; they went back to their beds.

The morning came up sunny and bright. In spite of the disturbed night they were up at dawn; there was a great deal to be done if they were going to leave next day. They got the children up and cooked the breakfast; as they were washing up Joan sounded the water-tank.

'We'll want some more today,' she said. 'Could you get that when you go on shore?'

He nodded. 'I'll take the water-bag with me.'

He went off shortly afterwards, pulled the dinghy up upon the hard, and walked into the inn. The barman was there, polishing the glasses. 'I want a bag of water,' Corbett said. 'Can I go through and get it?'

'Tap ain't running.'

Corbett stood and stared at him. 'There isn't any at all?'

The other shook his head. 'Go and try if you like. It wasn't on five minutes ago.'

'Has it been like that for long?'

The man shrugged his shoulders. 'All right last night, it was. Then this morning there wasn't none of them running. It's the same all through the village.'

'Do you think the mains are bust?'

'Aye, that'll be it. They was all around last night, between here and Southampton, dropping their bombs. Did you hear them?'

'Did I not!' He paused. 'There was one lot over at Warsash.'

'Aye, there was seven of them dropped there, but they didn't do no harm. They copped a packet at Bursledon, someone was telling me.'

'Was anybody hurt?'

'Aye. Fell right in among the boats, hauled out of the water in Henderson's yard. Knocked five or six of them right over flat, so they say – with the people in them and all.'

'That's bad.'

'It is, that,' said the man dourly.

Corbett went out to the yard and tried the tap; it was quite dry. He went back to the barman. 'Are there any wells here that I could get water from?'

The man said: 'I couldn't say. Far as I know, everybody takes the water from the main. You might find an old well in one of the cottages, but I don't know as I'd care to have a drink from it.'

'No,' said Corbett, thoughtfully.

He left the inn and went on to the sail store. The water would have to wait for a bit; he felt that he would like to think it over and have a talk to Joan before he started to get water from a disused cottage well. He started to carry sails and gear down to the dinghy; when he had a load he took it off to the yacht.

He told Joan about the water.

'That's another bad one,' she said quietly. 'Do you think we could get any over on the Warsash side?'

He was doubtful. 'That probably comes from Southampton, too. No, I think I'll take a run up to the aerodrome this afternoon and see if Collins could wangle some for us from their supply. He might be able to – if everybody else hasn't thought of the same thing. I'll take the car to bring the water-bag back in.'

'We'll have to get some more milk today, Peter. We're down to that one tin again.'

He sighed. 'I know. Look, I'll go off and get the rest of the stuff back on board. Then you can go and look around for milk while I start rigging the ship.'

He went back on shore and got a man to help him carry the boom of his mainsail down to the water's edge. He carried down the gaff himself and loaded up the dinghy with the rest of the sails and gear. Then he launched the spars into the water till they floated, and towed them behind the dinghy to the yacht. Joan helped him to unload the dinghy and get the spars on board; then she went on shore with the two children. Corbett got to work on deck with spun-yarn, marline-spike, and knife.

It was a couple of hours before Joan returned. She brought with her a quart of milk, which she had purchased at a farm, having left the children playing in the mud beside the dinghy.

'It was awfully difficult,' she said. 'I had to go about a couple of miles before I found a farm where they had milk to sell. I tried to get them to keep me some tomorrow, but they wouldn't do that. Everybody's after milk.'

They started to get lunch. 'You know that shop I went to the other day?' she said. 'Where they had all that tinned milk? I believe they've got it still. I went in, but the man was there, and he just shut the door in my face. He said they hadn't got any to sell.'

'You told him we've got a baby?'

'He knows that all right. I told him last time.'

After lunch Corbett left Joan to do the washing-up and put the children down for their midday rest, and went on shore to look for water. As he passed the inn the barman saw him carrying the water-bag, and called to him:

'The water-cart's just up the street, if you want any, Mr Corbett. Better hurry up, or it'll be gone.'

He went back to look for it. It was a horse-drawn tank-cart used for carting water to the animals upon some farm; it was halted in the middle of the road with a crowd about it. The man in charge was selling water at sixpence a bucket.

Corbett pushed his way into the crowd. He asked the man: 'Where did you get the water from?'

'Old reservoir,' the man said. 'All clean and fresh. Best water round about these parts. Take your turn, Mister.'

Corbett withdrew as if to take his turn. He withdrew altogether. He was not squeamish, and the water looked beautiful, but he wanted to think about it for a bit before he drank the water from a cholera camp.

He walked down to the water's edge again, started up his car, and drove out to the aerodrome. At the entrance he was stopped by a guard; he asked for Flight-Lieutenant Collins.

'Which squadron, sir?'

'I don't know, I'm afraid.'

'Park your car here, and go and ask in Wing Head-quarters' office, third door on the right. They'll tell you there.'

He found the office and went in. A corporal was sitting at a desk talking into a telephone; there was much coming and going. Presently Corbett got a chance to ask for Collins.

The man looked up at him. 'Is it on business?'

'No. It's a personal matter.'

The man got up and went into an inner office. A few minutes passed before he returned; a flying officer followed him.

'What is it about Collins?' asked the officer.

'I'm a personal friend of his,' said Corbett. 'I came up to see him.' He paused. 'If it's not convenient, I'll just leave a note.'

There was a pause.

'It's not that,' the young man said awkwardly. 'But Flight-Lieutenant Collins – there was an accident, the night before last. I'm afraid you haven't heard about it. He was rather badly hurt.'

'I see,' said Corbett. He raised his eyes to the officer's face. 'Are you trying to tell me that he was killed?'

The other said hurriedly: 'Oh, no. He was a good deal knocked about, though. He had both legs broken, and there were one or two burns.... He's in hospital in Winchester.'

'Do you know how he's getting on?'

The young man shook his head. 'I haven't heard. We never do get any news of them, once they've left here.'

'How did it happen?'

The young man said: 'It was a collision in the air, just over the edge of the aerodrome here. Chap circling round to land took his tail off for him. They both piled up, of course. The other chap was killed.'

'Was it the weather?'

The other nodded. 'You can't help it, flying on these bloody rainy nights. The clouds were down to about three hundred feet that night.' He was silent for a moment. 'Still, that's what happened, I'm afraid.'

'I'm terribly sorry.'

The officer turned back towards his room. 'I've got a lot to do – I'm so sorry.... It wasn't anything of importance that you wanted to see him about?'

Corbett shook his head. 'Nothing important.'

He turned away and went back to the car; he drove down to the river and went on board again. Joan was there; he told her all about it.

Her lips tightened. 'I'm awfully sorry for Felicity,' she said quietly.

'I know.'

132

They sat in silence, smoking for a time, the discarded water-bag at their feet. In the end Joan kicked it with her toe. 'You didn't get any water, I suppose?'

'No. How much have we got left?'

'Very little indeed. We'll be out by breakfast-time to-morrow, if we wash up anything.'

He sighed. 'We'll have to get some more. I don't think I can go back to the aerodrome – they probably wouldn't give it to me, anyway. They'll be short themselves. If Collins had been there I might have got some as a favour.'

Joan nodded. 'I doubt if it's much good going back there.'

'Would you care for any of that water from the reservoir? There's typhoid, cholera, and God knows what, camped right beside it.'

She smiled. 'It sounds a bit insipid. Can't you find me a nice, fruity well?'

He rubbed his chin. 'Wells aren't so easy to find these days. We might try on the Warsash side. But if we get well-water you'll have to boil it before you give it to the baby.'

'I suppose I ought to.'

She turned to him. 'I'm sick of scouting about alone, Peter. Let's go on shore together, for a change.'

'How are you going to manage that?'

They did manage it. They took the baby in its cradle, fast asleep, and parked it in the kitchen of the inn on the Warsash side, with half a crown parking fee. Then they set off up the road to look for water, the children following behind.

They did not have to go very far. They found a cottage where a woman made them free of her well. 'Nine 'ealthy children I've brought up on the water from that well,' she said comfortably. 'Seven still with us, and all of them 'ealthy as you or me, barring the goitre.' She would not take payment for the water. 'It's little enough that one can do to 'elp, these dreadful times,' she said. 'But pure well water – that one *can* share with other folks.'

They thanked her, and set off down the road carrying

the water-bag slung upon an oar. 'We'll have to boil every drop of the bloody stuff,' said Corbett when they were out of earshot. 'I don't want to get goitre.'

Joan laughed. 'I don't know that I know what goitre is,' she said. 'Sort of swelling, isn't it?'

'I don't know,' said Corbett firmly, 'and I don't want to know.'

He spent the evening boiling water in the pan that he had bought to boil the beef, and transferring it sterile to the water-tank. That night they had more trouble with the baby. The milk they had in hand was sufficient for only half a feed; they watered it to something like the proper volume, but the child cried continuously for two hours before it sank into a restless sleep.

When finally the noise ceased they got their supper, very quietly. Joan said: 'Peter, we've got to face up to this milk business. It's serious. I mean, I don't think we ought to leave here without a few tins more. We don't know what things may be like in the Isle of Wight.'

'I know. We do seem to be able to scratch along here somehow or other, a pint or so at a time.'

'That's what I feel. We might find ourselves landed without any milk at all.'

'If that happened, could we get along?'

She shook her head. 'I don't believe we could. Phyllis and John can eat anything: things out of tins, I mean. But Joan – I don't know. She's all right on tinned milk – we know that. But I tried her on that tinned soup yesterday, and she was awfully upset.'

He asked: 'Would she be any better on another sort of soup?'

Joan shook her head. 'It wasn't mulligatawny, or anything like that. It was consommé Julienne.'

'Babies do eat soup, though.'

'Of course they do. But you start them off on good stuff made out of very fresh meat, and you give them a lot of milk along with it, at other feeds.'

He thought about it for a minute. 'You mean this, really.

If we can't keep up the milk supply, we're going to have real trouble?'

She nodded. 'They go down so quickly. I'm afraid we might lose her, Peter.'

He smiled at her reassuringly across the table. 'We're not going to do that.'

They dropped the subject till the meal was over. But when the washing-up was done, he said: 'We'll have to get some of that tinned milk from your grocer's shop.'

She stared at him. 'You mean the one over on the Warsash side? You won't get any there. They won't sell it.'

'We'll have to make them sell it. They can't hog on to it, in times like these.'

She looked very doubtful. 'You'll have to go. They wouldn't pay any attention to me.'

'We'll go together. That woman at the inn would take the children for an hour or so.'

'All right.'

They went on deck and smoked for a little in the cockpit. Lights streamed from the inn at Hamble, cheerful and inviting. Joan asked: 'Are you going on shore?'

He shook his head. 'I think the less we go on shore the better, the way things are now. If we want exercise, let's get it on the Warsash side.'

They went to bed early, in preparation for a heavy day. They slept for an hour or so; then, punctually as an alarm clock, they were awakened by the raid. For a time they lay in their bunks listening to the concussions in the distance.

A salvo fell very close to them, on the marshlands behind Hamble. The children woke and cried a little; they got up to comfort them and turn them over to sleep again. They stood together in the hatchway for a while with blankets draped round them. Bombs seemed to be falling all over the countryside.

'I don't believe they're hitting Southampton at all to-night,' said Joan. 'They're rotten shots.'

Corbett nodded. 'They're getting wilder and wilder. I

don't believe they'll do much damage with this raid, except by a sheer fluke.'

Joan said: 'They couldn't miss London like this, though.'

'No, London's different. I bet they're getting hell up there.'

After a time, before the raid was ended, they grew bored and cold, and went back to bed. 'You'd better wake me if the ship begins to sink,' said Corbett. 'I'm going to sleep.' Inured to the concussions by familiarity they fell asleep, stirring and turning over now and then at the nearer explosions. Presently all was still again, and they slept quietly.

They did not sleep for long. The baby woke them shortly before five o'clock, crying and whimpering in her basket in the forecastle. Joan got up to settle her, but only succeeded in rousing her to bellow lustily, continuously. Corbett got up and found Joan rocking the infant in her arms. The baby was red in the face, and screaming at the top of her voice.

He said: 'I suppose she's hungry.'

'I think that must be it,' said Joan. 'We've got one tin of milk left. Shall we open it?'

He hesitated. 'I should think we'd better. That's the first thing we've got to tackle today.'

He reached for the tin and the tin-opener, and pierced it through.

'Now we've got nothing left at all,' she said quietly.

He was touched by the seriousness of her tone. 'Don't worry,' he said gently. 'We'll get some from that shop, somehow or other.'

They gave the baby a good bottle; it stopped screaming instantaneously and fell asleep immediately it had finished sucking. Tired and on edge they went back to their bunks in the grey dawn and dozed uneasily until the day was bright.

They breakfasted and washed up; then they were ready to go on shore. Corbett put on a raincoat, and slipped the automatic into his coat pocket. Joan saw him do it. 'Peter!' she said. 'You're not going to take that?'

He met her eyes. 'We've got to get some milk,' he

said evenly. 'There may be difficulties. I think I'll take it along.'

She said no more.

They went on shore together, taking the children with them and the baby in its cradle. They had no difficulty in arranging to leave the family in the kitchen of the inn for an hour; then they set out together up the hill towards the shop. They hardly spoke at all. There was a light drizzle of rain falling; Corbett walked with his head down, the cold metal of the loaded automatic hard against his hand deep in the pocket of his coat. It was incredible that he should be doing this.

Once he said: 'I'll offer up to five shillings a tin. But then, if I have to threaten them, you must be ready to go in and take it.'

'All right,' she said.

Twenty minutes later they came to the shop. It was a small general shop at a cross-roads; behind it was the dwelling-house. There was nobody about. Corbett went up to the door and rattled it; it was locked.

Joan said: 'We'll have to go round to the back.'

He turned, and walked round the building to a littered and untidy yard; Joan followed him. They came to a back door.

'This'll be it,' he said.

He knocked on the door. Inside there was a sound of movements, but nobody came. He waited in the rain for a minute, and then knocked again. There was no answer.

'There's somebody inside all right,' said Joan.

He put his hand to the door and tried it. It opened a few inches, and then stopped on a chain. He called out: 'Is anyone at home?'

What happened then was unexpected. A little girl of ten or twelve years old, a child in a dirty print frock and long black stockings, came to the crack of the door. 'What do you want?' she asked.

Corbett said: 'Good morning. I came to see if we could buy some milk.'

She said: 'The shop isn't open. We haven't got any milk to sell.'

'Look,' said Corbett, 'I see the shop's not open. But I've come a long way, and I need milk for my baby. If you'll sell me some, I'll pay you much more than you usually get for each tin.'

There was a pause. The child said in a frightened tone: 'We haven't got any to sell.'

She tried to shut the door. The solicitor was before her, and put his foot into the crack. 'Look,' he said, 'we need milk really badly. Ask your mother if she'll speak to me.'

The child said through the crack: 'She's not here.'

'Let me speak to your father.'

'He's not here, either.'

'Where have they gone to?'

'Swanwick.'

'When will they be back?'

'I don't know.'

There was a short pause. The rain dripped from the roof with little liquid noises. Joan said: 'Is there anyone else in the house besides you?'

The child did not answer, but tried again to shut the door. Joan turned helplessly to Corbett. 'What are we going to do?'

'Get some milk,' he said grimly.

He turned back to the door. 'Open the door and let us in,' he said. 'Then we can talk this over.'

For answer, the child tried to kick his foot out of the door. Corbett turned to Joan. 'We'll have to break our way in, or give it up. But there's nothing on the boat for the baby if we give it up.'

She hesitated. 'This is hateful.'

'I know. Still, we'll have to do it.'

He turned back to the crack. 'If you won't open I shall have to break the door down,' he said. 'Be a good girl, and open up.'

He heard her sobbing, struggling to close the door. 'You're *not* to come in.'

Corbett said: 'I'm coming in. Keep away from the door – I'm going to break it open. Keep right back, or you may get hurt.'

Joan got a piece of wood and wedged the crack open while he withdrew his foot. He took a short run and stamped violently against the door. At the third shot the staple of the chain tore from the woodwork; the door flew open and the child was thrown heavily against a sink at the far side of the scullery. With incredible agility she picked herself up and flew at them.

'You're *not* to come in,' she cried. 'You're *not* to! You're *not* to!'

She landed a well-directed kick on Corbett's shin, and a deep scratch on his cheek. He struggled with her for a minute, then overpowered her and held her arms pinned behind her back, kicking the air, tears streaming down her cheeks in impotent rage.

'You hold her if you can,' he said to Joan. 'Let's get this over.'

Joan took her from him and he went forward through the sitting-room into the shop, mopping his bleeding cheek. She followed him in a minute; the child had ceased to struggle and was sobbing bitterly, refusing all comfort. She found him stooping down behind the counter.

'Here it is,' he said. 'There's a crate nearly full. Over fifty tins.'

Joan released the child, but kept between her and the door; the little girl collapsed on to a sack of potatoes and crouched there, crying her heart out. Joan leaned across the counter to look at the milk. 'One of those will last the baby for a day,' she said. 'Take about fifteen – then we'll feel safe.'

Corbett nodded. 'May as well be hung for a sheep as a lamb.'

He put the fifteen tins out on to the counter. 'How much do these things cost?'

She said: 'Sevenpence.'

He calculated quickly. 'I make that eight and ninepence. I'll leave a pound – that's more than double the price.'

Joan said: 'Make it thirty bob. I mean, we won't do this every day.'

'All right.'

Behind them the little girl was sobbing hopelessly and bitterly upon the sack, in utter misery. 'I can't stand this,' said Joan.

She crouched down beside the child, and put an arm around her shoulders. 'Don't cry like that,' she said gently. 'You put up a grand show. Nobody could have done more than you did. It's not your fault we were too strong for you. And we had to have the milk for our baby.'

The sobbing continued unabated. Joan fumbled for a handkerchief and wiped the child's eyes. 'It wouldn't have made any difference, even if you had been a man. We had to get milk.'

The child lifted a tear-streaked face. 'You wouldn't have got it if my daddy had been here.'

'Yes, we would. This was a hold up, dear – a real one, like you see on the pictures.' She turned to her husband. 'Peter, show her your gun.'

He pulled it from his pocket, a little awkwardly. The little girl stopped crying and looked at it, awe-struck. 'Are you two gangsters?' she said at last.

Joan nodded. 'Yes, we're gangsters,' she said quietly. 'Tell your daddy from us that you put up a splendid fight. And look, here's the money. We've taken fifteen tins of milk, and here's one pound ten shillings to pay for it. Now, don't cry any more.' She held her handkerchief to the child's nose. 'Come on and blow.'

The little girl obeyed. Her eyes were still fixed upon the automatic pistol. She asked: 'Could I hold it for a minute?'

Joan nodded to Peter. He slipped out the magazine and gave the pistol to the little girl; she held it in her hands and turned it over. 'My!' she said. 'Isn't it heavy!'

They took it back from her and went towards the door, carrying their tins of milk. 'Lock the door behind us when we've gone,' said Joan. 'Then nobody else will be able to get in.'

She hesitated. 'Don't think too badly of us,' she said. 'One day you'll have a baby of your own, and then you'll know. . . .'

The child stood at the door and watched them as they went. 'Goodbye,' she said shyly.

They waved to her and went down the road towards Warsash, their arms full of tins. They went silently, immersed in their own thoughts. At last Corbett said:

'Well, anyway, we've got the milk.'

Joan said: 'I do hope she'll be able to make her people understand.'

They went on down the hill with heavy hearts. They found the children at the inn and went on board the yacht again. They stowed their precious tins of milk away carefully and made a survey of their other stores.

'I think I'll make a loaf of bread before we start,' said Joan. 'We've got time, haven't we?'

Corbett nodded. 'I'm going to go on shore and see if I can get some brandy at the pub,' he said. 'We've only got a little whisky here.'

He took the dinghy and rowed over to the Hamble side. The barman sold him two bottles of old brandy at a fantastic price. Coming out of the inn he met Lammermoor, who had helped him on the first afternoon at Hamble. The young man's features were a sort of ashen grey.

'I say, old man,' he said urgently. 'Where does the district nurse live – do you know?'

Corbett shook his head. 'I haven't an idea. I'm sorry.'

The young man shook his head despairingly. 'There must be a doctor or a nurse, or *someone* here. I can't get any help.'

'What's the trouble?'

'It's Sissie. She's been ill all night, and she's looking simply awful now. I must get somebody. . . .'

He ran off up the village street. Corbett went back on board.

'I'd like to get away as soon as we can,' he said to Joan. 'Let's make it snappy.'

They had a quick lunch, started up the engine, slipped the mooring, and stood away down river.

6

A BRIEF SHAFT of sunlight pierced the clouds as they got under way. Joan sat at the tiller, taking the vessel down the river that she knew so well; the children played around her in the cockpit. Corbett was forward in the bows, ranging cable ready for anchoring. The vessel chugged forwards towards Southampton Water under the power of her old engine.

'Mummy,' asked Phyllis, 'are we going to Seaview to have a bathe?'

'Not today.'

'Are we going to have a paddle?'

'No. We're just going to have a lovely sail.'

'We can have a bathe one day, can't we, Mummy?'

'One day,' said Joan.

Corbett came aft to the cockpit. 'Peter,' she said. 'Where are we going, anyway?'

He looked at her in surprise. 'I thought we decided on Wootton. We shan't do any better anywhere else. Unless you'd rather go to Cowes. But there's that fresh-water lake at Wootton, which would do for washing, anyway.'

She nodded. 'That's all right. I only wanted to know.'

They stood down the Hamble river and out into the middle of Southampton Water. Here Joan headed the vessel up into the wind while Corbett got the mainsail up; they had worked a boat together for so many years that they had little need to talk about the jobs. He swung upon the halliard to tighten the luff; then she laid the boat off on her course towards the Solent, slacked sheet and runner, and settled down at the helm. Corbett set the jib and foresail, came aft and stopped the engine. The vessel slipped forward under sail alone, the dinghy towing behind.

Joan sighed. 'It's good to get away from Hamble,' she said. 'It was beginning to get on my nerves.'

He nodded. 'I know. Still, I'll feel better when we're settled down in some new place.'

She glanced up at him in surprise. 'But Wootton will be all right. There won't be any bombing there, or cholera. And there ought to be plenty of milk in the island.'

He nodded. 'It ought to be all right. I only hope there isn't any catch in it.'

She laid her hand upon his arm. 'Don't worry – we'll come out all right. If it comes to the worst we can always go back to Hamble.'

He nodded.

Presently she said: 'Did you do anything about the car?'

'No – I just left it parked where it was. Nobody will pinch it, because there isn't any petrol. And anyway, it's not worth pinching.'

She sighed. 'We're leaving a good bit of our property around the countryside. First the house and all our things, and then the car.'

He smiled. 'We'll be back home again before very long, and then we'll have a fine time picking up the bits.'

She said quietly: 'I wonder.'

Wootton Creek lies towards the east end of the island, not very far from Ryde; a car ferry runs to it from Portsmouth. They had a fair wind but a foul tide; it was about four o'clock in the afternoon before they reached the booms marking the entrance to the channel. Here they started up the engine again and brought the vessel head into the wind to lower the mainsail before going in.

A speed-boat of the type used from beaches in the summer for joy-riding came from the creek to meet them, throwing the waves magnificently aside. There was a policeman in her and two special constables; Corbett noticed with uneasiness that there was a service rifle beside one of them.

'Here's trouble,' he said to Joan.

The boat ranged up to them, lost way, and lay rocking on the water half a dozen yards away. The constable stood up and hailed them. 'Where are you from?'

'Hamble.'

'Have you got a Bill of Health?'

'No,' said Corbett. 'We've not been abroad. We've come from Hamble – Hamble, near Southampton.'

'You want a Bill of Health, coming from Hamble. That's in the infected area.'

'How long has this been in force?'

'Thursday last. Nobody can land in the Isle of Wight without the vessel has a Bill of Health. I'm sorry, sir, but you'll have to go back.'

'Can I lie in Wootton for the night if I don't go on shore?'

'No, sir, you cannot. If you want to anchor you must go to quarantine.'

'Where's that?'

'Southampton Water, just down below Hythe. You'll see it marked with a big yellow flag. When you get there, report to the Port Sanitary Office – the launch will come out to you. Then when you've lain there for the statutory time, they'll give you a clean Bill of Health, and you can come on here.'

'How long will I have to stay there?'

'I couldn't rightly say – they'll tell you when you get there. I did hear it was seventeen days.'

Corbett expostulated: 'But that's absurd! I'll get bombed to hell each night I anchor there.'

'I'm sorry, sir, but them's my orders.'

'Isn't there anywhere else that I can go to go into quarantine?'

'Not in the Solent, sir. Of course, you could go back to Hamble. You won't be able to go into Portsmouth. I should go back to Hamble, if I was you.'

There was a short silence. At last Corbett said: 'All right – I'll go back.'

'One more thing,' said the constable. 'I know you're a responsible gentleman, sir, and you wouldn't go doing anything silly. But I have to warn you that no landing whatsoever, under any pretext, is permitted on the island except at Wootton, Ryde, Cowes, and Yarmouth, and then only on a Bill of Health. Any attempt to effect an unauthorized landing after receipt of this warning will be treated as an offence under the Defence of the Realm Act.'

The solicitor pricked up his ears. 'When did that Act come to life again?'

'Tuesday of last week, sir.'

'And what does all that mean, if I try to land?'

'You might get shot at, sir. In any case, you would be liable to a maximum penalty of imprisonment for five years.'

'I see,' said Corbett. 'I don't think I'll try it on.'

The man smiled. 'I'm sorry for your sake, sir, and the lady. But if I was you, I should go back to Hamble for the night.'

The speed-boat sheered away and went to intercept a little rowing-boat. Corbett turned the vessel from the creek and stood out to sea; in silence they got up the mainsail and jib again. He laid her to the wind for the beat back to Hamble, and sheeted the mainsail home.

Phyllis asked: 'Aren't we going to Seaview, Mummy?'

'Not today,' said Joan quietly. 'We'll go another day.'

Beating against the March wind, the children very soon became cold. Joan took them both below and wrapped them up in blankets in their berths with toffee to suck. Then, working under difficulties in the reeling forecastle, she heated milk over the Primus stove and gave a bottle to the baby. She came on deck after three-quarters of an hour feeling dazed and sick, glad to take the helm, up in the open air.

Night was falling; they were about half-way back to Southampton Water. From time to time a sloop or destroyer passed them in the fairway; once three motor torpedo-boats coming from Portsmouth passed them at a great speed, travelling in the direction of the Needles. Apart from these occasional ships, the Solent was completely empty; there were no liners or cargo vessels to be seen at all. The wind was cold enough, but not unbearable; they huddled in their oilskins and mufflers in the cockpit.

Joan said: 'Where are we going, Peter?'

He shrugged his shoulders. 'I'm not particular. Do you want to go back to Hamble?'

She shook her head. 'It gives me the willies, now.'

'I know. But I don't want to go to that quarantine anchorage – not tonight, anyway. We might not be able to get out again, once we got in. We might have to stay there, whether we liked it or not.'

'Being bombed all the time? They couldn't do that to us, Peter.'

'I'm not so sure. Anyway, I don't want to go there to-night.'

'We could just anchor somewhere for tonight and think about it, couldn't we?'

He nodded. 'We'd be all right anywhere on the west side of Southampton Water, in this wind. We'd be in the lee there.'

'We'd be out of the way of the bombs there?'

'I think so, if we didn't go too far up.'

They beat up to Southampton Water in the failing light. It was pitch dark when he dropped anchor in two fathoms a mile or so above Calshott. Below them the flying-boats swung at their moorings; a flare-path was laid out on boats upon the surface of the water. There was much going to and fro in motor-boats to the aircraft at their moorings; now and again one of the machines slipped away, taxied to the end of the flare-path, and roared off into the night.

Corbett stayed for some time on deck, stowing the sails and making all secure. Then he went down into the lamp-lit cabin. His wife was in the forecastle, busy over a stew upon the Primus stove; his children were sleeping quietly in their bunks. He had a great feeling of security, of domesticity.

He began to lay the table for supper. 'I tell you what,' he said. 'If we find we've got to go into quarantine, I'd rather do it in some other port. If we could get down to Weymouth, now – or even Plymouth. We might be able to do it there without being bombed all the time.'

She did not answer.

He asked: 'What do you think about that?'

She said: 'Supper's ready. Let's eat this while it's hot. We can talk about our plans afterwards.'

They were both very hungry. Half an hour later, fully gorged, Joan leaned back against the cushioned settee and blew a long cloud of cigarette smoke.

'Peter,' she said, 'where *are* we going to from here?'

'What do you mean?'

'Well, we were going to the Isle of Wight. We can't get into the Isle of Wight now unless we go into quarantine at Southampton for a good long time, and I'm not struck on that. You said we might sail down to Plymouth to do quarantine. But when we've done it, you wouldn't suggest that we sail back here again with our Bill of Health and get into the Isle of Wight?'

He rubbed his chin in perplexity. 'Seems sort of silly to do that.'

'Do you think the Isle of Wight is a very good place to go to? I mean, it's all right now. But with all this disease just over the water on the mainland, do you think they'll be able to keep it out of the island?'

He said: 'They're making a good stab at it. But – no. I think they'll fail.'

'Well then, it's not such a good place to go to.'

That seemed to be unanswerable.

She said: 'I mean, it's not much good going to another place we think will be all right, and then having to turn out again in a week's time and move on. We're on the move now, and so far the children have kept well. I'd rather move to some place where we know we shall be safe, and get it over.'

He nodded slowly. 'I don't know where that would be.'

There was a silence. Presently she said: 'Have they got these diseases down in Devon, or Cornwall? I mean, we might get a cottage there, somewhere.'

'I don't know how far the disease has spread. I think we've got to reckon that the whole of the south coast will be unhealthy. You see, it's the evacuation of the towns does it. . . .'

'You mean, it'll be like Swanwick? People mucking about in cars, all over the place?'

'It may be.'

'It doesn't look so good, Peter.'

'It doesn't.'

'Let's have a drink.'

He poured out whisky and lime-juice for them both; they sat smoking in meditative silence. Presently he said:

'There's always Canada.'

'I know.'

They sat there very still, immersed in their own thoughts. Over their heads the wind sighed through the rigging of the little boat, the water lapped on the topsides. He had a married sister in Toronto.

He said: 'Monica would love to have you and the children. And we've got a little bit of money in Canada, too – those railway shares.'

She said very quietly: 'I know.'

'It's the only really safe thing for the kids.'

For the third time she said: 'I know.'

She raised her eyes to his. 'You'd come over with us, Peter?'

He hesitated. 'I think I'd have to stay and do something in the war.'

She nodded. 'I know ... I'd want to be nearer you than Canada, Peter. Toronto's such an awful long way away.'

He leaned across the table and took her hand. 'You could take the kids over there and come back again when they were settled in. Monica would have them – I know she would. Especially at a time like this.'

She shook her head. 'It wouldn't be fair on them,' she said slowly. 'They're too little to be left. They'd be awfully unhappy without either of us.'

There was a long, thoughtful silence.

'There's no need for us to settle anything tonight,' he said at last. 'Let's sleep on it.'

'All right.' She got up and went through into the forecastle. And then she said: 'I do want to get some more water, if we can, tomorrow. There's a whole heap of the baby's things here to be washed out.'

He went on deck and looked around. There was still activity around the seaplanes; but for that, the night was quiet. It was heavily overcast, but no rain was actually falling. Over in the direction of Portsmouth there were searchlights playing in the sky.

He moved back to the hatch. Joan was there, standing and looking out into the night.

'Peter,' she said in a small voice. 'If we were to go to Canada, where would we go from?'

He rubbed his chin. 'I don't know. I don't believe there are any ships at all coming to Southampton now. They must have been diverted – farther west.'

'You mean, to Plymouth or Falmouth, or somewhere like that?'

'I imagine so.'

'We'd sail down there, would we?'

'I think that would be the best way to go. I don't much fancy trying to go by land.' He turned to her. 'What's in your mind?'

'I was thinking: it would take some time to get there. We wouldn't be sailing for Canada at once. And something might turn up....'

'Of course it might. We don't need to make our minds up yet.'

He went below, and they turned into bed. 'I don't know what to do about the water,' he said sleepily from his berth. 'I don't want to go back to Hamble for it.'

'Not much,' said Joan. 'They'd give us some at Yarmouth, wouldn't they? Even if we *are* unclean.'

'I don't know. We might try.'

They slept.

Soon after midnight the raid began. They woke to the sharp crack of guns; there was an anti-aircraft battery located on the edge of the New Forest, not very far from them. The guns went on incessantly, monotonously; the guns had a sharp, piercing crack that hurt their ears. The children woke up, and began to cry.

'Hell,' said Corbett. 'Where's that cotton-wool?'

They pressed wool into the children's ears, and into their own. They could not get any wool into the baby's ears, so they put pads of wool on top and bound the little face round with a bandage while the child yelled and struggled. Then they had done all they could do; for a time they lay in their bunks listening to the detonations of the bombs.

Presently, exhausted by the whimpering of the children and the screaming of the baby, they got up and made tea, and sat in the saloon in the darkness with the children, drinking it.

Corbett said: 'It won't go on much longer.'

As he spoke, there was a rushing, whistling sound, and a great splash near at hand as something heavy fell into the water. What happened then was past description. The vessel seemed to rise bodily into the air beneath them, plucking at her anchor-chain with a great crack that shook her to the stern. She was lifted, and thrown bodily on to the surface of the sea on her beam-ends, with a crash. In the saloon they were all flung together in a heap on the low side, stunned and deafened with the detonation. On her beam-ends she was carried swiftly sideways towards the centre of the channel; then she seemed to strike the bottom with her top-sides, though she had been anchored in two fathoms. Slowly she rose till she was nearly on an even keel. Then a great avalanche fell upon her, smothering her down, pressing her underneath the tumult of the sea. A ton of mud and water poured down into the saloon through the half-open hatch; she was spun bodily around. Then she rose, streaming like a half-tide rock, and drifted out towards the middle of the channel.

Deafened and dazed, Corbett groped his way to the hatch and clambered out on deck. By some freak of chance the dinghy was still with them; sunk to the gunwales, she was still attached to the stern by her painter. The boom was trailing in the water, topping lift and mainsheet carried away. There was a tangle of loose gear at the foot of the mast that he could not stop to investigate; the glass of the cabin skylight was shattered. The anchor-chain hung straight down from the bow, broken off short; the vessel was slowly rotating out into the middle of the channel. She was much lower in the water than usual; the decks were deep in slime.

He hurried aft to the sail-locker, got a warp, and bent it to the kedge-anchor. Then he went forward and anchored her roughly with the kedge and warp; she brought up in about six fathoms. Coming back aft, he saw that Joan was in the cockpit, working at the pump.

'Are the children all right?'

'I think they are. Look, take over pumping, Peter, and I'll go and see to them. There's over a foot of water in the cabin.'

He went to the pump. 'Mark the level in the cabin, and tell me if I'm getting it down at all.'

He settled to the pump. In the cabin he could hear her sloshing about in the water, could hear her comforting the children. Presently he heard the roaring of the Primus stove. He pumped on steadily. On shore the battery was still throwing its barrage to the sky; bombs were still falling round about. At the end of twenty minutes Joan said:

'You're getting it down, Peter. It's an inch lower than it was – an inch to an inch and a half.'

He rested for a minute, and began again. Presently, having soothed the children, she came to him with a cup of Bovril; he drank it gratefully while she relieved him at the pump.

He asked: 'Do you think she's making water?'

'I don't believe she is. The level's going down all the time. I think it's only what came into her by the skylight and the hatch.'

'Lord,' he said, 'we don't want another one like that.'

'What about that quarantine anchorage, now?'

'They can keep it.'

He busied himself with the boom. When that was inboard he went round the deck assessing the damage. It was not so bad as he had feared. The little yacht was injured, but she was not incapacitated; there was nothing there that he could not patch up and repair himself, given the time. He went aft and pulled the sunken dinghy up to the counter. Joan left the pump and went to help him; together they hauled it out of the water, emptied it, and put it back afloat. Then Corbett went back to the pump, and Joan went down below.

'The water's practically off the floor,' she said. 'I don't believe she's leaking more than usual. I'm going to change the kids into dry things.'

'Are there any dry things.'

'Oh yes. The things in the top drawers are quite all right.'

An hour later, the pump sucked. Corbett went below, exhausted and with a violent headache; he was amazed at what Joan had done. Regardless of the air-raid, which now seemed to be over, Joan had lit the lamp. She had changed the children into dry clothes and put them to rest upon the driest of the two settees; she had wiped over the floor and the paintwork. The saloon was looking almost normal, though it was smelling very bad.

He poured himself out a stiff whisky, and gave one to Joan. 'We'll get away from this bloody place as soon as we can,' he said wearily.

'Is the boat all right to get away?'

'I think so. I'll have to go and find the anchor. But it's got a buoy on it.'

He made her lie down on the other settee. Then he changed into dry clothes and put on his oilskins, spread a sail doubled over Joan's sopping bunk, pulled the wet blankets over him, and fell into a heavy sleep.

When he awoke, three hours later, it was daylight. He got up stiffly and took off his oilskins; Joan and the children were still sleeping. He went on deck, got a bucket, and started to swill away the slime that covered the vessel.

The morning came up sunny and bright. Joan heard him moving about on deck, got up, and came to the hatchway. She wrinkled up her nose at the mess on the deck; then she went back and started to get the children up. Corbett went off in the dinghy, found the anchor-buoy, and raised the anchor with ten feet of broken chain attached to it. He took it back on board and shackled it on to the remainder of the chain.

A couple of hours later they had more or less recovered from the incident of the night. They had had a good meal and had washed up; their clothes, their blankets and their bedding were laid out on deck and drying in the sun. Corbett was drying the magneto of the engine in the oven, and Joan, with sail-needle and palm, was repairing a long slit in the mainsail.

They worked all morning in the sun; by noon they were ready to get under way.

They were dead tired, and both confessed to headaches. The children were fretful and exhausted. Still, it was necessary to move on; they got the bedding down below again and put the children down to rest with a full meal inside them. For themselves, they took aspirin and a little food, and faced the future.

'There's one thing certain,' Corbett said. 'We've got to get away from here before tonight.'

Joan said hesitantly: 'Do you think we might go to Yarmouth?'

'That's in the Isle of Wight. They wouldn't let us in.'

She sighed. 'They're always so nice there.'

'We'll try it, if you like, but I don't think there's a hope. Still, they might let us have some water.'

She nodded. 'If they wouldn't let us stay we could go over and anchor for the night off Keyhaven, on the mainland side. We'd be out of the way of the bombs there, anyway.'

They got the dinghy up on deck and capsized her over the broken skylight in her sea-going position; then they set up the mainsail and got the kedge-anchor. There was a light breeze from the south-west as they sailed out of Southampton Water; the day was only partially overcast, so that there were patches of bright sun to warm them. They laid the vessel to wind for the beat down towards the Needles; Joan went below to sleep.

An hour later she came up on deck and relieved Peter at the helm; in turn he went below, and fell asleep at once.

He woke later in the afternoon, refreshed and well. He came up to the cockpit and took the helm from Joan, who went below and made tea. They got the children up on deck and all had tea together in the cockpit; by the time they could lie Yarmouth in the late afternoon they were cheerful and in good shape.

As they approached the little town at the entrance to its narrow creek they got the sails down and went forward under engine. A motor-boat came out to meet them, as at Wootton; before it had time to intercept them Corbett had anchored with his kedge-anchor and warp.

The boat came alongside. This time the sergeant of police in the boat was more truculent.

'Let's see your Bill of Health.'

Corbett said: 'I haven't got one, I'm afraid.'

'You can't anchor here without a Bill of Health.'

'I'm sorry about that.'

'Where are you from?'

'Hamble.'

The sergeant began upon a long, stereotyped harangue about quarantine, and the powers granted to the Local Authority under the Defence of the Realm Act to combat the spread of infection. Joan stood by the mast, aside. Out from the harbour entrance came an aged rowing-boat, rowed by a stocky figure in an old blue reefer and a seaman's hat. There was a black retriever dog perched in the bows.

Joan watched the boat as it drew closer. Then she interrupted the discussion.

'Oh, Peter!' she said. 'Here's Mr Low coming!' He was the Harbourmaster.

The police sergeant turned and looked with disapproval at the approaching boat. 'He's got nothing to do with this,' he said. 'Outside of his province, this is.'

Joan called out: 'Mr Low, do come and help us. We don't want to land. We only want some water.'

The Harbourmaster bumped his row-boat unceremoniously alongside the police launch. He beamed at Joan. He spoke slowly and without concern. 'Why, Mrs Corbett,' he said, 'quite a pleasure seeing you, this early in the season. And Mr Corbett, too.'

Joan said: 'Mr Low, they won't let us stay here. We know we can't land, but we want some fresh water. We've got the baby on board with us, and I must wash out her nappies.'

The sergeant said: 'They can't stop here. They got to go to quarantine.'

In the Harbourmaster the slow anger rose. 'Who says they can't stop here. They can't land – that I do know. But who's to say they can't anchor here, or anywhere they likes? Free for all, the sea is, below low-water mark.'

The sergeant, unaccustomed to marine law, hesitated. 'I got my orders,' he said a little weakly, 'and I got to see them carried out.'

The Harbourmaster followed up his attack. 'It don't say nothing in your orders about Mrs Corbett not anchoring here to get a drop of water, nor in the Defence of the Realm Act, either.' He snorted. 'Fine goings on, I do say!' He turned to the sergeant: 'All you want to know is that they're not going to land. Well, I've known this boat, and Mr and Mrs Corbett, these five years past. They come here regular, all through the summer. They won't land if you tell them not.'

'I don't want to land,' said Corbett. 'But I want some water now, and perhaps some more in the morning. I'd like to stay at anchor here for the night.'

'Where are you bound for?' asked the Harbourmaster.

'Plymouth, if I can get there.'

The sergeant said: 'All right,' and pushed off from the bow. He turned to the Harbourmaster: 'And don't you go on board of them, either. We don't want none of that cholera in Yarmouth.'

The Harbourmaster said disgustedly: 'Ah, get on out of it. Don't talk so soft.' The driver of the launch let in his clutch, and the boat slid away. The Harbourmaster beamed up at Joan. 'Got the baby with you, have you, Mrs Corbett? And the other two as well? My, don't they look well! A proper handful for you, they must be.'

Joan said: 'It's awfully good of you to let us stay the night. They wouldn't let us even anchor at Wootton.'

'Ah, stay as long as you like. You don't want to pay any attention to him. And there won't be any harbour dues, anchoring out here. But don't go on shore – not without he says you may.'

'We don't want to. All we want is some water, and then we'll be able to do the washing.'

'I'll get you the water – give us your bag.' They passed him the water-bag. 'How are you going on for milk?'

Joan said quickly: 'Could you get us some? Fresh milk?'

'Surely, Mrs Corbett.'

'Two quarts?'

'Surely. Do you want anything else – meat, or vegetables, or bread?'

Corbett said: 'We're quite all right for bread. We've got plenty of tinned things, but we've got no fresh meat or vegetables at all.'

'I could bring off two or three cabbages out of my own garden. What about a nice leg of lamb?'

Joan said unevenly: 'A nice leg of lamb. You don't know what you're saying, Mr Low.'

He smiled, and said: 'Suppose I bring you off a little bit of meat that you could cook yourselves, and have it hot for tonight. Then I could buy a nice big leg of lamb tonight and get the wife to cook it for you, and bring it off cold in the morning.'

Joan said: 'That would be splendid. You're ever so good, Mr Low.'

He said awkwardly: 'Ah, it's nothing, Mrs Corbett.' He pushed off and rowed back towards the quay. Joan turned to Peter, and her cheeks were wet with tears. 'I know I'm a damn fool,' she muttered. 'But it upsets one – when people are so kind.'

Half an hour later the Harbourmaster appeared again, still rowing with the dog perched in the bows. He brought them a bag of water, four cartons of milk, a little round of beef, and a cauliflower. They emptied the bag into the water-tank and gave it back to him to bring off full again in the morning. Corbett gave him money, but he would take nothing beyond the bare peace-time value of the food.

They spent the evening washing nappies, putting the children to bed, and preparing a great meal. It was after ten o'clock when it was finished and washed up; they sat on deck for a short time, smoking and looking at the lights across the water. From time to time a shadowy form, a warship or auxiliary vessel of some sort, went secretly past them without lights.

Corbett stirred. 'I knew that there was something wrong,' he said. 'I couldn't place it. The lighthouse at Hurst Castle isn't functioning.'

She looked towards the Castle in the black night. 'Is that because of the war?'

'I suppose it is. They turned out most of them in that last war, because they might have helped the submarines.'

'Do you think there are submarines in the Channel now, Peter?'

He rubbed his chin. 'I don't know. I don't think they'd bother much about us. We're too small.'

'I don't want to get submarined.'

He laughed shortly. 'If we stick around here, we'll get sent back to Hamble sooner or later. I'd rather go to sea and try and get down west. I don't think there's much risk.'

She nodded. 'You're right. I'd rather take that sort of risk than get sent back to Hamble.'

Presently they went to bed. In the night the distant thundering of bombs and the sharp crack of guns went on continuously from Southampton; it did not wake them. They slept peacefully and heavily all night; it was not till daylight that they woke again.

All that morning the ship was festooned with the baby's

washing and their own, hanging out to dry. The Harbour-master came off with the leg of lamb, fresh vegetables, more water, and more milk. He brought also a couple of loaves of bread to supplement the bread that Joan had baked, and a little bottle of boiled sweets for the children.

He asked: 'When are you getting under way, Mr Corbett?'

'This afternoon, I think. The weather looks all right.'

'I'll ring them up at Hurst Castle and tell them at the boom.'

'What boom?'

'They got the Needles channel closed with a boom, same as they did in the war – the last war. Because of the sub-marines, and that. All ships come in by Spithead now – we don't get none through here. But they'll let you through if they know. You go through on this side, right up against the shore. You'll see the mark boat there.'

He considered for a minute. 'I don't think they'll make any trouble. Another gentleman went through, day before yesterday, and they didn't make no trouble with him. They'll want to know where you're bound for.'

'Say Plymouth.'

'I'll arrange it for you, Mr Corbett. They won't make no fuss. I hope you'll have a very pleasant trip.'

Joan said: 'Goodbye, Mr Low. I'll never forget what you've done for us.'

He looked uncomfortable. 'That's all right, Mrs Corbett. We shall look forward to seeing you back in Yarmouth again.'

He rowed back to the town, the dog still perched im-passively in the bows of his boat. They watched him till he reached the quay.

'I knew we'd be all right if we came here,' said Joan.

They turned away, and started to get the boat ready for sea. They had baked a quantity of bread; with the two loaves the Harbourmaster had brought they had sufficient for a passage of two or three days. They had made a large meat stew and left it in the saucepan on the gimbals; they would get two meals out of that. They had a full water-tank, and some water still left in the bag.

They cleared the decks, gathering in the washing and stowing it away. Then they had lunch, washed up, and gave a feed to the baby. Finally at about three o'clock they were ready to go.

The day was overcast and cold, with a moderate easterly wind, fair for their passage. They got up their anchor and set sail towards the narrows; very soon they saw the mark boat with a small launch standing by. The launch ranged up alongside them; it was a naval boat, manned by two seamen and an RNR sub-lieutenant.

It passed under their stern to read the name. The officer hailed them.

'*Sonia*. Where are you from?'

'Hamble.'

'Where are you bound for?'

'Plymouth.'

'How many people on board?'

'Five. Myself, my wife, and three children.'

'Are you armed?'

'I've got an automatic pistol.'

'You'd better not try and use it. You can go through – between those two buoys. If you see any foreign submarine activity, or anything else that you think significant, put into Portland or Dartmouth and report.'

'I'll do that.'

'Good luck.'

The launch slid away, and they sailed forward through the boom.

Corbett touched Joan upon the shoulder. 'Go down and get some sleep. Put the children down, too. We shall be tired enough before we're through with this.'

She went below and slept. When she came up again it was five o'clock; the light was fading, and the sea was a dirty grey. Corbett smiled at her from the helm.

'The wind's getting up a bit,' he said. 'We're getting

along fine. Come and take her for a bit; I'll get a reef down before dark.'

She came to the helm. He went forward and took a couple of rolls down in the mainsail and stowed the foresail; the little vessel went more slowly but more easily. He came aft again.

She asked him: 'Where does this course take us to?'

'Seven miles outside Portland Bill – that leads us well clear of the Race.' He looked at the patent log. 'We've made a good five miles from the Needles. Getting along fine.'

She looked around, a little apprehensively. The sea was grey and angry looking, the dusk was falling. Behind them in the murk she could still just distinguish the high land of the Island; apart from that, there was no land in sight. It was unutterably lonely. She shivered a little.

He divined her thoughts. 'It's better than getting cholera.'

'I know.'

He smiled. 'Go down and make some tea – or I will, if you like.'

She went below and prepared the tea; then she relieved him at the helm while he went down and made a heavy meal. He came up and took the helm again while she gave the children tea; the bright lamplight made the little cabin seem homely even though everything was rocking on a slant, and she forgot her fears. She put the children to bed again when they had had their meal; finally she gave a bottle to the baby. Then she came up on deck.

'I'll take her now,' she said. 'You go down and get some sleep.'

He stood up and looked around distastefully. The wind was stronger, and the little ship evidently had all the sail that she could carry. The log showed thirteen miles from the Needles. 'I'll reef her down some more, and put on the little jib.'

It took him half an hour of heavy work, but the vessel went more easily under the reduced sail. He came aft, and looked again at the weather. The wind had backed in to the north and was freshening; in the saloon the barometer was falling slowly. A cross sea was getting up, giving an awkward motion to the little vessel.

'I hope this doesn't make the children sick,' he said.

'There's no sign of it yet,' said Joan. 'I kept them sucking sweets.'

'Glucose,' he said. 'I know.'

She turned to him. 'You go on down below and get some sleep. I'll be all right.'

'Sure?'

'Of course. Go on down.'

'All right. Call me at midnight, and I'll take over then. I shan't undress. Call me if anything happens, or if the wind gets up any more.'

He went below and lay down fully clothed upon the lee settee. In a few minutes he was asleep, warm and at rest. The vessel tore on through the darkness in the rising sea; at the helm Joan sat struggling with the tiller and fighting her fears. She told herself that there was nothing in the darkness to be afraid of. She was not a child. Peter was within call. When the sea made that noise it wasn't really dangerous. It was only strange. There was nothing to be frightened of. They were making a splendid passage down the coast. It would be a shame to call Peter before he had had a decent sleep. It was quite all right.

Presently a wave-top slopped up on the deck and brought her heart into her mouth.

A quarter of an hour later she heard a new noise in the darkness; the dinghy was moving about on the cabin-top. One of the lashings had slacked off with the motion of the vessel; with every lurch the ship gave the boat rolled upon the deck, looser at every minute. It might go overboard and be lost. She lashed the helm in the way that Peter did it, and in the darkness forced herself to leave the shelter of the cockpit and venture forward up the cabin-top till she could reach the loosened rope and get a heave on it. She made it fast, and looked around before she crept back to the cockpit. The vessel was rushing forward in the pitch darkness, lying well over; the sea was getting terribly rough. How awful it

161

would be if she were to fall overboard! She would be swept astern and nobody would hear her cries, for they were all asleep. The vessel would sail on and leave her, and she would be left swimming in the darkness in the terrible waste of sea, to perish, drown, and die.

She gripped the hand-rail on the cabin-top very hard, and crept back to the shelter of the cockpit.

An hour later the foresail flapped suddenly; the wind was heading her. She pulled the sheets in as hard as she could manage, and the vessel lay over on her beam and began tearing through the water in a smother of spray. The sea seemed to have become much rougher. She glanced at the binnacle; she could not lie her course. She was heading much too far south, and the yacht was over-powered, her lee rail under.

She leaned in at the hatch and cried out: 'Peter!'

He was on deck at once. She said: 'Peter, she won't lie her course. I think she's got too much sail up.'

He took a quick glance at the binnacle. 'All right, we'll lie her to.'

He put the helm down and hauled the jib sheet to windward; after a little experimenting she lay quietly on a more even keel. He slipped below and took a quick glance at the barometer. Then he was on deck again.

'Is it going down, Peter?'

He nodded. 'It's not quite so good. We'll stay like this till dawn.' He touched her on the shoulder. 'Go down below and get some sleep.'

'What time is it?'

'Half-past eleven.'

She sighed. 'I thought it must be nearly dawn.'

'No such luck.'

She went below and lay down on the settee. In the darkness on deck, Corbett settled down in the cockpit on watch. It was bitterly cold. There was nothing to be done, except to watch the vessel and to be ready for eventualities. Throughout the night the wind continued rising.

At three o'clock the vessel would not lie to any more;

continually she fell away from the wind, heeled over on her beam-ends, and came up to it again with the sails flapping madly. He called for Joan; in the turmoil she had been lying awake upon the lee settee, and came on deck at once.

He said: 'This isn't working any more. We'll have to get the sails off her, and run her off before it.'

'All right.'

He started up the engine to help the manoeuvring; then he got out of the cockpit in the darkness and went forward to take in the jib. Immediately he was soaked to the skin in the blown spray. He got the jib down without tearing it, brought it aft, and threw it down the hatch into the saloon. Then between them they got the mainsail down, got lashings round the wildly swinging gaff and boom, and lowered the lot down on to the deck. Corbett made it all fast in that position. Then they let the little vessel swing around and run in a south-easterly direction dead before the wind, under bare poles. He stopped the engine, and they went forward at about two knots.

The gale sang and whistled through the rigging in the darkness. The boat lay easily and safely, but with an appallingly violent motion in the rough sea. Below they could hear the children crying; Corbett stuck his head in at the hatch and spoke a word of comfort to them.

Joan said suddenly: 'Peter, I'm going to be sick.'

He said: 'So am I.'

They huddled together in the cockpit for an hour, drenched and cold, and vomiting from time to time. By experiment they found that they could retain brandy and barley sugar; no other food would stay with them. The children, lying in their berths and sucking barley-sugar, were not unwell; Joan resolutely kept them lying down. The baby, mercifully, slept through it all.

Presently Corbett made his wife go and lie down in the saloon.

The dawn came at last, grey and cheerless. The gale had not abated; the sea, now that it could be seen, was running very high. Corbett was not particularly alarmed. The little yacht was behaving well; she did not seem to be taking in very much water. He had only a rough idea where he was; he thought that they were heading more or less for Cherbourg, with eighty or ninety miles to go. The wind would drop, he thought, before they ran that distance. He was most concerned lest their strength should give out with the repeated vomiting.

He called Joan at about eight o'clock, went below himself, and fell into a doze. Joan settled down at the helm with the sweets and brandy flask, chilled and fatigued, but not uncomfortable. There was nothing to be done but to steer the yacht before the seas; since that was her natural direction it required little effort or attention.

Presently a new sound attracted her attention. On looking up, she saw a flight of aeroplanes circling overhead.

She watched them idly; they were in a different world. There were men up there looking at her vessel, but they could not help her, nor could she communicate with them. They turned and flew ahead of her; following their flight she saw a vast, ungainly block emerging from the mist. For one hideous moment she thought that it was a headland of the coast of France, that they were being driven dead on shore. Then she saw it more clearly, grey and menacing. It was an aircraft-carrier.

It was perhaps three or four miles away, down wind and to the west of them, heading on a course roughly parallel with their own. It seemed to be going at a great speed. She bent down and called to Peter; he came up on deck.

He studied the ship earnestly through field-glasses. 'It's either the *Courageous,* or the *Victorious,* or the *Glorious,*' he said. 'I can't tell them apart.' He paused. 'Look, they're taking the machines on board.'

They watched her for a time. The machines were circling round her, small as flies in the misty distance. They showed up clearly as they banked to turn; in straight flight they were little more than smudges in the sky. One after the other dropped down on a long slant towards the ship, flattened tangential to the deck and disappeared. With the fourth there was a difference. The plan form of the aeroplane showed suddenly and clearly at the end of the deck, poised for a moment, and then vanished.

Corbett smiled. 'They piled that fellow up, I think.'

Joan shook her head. 'It couldn't have been a crash. Look, they're going on just the same.' Another machine slid down to the deck and disappeared; the carrier steamed on.

'It was a damn funny landing, anyway,' he said.

Abruptly, from the bridge of the carrier, a bright light flashed. It flickered intermittently in flashes of Morse code. They watched it for a minute.

'I believe that's for us,' said Corbett. 'They're signalling with a searchlight.' He glanced behind him; there was no other ship in sight.

'What do you think they're trying to say?'

He shook his head. 'Blowed if I know. I can't read Morse,' The searchlight went on flickering.

The last machine slid down on to the deck. The carrier altered course and swung towards them, still steaming at a great speed. 'She *is* a thing . . .' said Corbett wonderingly.

Joan said: 'Like Broadcasting House going for a walk down Regent Street.'

As she drew near, two strings of brightly coloured flags broke from the yard on her short mast.

Corbett smiled faintly. 'Too bad. I can't read those, either.'

Quite suddenly she altered course away from them. For three or four minutes she zigzagged upon different courses, crazily, then with a swift dash she bore down on them. She passed behind them less than a hundred yards away, towering above them, confusing them with her immensity, blanketing them from the wind. In the lull they heard the sighing of the wind over her bulk, the shrill whine of her fans, the clamour of her passage.

A voice spoke suddenly from her loudspeakers, the bellowing of a husky giant. Joan started violently.

'Yacht ahoy!' The enormous voice spoke in measured tones, each word separate and distinct. 'There is a wrecked aeroplane lying on the water, bearing fifteen degrees on your starboard bow, distant two miles. Go and pick up the crew. Raise your right arm if you understand, and if you are able to rescue the crew.'

Mechanically Corbett threw his arm above his head.

'Thank you.' The voice repeated, measured and distinct. 'The aeroplane is fifteen degrees on your starboard bow, magnetic bearing south five degrees west from you, distant two miles. Land the crew in England if possible. You will be paid compensation for the deviation from your course. Goodbye.'

She swept past them and away; they were enveloped in a choking cloud of fumes. Through the smoke the gilt letters of her name, VICTORIOUS, shone out above them on a background of her dark grey hull. Then she was gone; her wake made a slick in which the sea was momentarily smooth.

Corbett was peering into the binnacle. 'Fifteen degrees – that comes to just about south five degrees west,' he said. 'Steer south fifteen degrees west, to allow for us being blown down. There. Take her, and I'll start up the engine.'

Joan took the helm and he went down below; presently the engine began coughing into the sea. He came on deck again.

Joan looked wistfully at the departing bulk of the great ship. 'She isn't rocking a bit.'

Corbett propped himself against the cabin-top and the boom, and stared ahead through the glasses. 'I can't see any sign of this aeroplane,' he said. 'We'll have to go on for a bit yet.'

The motor chugged steadily beneath their feet; they went forward slightly across the sea. The motion was worse than ever; the fumes of the exhaust blew nauseously from the stern over them in the cockpit. Corbett leaned suddenly aside and retched impotently; presently he sat up, white and shaken.

Joan said: 'Come and take her,' and slid from the helm. It was better to steer when one was sick. She took the glasses and peered forward; presently she said: 'Peter, what's that over there?' She pointed ahead.

He looked where she was pointing. 'That's her, all right. That's the tail sticking up.' He altered course a little more to windward and went on; from time to time they saw the tail of the machine again.

Joan asked: 'What'll we do, Peter?'

He rubbed his chin. 'It's not going to be easy. If we get down to leeward of her, we'll never get back against this wind. I don't want to get too near to her, either. We might get stove in.'

He gave the tiller back to Joan and got a warp out of the sail-locker. By this time they could see the wrecked machine practically all the time; she lay right side up, the top plane just clear of the water, the tail lifted high. There were two men standing in the aft cockpit, up to their waists in water. Down to leeward portions of the machine were drifting away; she was breaking up.

Corbett said: 'Keep straight for her. I'm going to try and get a warp on board her, and moor to her by the stern.'

He tied a light heaving-line to the warp. As they drew near he held it up, showing the line and warp; in the cockpit one of the men raised his hand. Corbett took the helm from Joan. 'There's no second shot,' he said quietly. 'I'll take her up as close as I dare. Then I'll hand over to you and chuck the line. When you take her, turn away down wind and put the engine in reverse.'

He headed for the smashed and broken wing-tip. He held on till the very last moment, till his bowsprit was stabbing the air behind the wing, then he jumped aside. 'Hard over now,' he said to Joan. 'Put her in reverse.' He jumped up on to the cockpit seat, collected himself, and flung the line. It fell across the fuselage; one of the men got hold of it.

Corbett shouted. 'Heave in the warp!' As he did so there was a heavy blow forward; he turned to see the tail plane rising from the deck, poise for a moment in the air, and crash down on them again. He shouted to Joan: 'Put her ahead and pay out the warp. We've got to get out of this!'

He ran forward, caught the plane in both hands, and broke the force of the next blow. As the yacht moved forwards the plane caught the starboard rigging and went sawing up and down. He managed to push it clear, pinching his right hand cruelly; then they were free. He turned aft to the cockpit.

He shouted to Joan: 'Astern – put her astern again,' and looked to see what was happening on the machine. They had not made the warp fast. Instead, he saw for the first time an inflated rubber raft, or dinghy, lying in the water by the fuselage. They had made the line fast to that. As he watched one of the men lifted the other bodily, heaved him over the side of the cockpit, and dropped him down into this raft. In the raft the man moved feebly, ineffectively. The other jumped into the sea beside the raft and floated high in the water, supported by an inflated jacket. He waved to them from the water, holding on to the raft with one hand.

Corbett said: 'Head her over that way – pull them clear of the tail. Put her ahead a little bit. That's enough.'

He pulled in the warp; the craft came slowly to them. As it came alongside, Joan and Peter leaned down and helped the fit man from the water. Then with great difficulty the three of them got the injured man from the raft into the cockpit.

The stranger said: 'Good thing you came. She was breaking up pretty fast.'

Joan said: 'Your ship came and told us. Why didn't she stop and pick you up?'

The man said: 'This is a submarine area. She daren't stop. She's got to keep on going.' He wriggled himself out of his sodden flying-suit, and showed himself dressed in the uniform of a lieutenant-commander.

Corbett said: 'You'll find some dry clothes down in the saloon. Help yourself.'

The stranger said: 'Later. Can we get this chap down below and get his wet things off? He's pretty bad.'

The other man lay collapsed upon the cockpit seat,

stirring a little with instinctive reaction as the vessel rolled. Water was dripping from his sodden clothes and flying-suit. He had no hat or helmet on his head; a deep gash showed white and unpleasant in the side of his face. 'He's the pilot,' said the other. 'His name's Matheson. He hit his head as we went over.'

They looked at him in consternation. The injured pilot was a very young man, not more than twenty-two or twenty-three years old. The other was an older man, perhaps forty or forty-five. Joan said: 'Let's get him down below. We've not got a great many dry clothes, but we can wrap him up in blankets.'

The lieutenant-commander slid back the cabin hatch and glanced below; he saw the two children in the waterway bunks. He turned to Corbett in surprise. 'I say,' he said, 'how many of you are there on board?'

'Myself, my wife, and three children. My name is Corbett. We're from Southampton.'

The other said: 'Mine's Godfrey – Lieutenant-Commander.' He paused awkwardly for a moment, and then he said: 'I'm afraid we're going to be a frightful nuisance to you. Where are you bound for?'

'Plymouth.'

The other glanced at the binnacle. 'You're heading for Cape Barfleur now.'

'We've been running before it since midnight.'

Joan said: 'You can talk about that later. Let's get him down below.'

Corbett stayed at the helm. Joan and Godfrey stripped the flying-suit from the all but helpless body of the pilot, removed his outer clothes, and got him down into the saloon. They started to undress him. The children watched with interest from their bunks. John asked: 'Mummy, why are you putting that man to bed?'

Godfrey turned to him, and said: 'He tumbled down and hurt himself.'

Joan said: 'There's a pair of pyjamas in the top drawer –

there. Give them here. Lie down again, John – you're not to get up. Oh, God, I'm going to be sick again.'

She vanished up the hatchway into the cockpit. Godfrey was left alone. He got the injured man out of his underclothes, rubbed him with a towel, put him into pyjamas. He laid him on the settee, propped up his head, and covered him with blankets. Then he, too, made a dash on deck and to the rail.

Presently he raised himself. 'I say, I'm sorry,' he said apologetically. 'I haven't been in anything this size for years.'

Joan said weakly: 'That's all right. You're all square with us now. Have some barley-sugar and brandy.'

She passed him the flask and the screw-top bottle. Corbett explained: 'We can keep those down if we don't have to move about too much. Anything else comes up at once.'

Joan leaned in through the hatch and looked below. Phyllis was lying dozing in her bunk, clutching a Teddy Bear. John was lying on his back, playing with a bunch of coloured wools. In the saloon the sick man lay inert.

'I suppose it must be concussion,' she said doubtfully. 'We must do something for him. Does anyone know what the treatment is?'

The men shook their heads. 'All I know,' said Godfrey, 'is that you mustn't give them alcohol.'

Joan nodded. 'I've heard that. I believe he ought to have a hot-water bottle at his feet.'

Corbett said: 'That's a good idea. Take her, and I'll go and put a Primus on.'

Joan shook her head. 'I've got to go below and put one on for the baby's feed. I'll do it. I've just been sick, so I'm good for the next quarter of an hour.'

She went below again. Godfrey was shivering; on Corbett's advice he went below and changed into a miscellaneous set of clothes, not dry but drier than his own, which were in the saloon. He came on deck again.

'Let me take her,' he said. 'I can stand trick and trick with you now.'

Corbett gave him the helm. His hand was paining him a good deal; it was stiff and swollen where it had been pinched by the tail-plane. He asked the officer: 'Do you know where we are?'

The other considered for a moment. 'Must be about forty miles north-west of Barfleur. Is that about what you make it?'

'I hoped it was sixty or seventy.'

'I don't think it's as much as that. No, I'm sure it's not.'

'What's the weather going to do?'

The other thought hard for a moment, memorizing the barometric chart that he had seen at dawn that morning. 'The depression was over northern France, moving northeast. It should get better presently.'

He turned to Corbett. 'Tell me, how did you come to get out here?'

Corbett shrugged his shoulders. 'It just happened.' He paused, and then said: 'We couldn't stay in Southampton, where we live.'

'Why not?'

'We had to get out damn quick.'

'Because of the bombing?' The officer seemed genuinely surprised. 'Was it as bad as that?'

Corbett eyed him for a minute. 'Do you know what things are like on shore?'

The other shook his head. 'We've none of us been near the beach since war began. I know there have been raids.'

'Well, I'll tell you.' In short, unembellished terms, he told the naval officer what had happened to them since the war began. The officer heard him to the end.

'It's amazing. . . .' he said. 'We knew there had been raids on various towns, but we never dreamed that it was anything like that.'

He hesitated for a moment. 'You didn't happen to hear how things were going on at Alverstoke?' he said.

Corbett shook his head. He knew Alverstoke, a little place near Portsmouth, on the Solent. 'I don't know anything about conditions there,' he said. 'Why?'

'I've got a flat there,' the officer said simply. 'My wife's there now, with our boy.'

There was a silence. Corbett said at last: 'I should think they'd be all right.'

The other nodded, but did not pursue the subject. Presently he said: 'We knew there weren't any newspapers. We couldn't understand why.'

'There's been nobody to print them, or distribute them.'

The officer asked: 'Why is that? They aren't all in the army, yet?'

Corbett said: 'It's not that. But it's been the same with everything. Nobody's had time to do his job – whether it's been printing a newspaper, or driving a milk lorry, or shunting coal-trucks. You see, for the first few days we were all digging trenches in our back gardens. That had to come before one's job – otherwise one would just have been killed. And after that, in the evacuation period, no one worried much about his daily job. Everybody had his wife and kids to look after.'

The naval officer said quietly: 'Excepting us.'

7

JOAN CAME on deck, white and ill. She had been below for the greater part of an hour. She had given a bottle to the baby and she had put a hot-water bottle at the feet of the sick man. She had washed his face and dressed the wound upon his cheek; she had not been able to do more for him. He lay there breathing heavily, virtually unconscious and unable to take food.

She took the helm and immediately felt better. 'Peter,' she said. 'We must get somewhere soon. That man below will die unless we get him into hospital.'

He nodded. 'I know. I'm afraid there's nothing we can do.' He looked round the horizon. 'Blowing as hard as ever,' he said. 'She won't stand any sail yet.' He turned to Godfrey. 'What do you think?'

The other shook his head. 'I'm afraid I just don't know. I've never been in anything smaller than a destroyer, and I don't know much about sail. I should wait a bit.'

Peter showed his hand to Joan. It was much swollen, with a bluish look. She bent over it and examined it critically. 'I don't know what to do for that, Peter. Does it hurt much?'

'It throbs a bit.'

'I could put a bandage on it with some Pond's extract. I'll go below and get it.'

Godfrey moved to the hatch. 'Tell me where it is – I'll go.'

He went below and handed up the bottle and the bandages. Then he went over and examined the sick pilot. He was warm and apparently comfortable; there was nothing to be done. He went to the hatch and stood for a minute between the waterway bunks, watching Joan in the cockpit as she bandaged Peter's hand.

From the bunk beside him John plucked at his sleeve. 'Will you read this book to me?'

He turned. 'What's that, old man?'

Phyllis said from the other bunk: 'He wants you to read his book. I can read by myself.'

'Can you?'

She nodded vigorously.

He turned to John, took the little book from his hand, and settled down upon the engine casing. He glanced at the cover, and then opened it.

He read: ' "This is a fierce bad Rabbit; look at his savage whiskers, and his claws, and his turned-up tail." '

John leaned over. The lieutenant-commander showed him the picture. 'There's his turned-up tail – see?'

'Which are his savage whiskers?'

'There.'

'Oh.'

' "This is a nice gentle Rabbit. His mother has given him a carrot." '

The little vessel reeled and lurched over a grey sea; the low grey clouds flew past hardly above the mast. The wind droned and whistled in the rigging; from time to time a wave-top was blown off and flew over the boat, stinging the faces of the people in the cockpit. At the helm Corbett sat steering with one hand; Joan was bandaging the other one for him. Before she had finished, the bandage was wet with spray. In the alley-way between the bunks the naval officer sat reading steadily, pausing now and then to show a picture to the children.

He finished that book. He was pressed to read another, but refused, and came up on deck. He said to Corbett: 'Let me take her. You go below and get some rest.'

Corbett gave him the helm, stood up, and looked out over the grey rollers. 'If we go on like this we'll hit the coast of France some time tonight,' he said. 'In the dark. Are the lighthouses working?'

The officer shook his head. 'No. This is a submarine

area. I've been thinking about that, too. You've not got a sextant on board?'

'No. I never learned to use one. You see, we don't go outside the Solent very much, except in August. We go down the coast to Cornwall then, most years. But that's only day sailing.'

Godfrey nodded. 'Anyway, there's no sun.' He paused. 'I think it should let up a bit this evening.'

Corbett went below; and Godfrey settled down with Joan at the helm. She asked him: 'How did your accident happen?'

He shrugged his shoulders. 'He just landed short. I thought we were for it properly – going to hit the end of the deck. He pulled up before hitting it, and stalled her down on the aft end. Then she dropped a wing, and we did a cartwheel into the ditch. We never got to the wires at all.'

She pondered this for a moment, understanding only half of it. 'Is he a good pilot?'

Godfrey smiled. 'Not out of the top drawer. He's very young, of course.'

'Are you a pilot?'

He shook his head. 'I'm the observer.'

'Have you been in the Navy all your life?'

He nodded. 'I was a snotty in the last war.'

He asked her what they were going to do, why they were making for Plymouth.

She said: 'Peter thought that there'd be ships going to America from there. There aren't any ships coming to Southampton now – at all.' She paused, and then she said: 'He wants me to take the children to his sister, in Toronto.'

He glanced at her curiously. 'Do you want to go?'

She shook her head. 'I don't want to go a bit. But he's quite right. It's the only safe thing for the kids.'

'Is it as bad as that on shore?'

'It was where we were. It might be better in other parts, but how can you say?'

He did not answer; for a moment he was preoccupied with his own concerns, with thoughts of his own family. If this was what civilians thought about things, somehow or other he must get to know how things were going on at home, must help his wife in this emergency. But presently he said:

'Is Mr Corbett going over with you?'

She shook her head sadly. 'We haven't talked about it, but I know he won't come. He wants to do something in the war, enlist or something – as soon as he can get rid of us.'

He glanced at her; his eyes were very soft. 'It's a hard business, this.'

'It's hateful.'

He thought about it for a minute. 'He's doing the right thing,' he said at last. 'I suppose it would have been easy enough for him to go and enlist right away. But after what you've told me, I don't see how he could have left you to fend for yourselves until he'd got you somewhere safe.' He paused. 'It's different for us, of course, in the Navy. It's one of the risks we take when we choose the Navy as a career – that in time of war our families must scratch for themselves. I must say, I never realized what kind of risk it was.'

He said: 'You didn't hear of any cholera or typhoid round about Alverstoke, did you?'

She shook her head. 'Not a word. Botley was the nearest. That's about fifteen miles away, isn't it?'

'I shouldn't think it's quite so far.'

There was a silence. Presently he said: 'I don't believe you'll get a ship at Plymouth. That's been bombed just like Southampton, I believe. You might get one at Falmouth. But most of the ships have been diverted to the west, you know. Places like Cardiff, Milford, and Liverpool.'

'Is that because of the submarines?'

'Partly. Partly because of the towns and docks being bombed. And also, to get them out of the way of things like last week's show.'

'What was that?'

'Off the Thames, and round about the Goodwins. You heard about it, surely?'

She shook her head. 'What was it – a battle?'

'I suppose you'd call it that. I didn't see anything of it – we were up in the Irish Sea and the west coast of Scotland, waiting for them there. But this thing – they were trying to force the Straits, you know. We put it across them properly. Do you mean to say you didn't hear of it on shore?'

She shook her head. 'We were out at Hamble. There weren't any papers there – or nothing that had anything like that.'

'Wasn't it on the wireless?'

'It may have been. But there's been no electricity, you see – and so no wireless. Not many people have a battery set, these days. And anyway, you can't get the batteries charged when there's no current in the mains.'

He stared at her in wonder. 'I never thought of that.... It was a big engagement, though – a very big one. As big as Jutland. We lost two capital ships, the *Warspite* and the *Hood*. They lost about ten.'

'You mean that we won?'

He shrugged his shoulders. 'I don't know that you can say that anyone wins anything, these days – not quite like that. It finished up with our fleet much superior to theirs in capital ships, anyway. It's given them something to think about.'

Joan said: 'You must tell Peter when he comes on deck. He'll be awfully interested.' She reached for the screw-top bottle. 'Have a barley-sugar. They're full of glucose.'

The afternoon wore on. Corbett came on deck presently and Joan went down; she busied herself in the reeling forecastle with cups of Bovril for the children and a bottle for the baby. It took her an hour. Then, sick, dizzy, and exhausted, she lay down on the settee and fell asleep at once.

Shortly before dusk the wind moderated and backed more into the west. The sea was running very high, but in long, even rollers that the vessel had time to rise to and slide over. Corbett looked around. 'She'd stand a bit of sail on her now, I think.'

Godfrey said: 'It would be just as well. I don't know where we are – not within twenty miles. We'd better head up north; we can't be far from the French coast.'

Corbett nodded. 'We don't want to bump on that in the dark.'

They shipped the pump, and he began to pump the vessel out before setting sail. The working and the straining that she had been through in the last twenty-four hours had not improved her; there was a good deal of water in the bilge. They cleared her in twenty minutes' pumping, then turned to the sails.

'You'll have to do most of it for me, I'm afraid,' said Corbett. 'This hand of mine isn't much good to me.'

The naval officer said: 'That's all right. You tell me what you want done.'

In half an hour of shouted instructions and heavy work they got the mainsail set, a little close-reefed rag; they followed it with a small jib set up from the stem. With that sail the little yacht had all she wanted; she surged away to the north with the wind free, clambering up over the one side of the rollers and charging down the other side like a speed-boat. Immediately they felt relief from the incessant motion as she steadied to the pressure of her sails.

All square forward, Godfrey came aft to the cockpit. 'That's better,' Corbett said, bracing himself against the tiller. 'We're getting somewhere now.'

In the gathering dusk the little ship went bustling on, making perhaps three knots in the rough sea. Their spirits rose; they had a drink of brandy. Then Corbett, greatly daring, went below and fetched a few dry biscuits. They ate them, and retained them.

Presently it was dark. They sailed on through the night, the wind moderating all the time. After a while Corbett said: 'Should we be showing lights?'

Godfrey considered for a minute. 'Well, nobody else will be that we meet. Still, I think I'd put them up. They might stop someone from popping off at us for luck.'

Corbett went below to get the port and starboard lanterns, and lit the cabin lamp to see to them. The light woke Joan; she stirred and rubbed her eyes, and followed him on deck when he took up the lights. He set them in the rigging, glowing brilliant in the night.

Joan said: 'This is lovely, sailing along like this.' She reached out for the brandy flask and took a little drink. 'Where are we going to?'

Godfrey said: 'Back the way we came, on the reverse bearing. I'm afraid I can't say more than that.'

'That probably means Portland,' said Corbett.

The officer looked at him seriously. 'If that's all right by you, it would be a good place to put us off. *Victorious* is going there to fuel – or was when last I heard. We could get Matheson into the hospital on shore there, too.'

Corbett said: 'That suits us. The sooner he gets into hospital the better, I should say.'

Godfrey agreed. 'We ought to sight the coast tomorrow morning, probably. We'll have to see where we come out, and what the wind is doing. It might be better to go into Poole. We'll have to see.'

Joan stood erect, and looked out over the dim sea. 'I liked that nip of brandy,' she said unexpectedly. 'Peter, does anyone want anything to eat?'

They became aware that they were very hungry. 'It's not half so bad now,' said Joan. 'I believe we could cook something hot.'

She went below and emptied tins of beef and vegetables into a large saucepan. She put in a little water, heated it on the Primus stove till it was boiling, added Bovril and condiments, and carried it up to the cockpit with three spoons. They ate it gratefully, and retained it. Satisfied and encouraged, they sent Godfrey down below and settled down together upon watch.

Godfrey knelt by the pilot and examined him. He was still unconscious, breathing rather heavily and growing cold about the hands and feet. The officer went through into the forecastle and boiled a kettle, refilled the hot-water bottle, and laid it in the blankets at the sick man's feet. He raised the head a little with another cushion; then he had shot his bolt, there was no more that he could do.

He remained kneeling by the sick man, lost in thought. He thought of his flat in Alverstoke, of Enid, his wife, of Joe, their little son. They only had one child; it was a pity, but naval people mostly had to be content with one. If anything should happen to them . . . The thought tore his heart. He remembered the prayers he had not thought of since he was a boy; he could not quite remember all the words, but he said what he could remember.

Presently he went over to the other settee, and slept. On deck, Joan and Peter huddled together in the cockpit as the vessel sailed on through the night. It was colder, but the wind was dropping. Joan went below at midnight and cooked another stew; Godfrey awoke and went on deck. Together they shook out a reef and set the foresail; then Joan went below to sleep. When dawn came, Joan and Godfrey were on deck and Corbett was asleep.

It was full daylight when he came up to the cockpit. Ahead of them, in the far distance, land was showing as an isolated lump; over on the starboard bow it showed again. Godfrey nodded to it. 'St Albans right ahead. That's the island over there.'

Corbett stood for a minute, taking it in. 'Can you lie Portland?'

'Not quite yet. We may be able to before so long. The wind's backing all the time.'

Corbett thought for a minute. 'We've got about six gallons of petrol left. We'll keep a gallon to get into harbour with. I'll put the engine on; it'll help her along a bit.'

They sailed on all the morning, gradually raising the wedge bluff of Portland above the horizon. About noon a grey trawler, armed with a gun upon her forecastle and manned by a naval crew, closed up to them and hailed them, asking where they were bound. Godfrey slipped on his monkey jacket and hailed back.

In the early afternoon, five miles from the harbour near the Shambles lightship, a motor torpedo-boat ranged alongside, questioned them closely, and gave them the rather complicated sailing directions for entering the harbour through the mine-field.

At four o'clock they sailed in through the breakwater gap. The harbour was thronged with warships of every sort, with oil tankers, colliers, and a great multitude of smaller craft. In the middle loomed the flat, ungainly bulk of the *Victorious*.

Godfrey said· 'She's here before us. I thought perhaps she might be.'

They dropped sail, and went forward through the fleet under engine alone. The officer went forward to the anchor gear; they brought up in three fathoms at the south end of the harbour, near the stone jetty.

Corbett went below to stop the engine. When he came up again, he glanced forward; Godfrey was standing on the cabin-top, a handkerchief in each hand, sending a long message by semaphore. Corbett stared at the aircraft-carrier; on her bridge the mechanical semaphore wagged at the conclusion of each word.

The officer finished his message and came down from the cabin-top. 'What's happening?' asked Corbett.

'I told them we were here and wanted the doctor. They'll probably send off a boat.'

He busied himself with Corbett in stowing the mainsail. In a very few minutes a hard chine launch came swiftly to them from the carrier, throttled her engines, sunk into the water, and made fast alongside. A surgeon-commander, immaculate in uniform, stepped from the boat down on to the deck of the little yacht. Godfrey was there to meet him; they exchanged a few words, and he went below.

The pilot was put on to a stretcher and taken on board the launch; the surgeon turned to Joan: 'Has he had anything to eat or drink?'

'Nothing,' she said. 'I couldn't get him to take anything. I kept a hot bottle at his feet.'

'He's had nothing at all? That's quite all right – I wanted to know.' He glanced around. 'How long have you been at sea?'

Joan glanced at Peter. He said: 'Four days, I think. It might be five.'

'These children. Have they kept well?'

Joan laughed. 'They never turned a hair. I kept them lying down. The baby slept practically all the time.'

'Baby? Have you got a baby on board?'

'Come and see.'

She took him through into the forecastle and showed him little Joan in her cradle, lashed to the bulkhead above the water-closet. The forecastle was a wild litter of spilt food and paraffin, lamps, unwashed dishes, tins of food, petrol-cans, ropes, sails, and gear. The infant beamed up happily at them as they bent over it.

The surgeon-commander straightened up, bumping his head painfully against the deck beams. 'Not much wrong with her.' He stared around him at the litter in the forecastle, at the wet squalor of the saloon, at the two children in the waterway bunks. 'You had it pretty rough, the last two days?'

Joan nodded.

The surgeon glanced at her drawn, haggard face, the wet hair plastered over her forehead, the white salt crusted on her cheeks around her tired eyes. 'You've done a good job, Mrs Corbett,' he said suddenly. 'Your children are well and healthy, and that man will live.'

He went on deck and turned to the launch. He said to Godfrey: 'I'm taking him straight on shore, to the hospital. I'll send the boat back for you as soon as I've done with it.'

The lieutenant-commander asked: 'Do you know when we're sailing?'

'I haven't heard.'

The boat slid away and accelerated, rising on to the surface of the water at the head of a broad wake of foam. They watched her for a minute, then turned back to their own affairs. Godfrey went down below to change into his own clothes. Corbett leaned in at the hatch and said to John and Phyllis: 'You can get up now. Come out on deck.'

They scrambled out into the cockpit. With the coming of the evening the clouds had lifted; over the Chesil Bank there was a sunset in the west, all blue and rose colour. The grey forms of the warships became shot with gold; they took on a purple tinge against the background of the misty downs.

Phyllis asked: 'Where are we, Daddy? Daddy, where are we?'

John echoed: 'Where are we, Daddy?'

He was suddenly very tired. 'Portland,' he said. 'Did you think we were never going to get here?'

She nodded. John said: '*I* thought we were going to get here, Daddy.'

'No, you didn't, John. Daddy, he didn't, did he? Daddy, where is Portland? Is it near London?'

He shook his head. 'Not very. Look at all those battleships. Do you remember seeing them before, at the review?'

Phyllis nodded. 'Daddy, will there be fireworks on the ships tonight?'

'Not tonight.'

'There was at the review, Daddy.'

He sat down on the cockpit seat. He was beginning to grow cold; he became aware that all the clothes that he had on were clammy and damp. He thought with dismay that there was nothing dry on board. Clothes, blankets, mattresses, and sails – everything was wet, and night was coming on.

Joan came to the hatch. 'Come out on deck and look at the sunset,' he said wearily. 'I'll go below and light the Primus stove. We'll have a cup of tea.'

Godfrey heard him. 'Look here, don't do that. We can do better than that. We'll go to the *Victorious* and have a proper meal.'

Corbett laughed. 'With all the family?'

'Of course. Why not?'

Joan said: 'It's terribly nice of you, but we really aren't decent. I couldn't leave the baby, and I couldn't take her with me on your ship. No, we'll be quite all right here.' She hesitated. 'If you could send us off some fresh milk from the ship . . .'

The boat returned and slid alongside. The surgeon-commander stepped on board again. 'Mrs Corbett,' he said, 'I've seen the surgeon-captain in charge. He asked me to tell you that if you would care to take the children to the hospital for tonight, with your husband, he can accommodate you all.' He smiled. 'I think if I were you I should accept that offer. There's a hot bath attached to it.'

Joan said simply: 'I can't say no to a hot bath.'

Godfrey said to Corbett: 'You'd better do that. Then I'll get all your mattresses, blankets, clothes, and stuff taken on board *Victorious* and dried by the morning.'

He spoke to the coxswain of the boat and gave him his orders. 'I'll see the officer of the watch when I get on board.'

Half an hour later Joan and Peter were lying in hot baths in the bath-house, separated from each other by a green canvas curtain. The children had been taken from Joan by the sick bay stewards to be bathed. Even the baby had been taken from her; in the quiet efficiency of the place she was content to let it go. They lay luxuriating in the hot water, soaking the salt out of their bodies.

'Peter,' said Joan from behind the curtain. 'When did you have a bath last?'

'Good Lord! – I don't know.' He thought for a minute. 'Not since the war began.'

'Nor have I. How long is that?'

They tried to count the days, came to a different answer every time, and gave it up. 'I do hope they'll let us have another bath in the morning,' said Joan.

'They might. It's a bit of luck getting in with the Navy like this. We might not have got a bath for months.'

Presently they got out, still rocking with the motion of the boat, dressed in borrowed pyjamas and dressing-gowns, and went through to a small dining-room with a fire. A steward was waiting to serve them with short drinks, and a dinner of soup, stewed steak and vegetables, and a steamed pudding.

By the time they reached the coffee stage they were all

but asleep. 'Now I lay me down to rest,' said Joan. 'I do like the Navy, Peter.'

They went through to the room arranged for them, stumbling a little as they walked. There were three beds; in one of them the two children were already asleep. The baby was reposing in a drawer laid carefully upon two chairs. Joan and Peter climbed into their beds, turned over, and within five minutes were asleep themselves.

Corbett woke at dawn, slept again, and woke finally at about nine o'clock. Joan and the children were still sleeping; he got up very quietly, went to the bath-house and had a shower, and came back to dress. His clothes were laid out at the foot of his bed; they had been dried and brushed, but were sufficiently disreputable. He left the room before the others were awake, and went along to breakfast in the dining-room.

A signalman came to him as he was finishing. 'The surgeon-captain has had a signal from *Victorious*, sir. The captain would like you to go on board this forenoon. He'll send a boat in for you as convenient.'

Joan was still sleeping; the children were all right. Corbett said: 'I can go at once.'

'Very good, sir. I'll tell the surgeon-captain and he'll send a signal for the boat. Down at the jetty, sir.'

It was a sunny morning late in March; there was a fresh wind from the Channel. Corbett left the hospital and walked down the road to the jetty; in the harbour the fleet lay spread out before him, bright and cheerful in the morning sun. He sat for a time upon a block of stone upon the jetty watching the traffic of the harbour; presently the boat slid up to the steps.

He got down into the stern-sheets and was carried swiftly to the carrier. As he went, he was distressed about his clothes. In spite of the attention that had been given to them at the hospital they were not very good. He was wearing a very old tweed coat with a torn pocket; though the salt had been brushed from his trousers, traces of motor grease remained. On his head he wore a very battered soft felt hat; his collar had been clean before the war.

The boat drew up to the gangway; he went on board, turning to raise his hat to the quarter-deck. So much, at least, he knew about the Navy. Godfrey was there in a new uniform; he came to meet him.

Corbett said awkwardly: 'I say, I've not got clothes to come on board. I'm terribly sorry.'

'You're perfectly all right. The Captain said he wanted to see you. You don't mind?'

'Not if he doesn't mind seeing me like this.'

They went forward through the lower hangar, out into an alley at the side, up three flights of very steep steel steps, out on to the flight-deck, wide and unencumbered, and into the island bridge. At the door of the captain's sea cabin Godfrey knocked and went in. He came out in a minute.

'Would you come in?'

In the narrow little room, cumbered with berth and desk, there was barely room for the three of them. The captain rose and held out his hand, a broad, youngish man with curly red hair and a merry face.

He said: 'Mr Corbett? Good morning. I wanted to meet you to thank you for picking up Godfrey and Matheson. I hope it hasn't been too inconvenient for you.'

'Not a bit, sir.'

'Where were you bound for when we spoke to you?'

'Plymouth.'

'Plymouth? But you were running south.'

Godfrey said: 'It was a very strong wind for a small boat, if you remember, sir. I found that when I got on board. They couldn't carry any sail at all. They'd been running before it since midnight, waiting for it to moderate.'

'I see. So actually you haven't been taken much out of your way by coming back to land them here?'

Corbett smiled, and shook his head. 'I shan't put in any claim for compensation. Not after all the hospitality we've had.'

'They made you comfortable in the hospital? I'm glad of

that.' He turned to Godfrey. 'What's happening about their stuff?'

'The boat's away now, taking it on board. The commander sent off earlier in the morning to clean the vessel out for them, sir.' He turned to Corbett. 'I expect they'll have put everything in the wrong place. I'll come with you when you go.'

'It's awfully kind of you to take all this trouble,' he said.

The captain held out a cigarette-box. 'Not a bit. Where are you bound for now, Mr Corbett? Still for Plymouth?' He struck a match and lit the cigarette for him.

'I'd rather like to get your advice on that, sir.'

'Go ahead.'

'I'm trying to get my wife and children on a steamer for the States, or Canada. I can pay the passage, and I've got money over there for them to live on, for a time at any rate. Nothing's coming into Southampton now. I thought if I got down to Plymouth I might get a boat for them there.'

'But why didn't you go by train, or by road?'

Corbett smiled, a little bitterly. 'I don't think you quite realize what things are like on shore, sir.'

Godfrey nodded. 'Things seem to be much worse than I knew, sir.'

The captain eyed them keenly. 'In what way?'

Corbett said: 'Things are very difficult in the Southampton district now.' In short, unembellished terms he told the captain what had happened to them since the war began. At the conclusion he said: 'You see, I thought it would be easier to take my family down by sea than going any other way. I still think it's the safest thing to do.'

There was silence for a moment. The captain said: 'I see ...' He turned to Corbett: 'Do you know what things are like at Fareham?'

Corbett shook his head. 'I'm afraid not, sir.'

'No matter.' The captain turned to some papers on his desk. 'I'm very doubtful if you'll get a ship at Plymouth. The town's had a bad time with these repeated raids. Besides that, as a naval base we're trying to keep merchant shipping out of it and send them somewhere else. You might strike lucky and get a ship there, or you might have to wait a month. You'd probably do better at Falmouth.'

He explained: 'You see, so far as possible, and in principle, we're keeping all merchant shipping out of the Channel. The War Scheme's working out quite well. Everything's going to the west coast ports. So far as possible, as I say.'

Corbett said: 'You mean I'd have to get round to Bristol or some place like that before I could be certain of a ship?'

'That's right. Or else to Brest. If you can cross the mouth of the Channel in your boat, you'd get a ship at Brest any day.' He paused. 'You must understand, there are four main ports to which we send the whole of the North Atlantic merchant traffic, Mr Corbett. Brest is one of them, and it's probably the nearest one for you.'

'I see.'

Godfrey said: 'If he decided to do that, we could let him have a chart or two, sir?'

'Of course. Get him anything he wants.'

Corbett said: 'I'd like to think about that, sir. It's a longer passage than I'd reckoned I should have to make. We're not a very strong crew – only my wife and myself, and, of course, the children don't make it any easier. If I could go with Commander Godfrey and have a look at the chart, perhaps? It really is most kind of you to help us in this way.'

'It's the least that we can do. Yes, go along and have a look at it. If you can face the passage, it's what I should advise.'

He turned to Godfrey: 'You'll have to get through with it this afternoon. We may be sailing tonight.'

'I'll be able to give him the five o'clock forecast, sir?'

The captain nodded. 'We shan't be sailing before that.' To Corbett he said: 'For your purpose, we should be able to give you a good idea of the weather for the next thirty-six hours. Have a talk with the Met. officer.'

He smiled. 'We can't come with you, but we can do our

best to give you a good push off. What do you want in the way of stores?'

'I should like some petrol and fresh water, sir.'

Godfrey said: 'You've got the water. They were going to fill up your tank this morning.'

The captain said: 'We've got about seventy-three thousand gallons of petrol on board at the moment. How much do you want?'

Corbett smiled faintly: 'Could I have ten of them?'

'Put it on the chit, Godfrey. It's leaded fuel, you know – eighty-seven octane. You don't want to get it in a cut.'

'I'd like some fresh milk, and some bread, sir.'

'Right. Anything else?'

'I don't think so. If there is, could I tell Commander Godfrey this afternoon?'

'By all means. I want you to feel that you can draw on us for what you want, Mr Corbett.' He turned aside. 'I think the admiral would like to have a word with you, while you're here.'

He lifted a telephone and spoke into it. 'That you, Flags? Tell the admiral that Mr Corbett is in my sea cabin. Ask if he would like to see him.'

In a minute the buzzer sounded; the captain lifted the receiver. 'All right. Godfrey will bring him along now.'

He turned to Corbett. 'Godfrey will take you along to the admiral,' he said. 'I shall say goodbye. I want you to draw on us for anything you need in the way of stores or provisions, Mr Corbett. We're very grateful to you.'

He held out his hand. 'Goodbye.'

They went back through the ship between the aircraft parked in rows with folded wings in the flight-hangar, down a hatch to the ward-room flat, and so to the admiral's cabin at the stern. In the fore-cabin the flag-lieutenant got up from a table.

'I'll see if he's ready.' He went into the inner cabin and came out a moment later. 'Will you go in?'

They went in. Godfrey said: 'This is Mr Corbett, sir.'

Corbett saw a stocky little red-faced man, with grey hair,

rather stout. 'All right, Godfrey. You needn't wait. I'll send Mr Corbett along to the ward-room when I've done with him.'

Godfrey withdrew; Corbett was left alone with the admiral. The stocky little man looked him up and down. 'So you're the young man who was in the yacht! What were you running like that for? Couldn't you carry sail?'

'No, sir.' He hesitated. 'If I'd had a full crew of men on board, we might have sailed her. But I'd only got my wife. I thought I'd let it blow itself out a bit.'

'You'd got three children on board, they tell me. One of them a baby.'

'Yes, sir.'

'Well, I'm very grateful to you for picking up my men. How do you earn your living?'

'I'm a solicitor. In Southampton.'

'Public school boy, by the sound of you.'

'I went to Repton.'

'How long have you been yachting?'

Corbett hesitated. 'Well, I've lived all my life in Southampton. I've sailed boats ever since I can remember. I've owned this one for five years.'

The admiral stumped over to a large, square port. 'That's her, lying over there?'

'Yes, sir.'

'How many tons is she?'

'Five and a half tons register. About nine tons, Thames.'

'East coast boat, by the look of her.'

'Yes, sir.'

The other turned back from the port. 'How do you navigate her? Can you take a sight?'

'No, sir.'

'Compass and log?'

'Yes.'

'Know anything about signals?'

'Nothing to speak of.' Dimly Corbett began to perceive what this was leading up to.

'What compass variation do you put on?'

'Eleven degrees west, sir.'

'Do you know your buoyage? What sort of buoys mark a channel, starboard hand going in?'

'Conical ones.'

'What does a green buoy mean?'

'A wreck.'

The admiral crossed to his desk, and sat down. 'We need fellows like you for our auxiliary craft.' He stared Corbett in the eyes. 'I should like to recommend you for a commission as a sub-lieutenant in the Volunteer Reserve. Would you take it?'

There was a pause.

'I should like a minute to think that over, sir.'

'By all means. Sit down in that chair. I have some things to do here.'

Corbett did not sit down, but turned back to the port and stood looking out over the harbour, bright and sunny in the morning light. There was a boat alongside *Sonia*, and people moving about on board. If Joan saw that she would be wondering who they were. The morning was getting on; she must be up by now. Joan ... She would never be able to get to Canada alone, from Portland. This commission – it would be too tough on her for him to think of. And the kids ... He'd brought children into the world, and it was up to him to give them a square deal.

He turned back to the desk. He said: 'I'm afraid I can't do that. I'm sorry. But I've got my wife and children to consider.'

The admiral looked at him for a long moment, inscrutably. Then he motioned to the chair. 'Sit down, Mr Corbett. Take a cigarette.' He watched Corbett while he lit it. 'Now, let me understand you properly. You say you have your wife and children to consider?'

'Yes, sir. I couldn't go away and leave them.'

The older man gave him a hard look. 'Why not?' he asked directly.

Corbett did not answer at once. He blew a long cloud of smoke. 'Well, what would happen to them?'

'Send them home.'

Slowly the anger rose in Corbett. 'I see that you don't understand,' he said evenly. 'My home is a ruin and a wreck. There's no glass in any of the windows. The ground floor and the garden are flooded with sewage. There's no water to drink but polluted water running in the gutters of the road. There's no milk for my baby. There's no fresh meat for the children. It's in a cholera district. It's bombed to hell every night – for all I know it may have been hit by now. That's my home, sir. If you think I'm going to send my wife and children back to that while I join the Navy, you can bloody well think again.'

He got up to go. 'I'm sorry if I've been rude,' he said, a little hesitantly. 'But it's really quite impossible.'

The admiral said: 'Sit down again.' Corbett sank back into his chair.

He looked at Corbett for a moment.

'Well, young man,' he said. 'It's not every day that I'm called a fool in my own cabin, but I'm glad to have heard what you said. Out here, you know, we only see the bare bones of the situation at home. We don't get the whole story. All we know is that since the war began, recruiting has been slow – very slow indeed. A certain flow of young men to the colours, of course, but really nothing to signify.'

Corbett nodded. 'I'm not in the least surprised.'

'Your home is in Southampton?'

'Yes, sir.'

'And you feel that your first duty is to make proper arrangements for your wife and children?'

'Yes.'

'H'm.'

The stocky little man got up again from his desk, stumped over to the port, and stood looking out for a moment. Then he swung round on Corbett. 'Well, I'm going to tell one or two of the officers in my command what you've said. That I could bloody well think again!' He snorted, smiled, relaxed, and became quite suddenly a fatherly old man. 'It really is an assistance to us if we understand what the people on shore are thinking, and doing. It prevents bitterness. . . .' He left that subject, and reverted. 'Now about yourself, Mr Corbett. All these schemes for helping people in your position that I hear about from London. They provide for your family, don't they?'

'What schemes are those, sir?'

'This Rehabilitation Order.'

Corbett stared at him blankly. 'What is that?' He hesitated. 'I left Hamble five days ago, and I've heard nothing since then. And then there were no papers to speak of, and no wireless.'

The admiral nodded. 'A great deal has been happening in the last few days. The Government are very much alive to this problem.' He paused. 'Well, broadly speaking, the scheme seems to be that people in your position are accommodated in quarantine camps till they are proved safe from infection. In the meantime their homes have been rendered habitable for them on their return. It all seems to be going ahead.'

Corbett hesitated. 'I hadn't heard of this. Do you know where these camps are, or what they're like?'

The admiral shook his head. 'I suppose there's a good deal to be done yet.'

Corbett nodded. 'At first hearing, sir, I don't much like the sound of it. I know what things are like on shore.' His lips tightened. 'It sounds to me like this: You find a couple of thousand diseased people living in their motor-cars in a wood without any sanitation or supplies, put a fence and a guard of soldiers round them to prevent them getting out, and call it a quarantine camp. I'm not so stuck on sending my family back to that sort of thing. I think I can do better for them myself.'

There was a silence.

He said: 'I do appreciate your offer of the commission, sir. I'd like to have it. But this is my first job. I've got them safe so far, and I'm going to see them through. And if I send them back on shore, I think they'll die.'

The older man looked at him keenly. 'Very well, Mr

Corbett,' he said at last. 'I'm sorry, personally, because I think you would make the sort of officer we want. That's my first interest, of course. But I appreciate what you've said, and I understand your position. In your place I should probably do the same.'

'If my position changes – if I get them safe – may I get in touch with you again?'

The other smiled. 'By all means. I should be glad for you to do so.'

He stood for a moment, eyeing Corbett seriously. 'You must be quick,' he said quietly. 'You, and everybody like you. We reckoned on your help in time of war – you temporary sailors, soldiers, and airmen. We counted on you. We always have counted on you, and up till now you've never let us down.'

Corbett nodded. 'I know, sir. I understand all that.'

The admiral smiled, and held out his hand. 'Goodbye, then, Mr Corbett. Come back if you are able to. Where are you off to now?'

'The captain's been advising me to go to Brest. I want to get my people on a ship for Canada.'

The older man nodded. 'A very good place to go to. You can make it, in your little boat?'

'I can have a stab at it. It seems about the only thing to do.'

'Good luck.'

Corbett went out and the flag-lieutenant took him to the ward-room. Godfrey was there. 'I've seen the navigating officer and had a chat with him about your passage,' he said. 'He's looking out some stuff for you. We'll go along there presently.'

'It's very good of you.'

They drank a gin together. As they drank, Godfrey questioned Corbett closely about his stores.

'I told them that you'd want some meat,' he said. 'They've cooked you a round of beef. It should be cold by now – cold enough to take on board. Then there are these other things.' He had made a list; they went through it together.

At the end Corbett said: 'Well, I can't think of anything else. But look here – I'll have to pay for all this stuff.'

The lieutenant-commander smiled. 'The captain told me to put it down to the mess.'

'It's terribly good of him.'

They finished the gin. 'Let's go and have a look at those charts.'

In the navigating cabin in the island bridge they met the navigating officer, a lean, saturnine commander (N). He had his charts out ready for them; together they bent over the table. 'Well,' he said at the end of five minutes, 'there you are. From the Bill to Le Four is two degrees thirty-seven minutes, south forty-eight west. A hundred and fifty-seven miles. And then on to Brest through the Chenal du Four, about twenty-eight. And five from here to the Bill.' He totted up quickly on a writing-pad. 'Say a hundred and ninety miles in all.'

Corbett stared at it. 'It's the hell of a long way.'

'How long would it take you?'

'With a fair wind – fifty to sixty hours, sailing easily. And one couldn't push her for that length of time. With a head-wind – anything you like.'

He stood in silence for a minute. 'It's exhaustion that I'm worrying about,' he said. 'The boat would do it on her head. But I'm not used to passages like this. If I get too sick to work her when we get to all this rocky stuff round about Le Four, it'll be just too bad.'

Godfrey nodded comprehendingly. 'You'll have to sleep all you can – let Mrs Corbett do the work for the first part of the trip. But you'll make it all right.' He paused, and then he said: 'I wish to God my wife and kid were with you.'

The navigating officer laughed shortly, without merriment.

Corbett said: 'Well, I'd better have a crack at it.'

The commander said: 'Good enough.' He turned to the

charts. 'You'll want this one of the Channel – I've got a spare. Here's the one of the Chenal du Four and Ushant. You'd better take this one of the approaches to Brest and the Rade. It's out of date down here' – he scribbled rapidly upon it – 'but that won't matter to you. You can take these parallel rulers, and these pencils and rubber.'

He bent over the channel chart and drew quickly on it in pencil. 'Look, that line's your course from the Bill to Le Four. I've marked it off in ten-mile intervals. You've got a patent log on board, haven't you? Well, set it going at the Bill, and then you'll be able to see at a glance how far you've got.'

'It's awfully good of you.'

'Not a bit.' He went to a cupboard and produced a very battered, dog's-eared old blue book. 'You'd better take this volume of the *Channel Pilot*. I've got a later issue.' He operated quickly on the book with a pen-knife. 'These pages that I've cut the corners off deal with the Chenal du Four and the approaches to Brest. Look out for the Vierge light-house – there. You'll probably see that first.'

Corbett surveyed the little heap of information on the desk. 'You've made it very easy for me,' he remarked. 'I'm very grateful.'

'I don't think you'll have any difficulty. It's a rough sort of coast down there, but it's all beautifully buoyed.'

They went through to the meteorological cabin, where a bored young officer was translating long strings of coded figures into isobars. 'A sort of string of secondaries coming over France, so far as I can see,' he said. 'Look, like this.' He sketched rapidly in pencil on his chart. 'Easterly or south-easterly winds for a bit, not very strong. Say fifteen to twenty-five miles an hour.'

Corbett said: 'Fifteen's all right. Twenty-five will be all I want.'

Godfrey asked: 'How long will that go on for?'

The other shook his head. 'It's difficult to say. Might be twenty-four hours from now, might be for two or three days. But I really can't tell you.'

Corbett said: 'It's really pretty good.'

The Met. officer nodded. 'You ought to be all right.'

'I think I should,' said Corbett. 'I think I'll get away this afternoon, while the going's good.'

Half an hour later they were on board the little yacht. In the interval since Corbett had left her she had been transformed. The sails had been properly stowed and the ropes coiled down in beautiful Navy circles on the deck; below, she had been scrubbed out from stem to stern. She was very clean, and smelt aromatically of soap. The mattresses were dry, and the blankets, dry and fluffy, were folded neatly on the berths. Even the pillow-cases had been washed and were white and inviting on the pillows.

Corbett said: 'She hasn't been like this since she was built.'

Godfrey was pleased. 'Now all you want is your stores, and you'll be well away.'

Presently they went on shore. Corbett got out on to the landing-stage; Godfrey stayed in the boat to go back to the *Victorious*. 'I'll be here at two o'clock to take you off,' he said. 'I'll have your stuff with me.' The boat slid away, put up her bow, and made for the aircraft-carrier. Corbett walked up towards the hospital.

He met Joan with the children in the road outside and told her briefly what had happened. 'They are kind to us,' she said. 'Peter, do you know what they did at the hospital? They washed all the children's clothes last night, while they were asleep. And they've done all the baby's things for me, too.'

'I know,' he said. 'We'll be starting off this afternoon with stores for a little liner.'

She asked: 'Peter, how far is it to Brest? How long will it take us?'

He told her.

'I think we can do that all right,' she said. 'I'm sure we can. I mean, it's very different starting off like this, with everything done for you.'

'You're not afraid of it?'

She shook her head. 'I'd be much more afraid of going back to Hamble. I mean – this is a clean and decent sort of risk. Not like the other.'

'I know,' he said. 'I feel like that about it, too. In that case, we'll get away this afternoon. The tide will take us round the Bill.'

They took the children back into the hospital and lunched in the same room; one of the sick bay stewards took the baby away and gave it its bottle. By two o'clock they were thanking the surgeon-captain for all that had been done for them; then they went down to the jetty.

Godfrey was waiting for them in the boat, with a considerable heap of stores and petrol. They were carried swiftly to the yacht; the boat stood by while the lieutenant-commander helped them to stow the petrol and the stores. Finally Corbett started up his old engine and together they got the anchor up.

Godfrey turned to Corbett. 'This is goodbye,' he said a little awkwardly. 'Let's have a post-card when you get to Brest. Send it to the ship, care of the GPO.'

Corbett nodded. 'I'll do that. I can't tell you what you've done for us.'

The officer moved down to the cockpit. 'Goodbye, Mrs Corbett. Don't let him stand every watch. I think you're going to have a good passage.'

Joan said: 'Look, Commander Godfrey. This will be our address in Toronto, when we get there. If your wife goes to Canada – if you think that's the best thing for her to do – do let me help her.' She said: 'I mean, it's all we can do to repay you for what you've done for us. Let us do that.'

He took the slip of paper. 'I'll remember that, Mrs Corbett.' He got into the waiting motor-boat. 'Good luck.'

Corbett put his engine ahead, and the vessels separated. The launch turned back to the *Victorious,* and Corbett headed for the harbour entrance. Near the breakwater he put the yacht up into the wind, Joan took the helm, and he went forward and got up the mainsail. Then they headed for the open sea, and left Portland behind.

Phyllis asked: 'Daddy, are we going to have another sail?'

'That's right,' he said.

'Is it going to be rough, Daddy?'

'I hope not.'

'It was rough before, Daddy.'

John said: 'I like it when it's rough.'

Joan said: 'Come on down, both of you. You know you can't stay on deck when it's rough. Come on and get to bed, and I'll read to you while you have your tea in bed.'

The wind was in the east. Corbett, alone in the cockpit, laid the vessel on a course along the Bill towards the south and put on another sweater. He settled down at the helm to steer; with the tide under him he made good progress down the land, half a mile on his beam. Very soon the bluff hid the harbour, the breakwaters, and the battleships from his sight.

As they approached the end of the Bill he got the patent log from its case and made it ready; then he called Joan on deck to help him in the actual passage round the land, inside the Race. For a quarter of an hour they were in rough water. Then they were through; away on their beam they saw the sharply breaking water of the Race. He streamed the log, set it to zero, and settled down again at the helm; Joan went below to finish off the children. It was then about four o'clock in the afternoon.

He put the vessel on her course for Brittany. The wind was on her quarter, moderate in strength; as they drew away from the land and the rough water round the Bill the yacht settled to a restrained, easy motion that was not unpleasant. The sun set in a glory of rose-coloured cloud flecked with patches of pale sky; the dusk grew on. In the hatchway he could see Joan's head and hear her reading *Jemima Puddle-Duck* to the children; from time to time a wave-top tumbled near them, drowning her voice. He sailed on; he was happy.

Presently she stopped reading and came on deck. 'How is she doing, Peter?'

'Going fine.' He stooped to look at the log. 'Three and a half miles from the Bill.'

She looked around. 'Is that the Bill back there?' She pointed to the land, seen dimly behind them in the dusk.

'That's it.' He hesitated for a moment. 'Take a good look at it,' he said gently. 'You may not see England again for some time.'

'Oh, Peter . . .' She was startled and appalled. While they were on the yacht the thought of leaving England had not been real to her; the yacht was a part of England, part of Hamble, part of their life together. Now, that dim wedge-shaped bit of land was England, perhaps the last of England that she would see for years. Gone was the pleasant, semi-detached house that she had married into, had her children in. Gone was their well-loved, battered Austin car. Gone were the happy summer week-ends, bathing at Seaview or Newtown. Gone was the cinema, two streets away from them, where they knew the manager and the cashier by their names. Gone were the occasional, economical trips to London. Gone were their friends, the Gordons and the Hutchinsons and the Littlejohns – all gone. Gone were the shops she loved, the one that had the puppies in the window, the one that sold the radiograms that they could not afford, the piano that they would have had when they were very rich. All these were gone. That rocky point with the white lighthouse, unlit and hardly visible behind them in the mist, was the last of all these things. When that went, England would be gone.

He took her hand. 'Never mind,' he said quietly.

She said: 'I hadn't realized what we were doing. We'll come back again, Peter, won't we? We shan't have to live in Canada for ever?'

He drew her down beside him in the cockpit, and put his arm around her. 'Of course not. We'll be back in Southampton as soon as ever the war's over. But Canada's a great country, I believe. People like living there.'

She nodded. 'I don't want to be silly about it. I believe

it's going to be all right. But – it's not like England, Peter. England's our own place.'

He said: 'I know. I promise you that we'll come back again.'

They sailed on for a long time in silence after that, his arm around her shoulders. Presently she took the helm, and he went down below to get supper.

The motion of the boat was easy; they were able to have a good meal of cold beef, potatoes, tinned fruit, and coffee. After that Joan went down below and gave a bottle to the baby, came on deck again, and took the helm. It was about half-past eight, and a fine, starry night.

She said: 'Go down and get some sleep, Peter. I'll be all right.'

He looked around. The breeze was moderate from the south-east; in the cabin the glass was steady. The vessel was running easily; the sailing lights shone forward into the darkness, red and green. The little lamp in the binnacle was glowing steadily. 'All right,' he said. 'You take her till midnight, and give me a call then. Give me a shout if the wind freshens, or if you can't hold the course.'

She said: 'I'll be all right.' He fetched her up a coat and a blanket to wrap round her, saw her settled comfortably at the helm, and went below to sleep.

She sat there in the darkness steering through the night. England was lost behind her, strange unknown things lay ahead. In the darkness and the waste of sea she seemed to be in limbo, forgotten in the wilderness. She was filled with a great regret for the lost past. She felt that on passing Portland Bill a part of her life, the first part, possibly the best part, had been closed. That part contained her childhood, her days at her boarding-school, her short time as a secretary, her marriage to Peter, their happiness together, their children. The history of that part was written now, the last sentence was complete, the book was closed, the covers latched together. It was final – nothing could be added to that history, or taken away. Before her lay a new period of her life, divorced entirely from the other. She felt that the new period could not be happier. It might be much less happy; it could never be the same.

The vessel sailed on through the night under the brilliant stars; she was the only one awake. It was not necessary for her to watch the binnacle intently; Peter had trimmed the sails for her and the ship was light to steer, holding her course very nearly by herself. She thought again of the life that she had left behind. She had no regrets for lost opportunities, for mistakes. The best that one could do was to live happily and cheerfully, help Peter all she could, and bring children into the world. She had done her best in all of that; she had no regrets. She felt a deep sadness that that happy time was over. There should have been more of it.

She sat there steering all night long, immersed in her thoughts.

Peter woke suddenly in the grey light of dawn. He rolled over on his settee and looked at his watch; it was half-past five. He got quickly to his feet and went to the hatch; in the cockpit Joan was sitting at the helm wrapped in a blanket, her face white and drawn.

'You are a mutt,' he said kindly. 'Why didn't you call me?'

She said: 'She was so light to steer, I thought I'd let you sleep. We'll have another night out, won't we?'

He slipped on a coat and took the helm from her. 'I suppose so. How has she been getting on?'

She got up and stretched stiffly. 'She's been going just the same all night.'

He looked at the log; it showed forty-six miles. 'About four knots,' he said. 'That's all right if we can keep it up.' He lashed the helm and made the vessel sail herself; then he took Joan below and put on a Primus stove.

Half an hour later she was asleep on a settee, a hot meal of baked beans and bread and cheese and cocoa inside her, a hot-water bottle at her feet. He covered her with a blanket and removed a smouldering cigarette from her unconscious fingers; then he made breakfast for himself and for the children. He kept the children in their bunks; the baby was asleep, and he left well alone. After an hour he was able to go on deck, light a pipe, and settle at the helm, getting the little ship upon her course again.

They sailed on all day uneventfully. The wind blew in to the north and grew colder, but it did not strengthen. In the middle of the morning a flotilla of destroyers passed near them at high speed taking no notice of them; all through the day there were aeroplanes in sight, patrolling the mouth of the Channel. One came down low to have a look at them; apart from that they were ignored. They saw two steamers on their way up Channel from the direction of Ushant; neither passed very close to them.

Joan came on deck at about ten o'clock, had a look round, and went below to give a bottle to the baby. They had a meal then with the children and let them up into the cockpit for an hour, while Corbett pumped the vessel out and filled the lamps again. Then he went down to sleep for a time and came back on deck again in the late afternoon. The log read ninety-seven miles.

At eight o'clock he gave the helm again to Joan, with definite orders that he was to be called at midnight. 'We shall be getting on towards the coast of France by then,' he said. 'If we're going to bump on anything I'd like to do it myself.' He went below and slept; at midnight she called him and he came up and relieved her. The vessel was still running in a northerly wind.

Joan woke at six o'clock. She came on deck in the grey light and looked around. She saw a rocky coast four or five miles away on the port bow, and nearer at hand a lighthouse standing on an isolated rock.

Peter said: 'That's Le Four.'

8

THE DAWN came up grey and squally; the wind had backed in to the north-west, and was a good deal stronger. Corbett said: 'We've had the best of the weather. Still, we've had great luck in carrying it so far.'

It took them all that day to sail the last twenty-five miles in to Brest. The tide was foul against them in the Chenal du Four until the middle of the morning and they made no progress; then they began to move southwards in a fresh wind and an uneasy sea. Slowly the intricate pattern of towers and buoys unrolled before them, but it was not till early afternoon that they rounded Pointe St Mathieu and bore up for Brest, twelve miles farther on.

Till then they had seen very few ships. In the Chenal du Four and off Conquet they had met fishing smacks and small boats hauling lobster pots; now as they approached the Goulet they came in to a considerable mass of traffic. Three French destroyers first came out of Brest, followed by a British light cruiser. An oil tanker and a big tramp steamer passed them going in, and a small liner came out. As they neared the Goulet a smart white steam yacht flying the white ensign and manned by naval personnel came past within a hundred yards of them; they rolled for a few minutes in her wash.

In the Goulet itself, the narrow entrance to the wide natural harbour, they came upon intensive submarine precautions. Half of the entrance was shut off with nets; a launch ranged up to them, asked a few questions in mixed French and English, and directed them between two buoys. They passed through the barrier, past half a dozen motor-boats attending to the nets, and so came to the shelter of the Rade.

The Rade de Brest is a wide inland sea, approximately

five miles square. That day, it was a mass of anchored ships. Near to the town there were British and French warships lying at anchor; farther away there were liners, transports, hospital ships, oil tankers, and tramp steamers of every shape and size. Corbett was amazed; he had never seen such a collection of ships assembled together.

'Peter,' said Joan. 'What are we going to do now?'

He had the chart with him in the cockpit. 'We want to get inside the breakwater' – he pointed to the chart – 'this thing they call the Rade-Abri, and drop our anchor. That is, if they don't stop us first. I'm not quite sure what you do then. I believe the thing to do is to hang up an ensign and a yellow flag.'

'Have you got a yellow flag, Peter?'

He stared at her blankly. 'No, I've not. You've not got anything yellow?'

She shook her head. 'You know I don't wear yellow.'

'We'll just have to hang up an ensign at the masthead, then.' He thought about it for a minute. 'As a matter of fact, that may be better. They may not want to put us into quarantine if we don't ram it down their throats.'

He went below and started up the engine. It was about five o'clock when they passed through the harbour entrance into the Port du Commerce and dropped anchor near some other yachts beside the breakwater. Corbett went below, found a red ensign, and hoisted it to the mast-head in place of the burgee.

He came aft to the cockpit. 'We might as well let the children up on deck,' he said wearily.

He dropped down on to one of the seats and lit a cigarette. Around them swarmed the traffic of the harbour; the water was alive with boats and pinnaces of every sort going back and forwards to the ships in the Rade. The children climbed on deck and stared around them.

Phyllis asked: 'Daddy, will you buy me a green hairribbon when we go on shore?'

He said: 'If Mummy says you can have it.'

'Oh yes, because you see she was going to get it for me at

home, ever such a long time ago, before the bangs. Cecily's got a green hair-ribbon, Daddy.'

'Has she?'

John asked: 'Are we going home now, Daddy?'

His sister rebuked him. 'You are a silly, John. We're ever such a long way from home. This is Portland.'

Corbett said: 'No, it's not. It's a place called Brest, in France. Where they talk French.'

'Like Mademoiselle?'

'That's right.'

'What do they do that for, Daddy?'

Joan came on deck with the baby in her arms; she was looking very tired. 'She slept almost the whole way,' she said. 'We've really had a wonderful passage, Peter.'

He nodded. 'Not so bad. It's been much easier than I thought it would be.'

'We've had great luck with the weather. I think we've got a lot to be thankful for.'

'I think we have.'

A little motor-boat came across the harbour towards them; on its bow it bore the legend, SERVICE DU PORT. It ran round under their stern and read the name; then it drew up alongside. Two men in shabby uniform stepped on board. The senior of them was a man of about fifty, black-haired, stout, and badly shaved.

'*La Douane,*' he said impassively. He produced a black notebook. 'You are English – yes?'

Corbett nodded. 'That's right.'

'*Bien.* Where have you now come from?'

'From Portland.'

The stout man glanced at him keenly, from little beady eyes. 'Portland – *c'est un port militaire* – only the Royal Navy. You 'ave come from Portland?'

'I put in there for a night on the way. That was my last port.'

'*Bien compris.* Before Portland, where have you then come from?'

'From Hamble, near Southampton.'

'Ah, Southampton.' The man looked at him woodenly. '*La patente de santé*, if you please – the Bill of 'ealth.'

Corbett shook his head. 'I haven't got one.'

'*Non? On ne peut pas passer la Manche sans une patente de santé.*'

'I've done it,' said Corbett wearily. '*Je l'ai fait.* And I'm not going back for you or anybody else.'

'*C'est bien serieux, M'sieur.*'

Corbett pulled himself together. 'I know,' he said. '*Je prie votre pardon, M'sieur. Nous sommes échappés des choses terribles en Angleterre, et je suis très fatigué.*'

'*Ne dérangez-vous pas, M'sieur.* You must not go on the shore. Tomorrow I will bring to you the Doctor of the Port. Tonight you rest here, but not to go on shore. And not to allow the visitors to land on your boat, here. You understand?'

Corbett nodded. 'Perfectly.'

'*Bien.* Now, M'sieur, the certificate of registry of the ship.'

Corbett shook his head. 'I haven't got it with me.'

'No?' The stout man raised his eyebrows. '*Alors*, your passport.'

Again Corbett shook his head. '*M'sieur, je suis désolé. Je n'ai pas des papiers – rien de tout.*'

'No papers – nothing at all?' The stout man clicked his tongue. 'This is ver' bad, M'sieur. Where is the crew?'

Corbett stared at him. 'I haven't got a crew.'

The stout man stared back. '*Vous avez traversé la Manche tout seul?*'

'*Mais non. Madame et les enfants étaient avec moi.*'

The stare broadened to a smile. '*Et aussi le bébé?*'

'*Oui, M'sieur.*'

'*Incroyable . . .*'

He turned back to business. 'It will be necessary that you visit your consul.'

'May I go on shore to see him?'

'Not at all. You rest here. I telephone to him. What name have you?'

Corbett told him. There was a long hiatus then, while he

wrote Corbett's name carefully in his book, and Joan's name, and the names of all the children, having a good deal of trouble with the spelling. But finally he said:

'From here, where do you go to?'

'I want to send Madame and the children to Canada by ship. To Canada, or to America.'

The man nodded. '*Vous avez de l'argent?*'

'*Oui.* I have enough for their passage, and more in Canada.'

'*Et vous, M'sieur?*'

'I shall go back to England. I may want to leave the yacht here – to lay her up.'

'*Bien compris.* Now, M'sieur, what 'ave you to declare?'

He examined their small stock of spirits and tobacco, passing them with a smile. 'You 'ave left Southampton, when?'

'We left Hamble seven days ago.'

'Seven days.' He made a note in his little book. 'I think it will be necessary that you rest some days in quarantine.'

Corbett said: '*Bien, J'ai grand besoin de sommeil.*'

The man smiled, and looked up and down the boat. 'She is ver' small to cross la Manche.'

Joan said: 'Peter, ask him if we can get some milk.'

He turned to the *douanier.* 'M'sieur, I need fresh milk for the baby, and the children. Also, in the morning I shall need water.'

The man smiled at Joan. '*Soyez tranquille, Madame.* I myself will bring milk, in one hour.'

He got back into his motor-launch and went away towards the quay. Joan turned to the children. 'You can have your tea on deck here, in the cockpit,' she said. 'After that you must go to bed.'

She went below and lit the Primus stove. Corbett busied himself on deck, stowing the sails and gear.

An hour later the children were in bed; Joan and Peter were smoking together in the cockpit. It was not warm; the evening was overcast and grey, with a rising wind from the south-west. Corbett looked at the weather.

'Made it just in time,' he said. 'We'd never have got here against this wind.'

'We've had terribly good luck.'

He nodded. 'It was the weather report they gave us on the *Victorious* that did it. We'd never have got here without their help.'

'Well, after all, we did fish them out of the sea.'

Two Breton fishing-boats slipped past them in the dusk, sailing up to the fish quay; in the small boat traffic of the harbour they saw the *douanier* in his launch heading towards them. He brought his boat alongside and came on board; he had with him a very large bottle of milk. Corbett gave him two English shillings for it.

'The Doctor of the Port, he comes in the morning,' he said. 'Also your consul, he comes in the morning. Now you must lift up the anchor, and I will take you where you must go.'

He explained. 'The place for quarantine is outside in the Rade. Tonight, it will be bad weather. In the Rade the waves will be gross. For such a small boat that is not good. I will put you in another place. I will show you.'

Corbett started up the engine and went forward to get up his anchor. The *douanier* made fast his motor-boat astern and they moved to the north-east corner of the Port Militaire, opposite the back door of the Bureau du Port. They dropped anchor again.

'Here,' said the man, 'it will be good.'

Corbett nodded. 'Can we stay here all the time of quarantine?'

'The Doctor of the Port will say. For me, I do not think that you are ill, or Madame, or the children, or *le bébé.*'

He paused for a minute. 'It has been bad in Southampton?'

Corbett nodded. 'Very bad. It is no longer possible to live there.' He indicated the boat. 'This is now my home.'

'It is terrible, that.' He got in to his boat. 'In the morning, I return with the doctor.'

They cooked themselves a large meal, went to bed, and

slept heavily, dreamlessly, all night. Corbett was up and shaving early in the morning; they had breakfast early, washed and dressed the children, and were all ready for the doctor by nine o'clock.

They waited all morning. 'The fact of the matter is,' said Corbett after two hours had elapsed, 'there's a war on, and we're a ruddy nuisance.'

In that he was not far from the truth. The motor-boat arrived at a quarter past twelve bringing the doctor, who was obviously in a hurry to get back to *déjeuner*. He took a cursory look at them and at the boat.

'You are in good health – yes?' he inquired. 'But you are come in from where there is both cholera and typhoid. It is since seven days that you departed. Twenty-three days is necessary. You rest here for sixteen days.'

Corbett asked: 'Is that for cholera?'

'I do not think you have the cholera. By now you would be dead. Also, I do not think you have the typhoid, but for that is necessary twenty-three days.'

Joan asked him: 'Must the children stay on board for the whole time?'

He did not answer that at once, but questioned them very closely about the water that they had drunk since war began. 'So,' he said. 'You have drunk nothing but the water from the town supply, except it has been boiled. You have been wise. No, I do not think it good for the little ones to stay on this small ship for sixteen days. Each day I will come to see if there are spots, or sickness. After I have seen, it will be possible for them to play on the breakwater between the Bureau du Port and the end.' He pointed to the shore. 'They must not pass the Bureau du Port.' He smiled. 'There is a window to my office. I shall see.'

Joan said: 'It's awfully nice of you to let them get on shore like that.'

He bowed to her. 'At your service, Madame.'

Corbett asked. 'How shall we get food, and water?'

The doctor shrugged his shoulders. 'I do not think it necessary that I should be severe. Each day, after I have

seen, you may go to buy food on the Quai de la Douane –
there. You must not rest there. You must come back quick.
In no case must you go into the town.'

He went away; a quarter of an hour later a young man
from the consul's office came to them. He heard their story
shortly. 'Well,' he said, 'you're fixed up here for the next
sixteen days. After that, you can come up to the Consulate
and I'll issue you with temporary passports. You'd better
not try to leave without them.'

Corbett shook his head. 'We don't want to.'

He went away, and was followed by a gloriously attired
Officer of the Port, who came to have a drink of whisky, to
gossip about the war, and to get Corbett to supply the
answers to the questions on a long buff form. They assured
him that they had neither rats, corpses, nor coffins on board;
he drank up his whisky and went away.

The next fortnight passed by in a dream of holiday idle-
ness. Each day the doctor came on board in the middle of
the morning, stayed for two minutes, and went away. After
that they went on shore and bought what food and wine
they needed, fetched water from the breakwater, and came
on board for lunch. In the afternoons they went on to the
breakwater with the whole family and fished with hand-
lines in the clear water of the harbour mouth for bass and
pollock, with a good deal of success. The weather was warm
and sunny; they sat smoking on the wall with the baby
beside them in her basket cot, dangling their lines and
watching for a bite, while the children played among the
litter of old anchors, chains, and buoys. Presently it would
be time to go back on board for tea, and to read a little to
the children from the well-thumbed books, *Ameliaranne*
and *Peter Rabbit*, before putting them to bed. Then they
would do the daily washing, cook the supper, and sit smoking in the cockpit till it was time for bed.

So the days slipped by.

In the harbour and the Rade, the pageant of nations at
war was staged before their eyes. It was unreal to them;
they seemed to have no part in it at all. Each day they got

a French paper and read about the progress of the war with
a small dictionary; vast things were happening in Europe
which they could not fully understand. They had no atlas,
and the names of places in the news meant little to them, nor
had they any chance to talk to other people. They were per-
petually bewildered by the progress of events. In some part,
however, the news which they read in the French papers
was translated to them by the movements of the ships. In
the Port Militaire and in the Rade warships of France,
England, and the Dominions slipped in, stayed for a day
and vanished in the night. In the Port de Commerce and
the east part of the Rade congregated the merchant vessels
of all countries taking their turn to unload at the quays;
by night the rattle of cranes and the clanking of goods
trains went on unceasingly under the glare of arc lights. All
these things flowed past them in their corner of the Port
Militaire; they did not affect their quiet life by an iota.

Towards the end of their quarantine, Corbett went on
shore one evening to buy bread. Returning to the yacht, he
stopped outside the café 'Abri de la Tempête'; he saw the
douanier who had met them on their arrival sitting alone
with a newspaper. He went in.

'M'sieur,' he said, 'is it permitted that you should drink
with me? There are two days only of the quarantine to go.
I do not think I have the typhoid fever.'

The man smiled. 'I do not think that you are ill. I should
be happy, M'sieur.'

Corbett sat down, and ordered Pernod for them both.
They talked for a time in bad English and worse French,
speaking very slowly to make each other understand.

The *douanier* raised his glass. 'To Madame, and *le bébé*,'
he said. 'They are well?'

Corbett nodded. 'Very well indeed.'

'Each day I see you make a walk with the children and *le
bébé*, and to catch fish.'

Corbett smiled. 'It is good to be quiet for a time before
entering the war.'

'Assuredly. Madame and the children, they go to Canada?'

'I hope to be able to get a passage for them on the *Lachine,* for Montreal. When does the *Lachine* sail?'

The *douanier* said: 'She comes to Basin Two tomorrow night, on the east side, but first the *Guinea Prince* is to unload. When the *Lachine* is unloaded, then she must coal, you understand. She goes to Quay One before departing. She may sail, perhaps, on Wednesday.'

Corbett nodded. 'That's all right. Our quarantine runs out on Tuesday night.'

'That will be convenient for you. You have friends in Canada?'

'Madame is going with the children to my sister, in Toronto.'

'And you, M'sieur?'

'I shall go back to England to take service in the Army or the Navy – I do not yet know which.'

The *douanier* said nothing.

Corbett asked: 'Is there any news in the paper tonight?' He indicated the *Paris Soir* upon the table.

'There has been bombing.' There was a momentary pause; then the *douanier* slammed his hand down on the table, rattling the glasses. 'It is madness – madness!' he said vehemently. 'In the papers, bombing, bombing – nothing but bombing! I'm sick of it.'

Corbett nodded without speaking.

The man leaned towards him. 'But, M'sieur, I tell you this. England will win this war, as together we have won the last war. She will win it because of the bombing.'

Corbett eyed him attentively. 'You think so?'

'Nothing is more sure. See for yourself. Here, in Brest, every ship, from every country in the world, brings doctors and nurses and supplies of every sort, to go to help England. I could not count, M'sieur, the number of doctors and nurses that have passed through Brest to England. Two days ago, the *Washington* from New York, the whole ship, only with medical help, M'sieur. Today the *Orontes* from

Sydney, with doctors and nurses and supplies, and very many young men to enlist to fight. It is so, every day. All the world comes to the aid of England, because of this bombing.'

'England needs all the help she can get.'

'Truly. But all the bombing – and what is it? Terrible, and devastating, to lose your homes. But no soldier yet has put a foot) in England except as prisoner, because your Navy has been strong. You hold the seas. The aeroplanes, they can do nothing but destroy your homes, blindly. They have not been able to destroy your ships. They have not hit your arsenals or factories, except by chance. In the air you are strong. They dare not come to bomb when they can themselves be seen, for then you can destroy them. They cannot bomb except from cloud. They can destroy your homes, and nothing else. *Je m'en fiche de tous les avions.*'

Corbett ordered another Pernod.

The *douanier* said: 'I tell you, M'sieur, it is a madness unbelievable that they should use their bombers so. Only a nation of no understanding, who did not know the world psychology, would make such mistakes. Very nearly have they brought in America to fight beside England. Not yet, because America is very careful, but – see for yourself! Every day the ships come from America, loaded with men, and money, and food, and military supplies – all for England. In your Empire, every Dominion has declared war, all are hastening to fight. Without the bombing, M'sieur, it would not have been so.'

Corbett nodded. 'That may be.'

The *douanier* drank his Pernod. 'England will now win this war.'

Corbett sighed. 'If we'd been a bit cleverer, we might not have had it at all.'

The other said: 'It had to come. Once in the history of the world this had to be tried, this blind bombing of the towns. But, M'sieur, I tell you this certainly – it has lost the war for them. This time, they will suffer a defeat and be smashed utterly. After that, I do not think that any Power will dare to do such things again.'

He got up to go. Corbett said: 'You think that?'

The *douanier* said with dignity: 'M'sieur, I still have hope for the world.'

Two days later their quarantine was up; Corbett went to the *Lachine,* saw the purser, and booked a passage for Joan and the children. The ship was due to sail next day.

That afternoon for the last time they went to the break-water with the children, the baby in its cot, and their fishing-lines. For a couple of hours they sat together in the sun, the children playing round about their feet. They caught nothing, perhaps because they were not trying very hard; it was their last afternoon. They sat dangling their idle lines into the water, saying little to each other but a good deal to the children, showing them different sorts of ships and boats, telling them what it was all about.

Presently they went on board for tea. They had a fine tea, as if it was a birthday, with strange French jam and bread in long sticks only half an inch wide, and little cakes, and *pain d'épices.* It was great fun. After tea Corbett read to them, while Joan washed them and put them to bed. He read for nearly an hour, right through *Nicodemus,* and *When Jesus was a Little Boy,* and *Ameliaranne,* and the *Story of a Fierce Bad Rabbit.* It took an hour because they had to stop at each picture while both children had a look at it, pored over it, and had it explained to them.

By seven o'clock they were asleep in their berths, tired out and happy. Joan finished off the baby and came up into the cockpit; Peter lit her cigarette. 'It's a pity we can't go on shore,' he said. It was impossible to leave the children alone on board. 'We should have gone somewhere, this last night.'

She shook her head. 'I don't feel much like it. I'd rather stay here.'

He nodded without speaking. Presently he said: 'It won't be for long. The war can't go on for long at this pace.'

She shook her head. 'That's what one tries to think,' she

said quietly, 'but it's not true. Wars seem to go on for ever nowadays. All these new things – tanks and gas and aeroplanes – don't seem to shorten wars a bit. They seem to make them longer.'

He shook her hand. 'It won't be so long.'

She said: 'It may be for years, Peter.'

'We mustn't let it be.'

They sat in silence for a time, smoking in the darkness. Over the water the shore ' lights made dappled tracks, shattered by passing boats, rejoining as the water stilled. A gentle little breeze blew from the west. She said: 'I knew that this would be the worst of all. So long as we could stick together everything was fairly all right. Even the bombs and cholera weren't so bad. This separating is the worst we've had to face.'

'I know.'

'We'll go back to Southampton when the war's over, won't we, Peter?'

'You want to go back there?'

She nodded. 'It's our own place. We'll be able to, won't we?'

'I'll try and make it so. I'll have to arrange with Bellinger to be on leave while the war lasts. I think he can carry on alone, for a time at any rate.'

She said: 'I want to go back just like we were before.'

He hesitated. 'We may not be able to do that. The house may be too bad.'

'Then I'd like to have another house in the same part. Do you think we'd have to have new furniture?'

He shrugged his shoulders. 'It depends what happens to the house. We might have to have a whole new outfit.'

'I believe that would be fun. The settee was awful, and the chairs weren't up to much. We'd have had to get some new furniture soon, anyway. And Peter, I do want a decent radiogram. The children are getting old enough to listen to good music now – just a little bit, now and again. I'd like to have a piano.'

'We might have to wait a bit for that.'

'We could have the radiogram, couldn't we? Even if we had to get it on the Never-Never.'

He pressed her hand. 'We'll have that,' he said, a little huskily.

'That'll be something to look forward to.'

They went below, and began to pack her luggage and the children's things. There was not very much; a suitcase and a kitbag held all that they had to take. When they had done all that was possible before morning they got themselves a meal; he had a bottle of Nuits St Georges on board, and they drank that. Then, for a long time they sat facing each other across the little table, littered with their plates and dishes. They sat smoking and drinking coffee, talking in little disconnected sentences.

'We're still young,' he said presently. 'We may lose a year together now – we may lose more. But we've got the rest of our lives before us.'

She nodded. 'But that will be different. You'll be a different man when you've been through this war, and I'll be different, too. We shan't be able to take up just where we left off. We'll have to start off new.'

He smiled. 'We shan't find that so difficult.'

'I don't think so. But this is the end of our young married life, Peter. We'll be middle-aged when we meet again.'

He was silent.

She said: 'I don't know if in passing through the world you leave a mark behind you. A sort of impression. I'd like to think so, because I think we must have left a good one. We're not famous people and we've not done much. Nobody knows anything about us. But we've been so happy. We've lived quietly and decently and done our job. We've had kids, too – and they're good ones. But I wish we could have had another boy.'

'I know,' he said. 'Too bad we didn't get time to have Little Egbert.'

She roused herself. 'Let's do the washing-up.'

They washed up and sat for a little in the cockpit, well wrapped up against the cold night air. And presently they went to bed. They did not sleep well; each in the night awoke from time to time and heard the other turning on the opposite settee.

In the morning all was bustle and confusion. They did the last of their packing, breakfasted, and washed up. Then they left the luggage ready in the saloon and went on shore in the dinghy with the children, carrying the baby. They went to the Port Doctor's office and got clearance; then they took a taxi to the British Consulate and got their passports. They turned back towards the Port du Commerce in the taxi; presently they came to a place where they had a wide view over the Rade.

Joan plucked suddenly at his arm. 'Tell him to stop, Peter – quick!'

He leaned forward and spoke to the driver, who pulled up. 'What is it?' he asked her.

She pointed to the mass of shipping in the Rade. 'Look, Peter – the aircraft-carrier! I'm sure it's the *Victorious*.'

He stared out over the sea, to where the white ensign blew lazily about the stern. 'It's one or other of them,' he said at last. 'It might be the *Courageous*.'

'Ask the driver if the *Victorious* is here,' she said. 'He'll probably know.'

With some difficulty Corbett did so.

'*Oui, M'sieur,*' said the man at last. '*Le bateau anglais là-bas? On a dit le nom* Victorious.'

Joan said: 'Peter, we must hurry. She may be going off at any time – they never stay long. Get us on board the *Lachine,* quick, and then you go and see the admiral.'

They went down to the quay. He left Joan and the children there while he went off to get the luggage from the yacht. Then, carrying the suitcase and the kitbag, they set off down the crowded quays and wharves for the *Lachine.* They found her without difficulty, her loading practically complete.

He took Joan and the family on board, found the cabin that he had engaged for them, and settled them in. She turned to him.

'We'll be all right now, Peter,' she said. 'You must go off, and get on board the *Victorious* before she sails.'

He said: 'There's no great hurry. You'll be going in an hour and a half.'

She shook her head. 'Please, Peter, go now. We're perfectly all right, and it's a chance you mustn't miss.' She hesitated, and then said: 'I want to think of you, being in the Navy.'

'I'd rather wait and see you off.'

'No, Peter. Please go now.'

He took her in his arms and kissed her. She said very quietly: 'I've been wonderfully happy all these years, Peter. As happy as a girl could be.'

He patted her on the shoulder, but said nothing. He kissed each of the children, tickled the baby's cheek. Then he was gone. Standing by the open port she watched him through a mist of tears, walking down the gangway and along the quay, out of her life.

He walked up through the town. In the British Consulate he made inquiries and was directed to the Naval Staff Office; he went there and got a signal sent to the *Victorious* without great difficulty. He waited half an hour in a bare waiting room.

'The admiral sends his compliments, sir. Will you go aboard. The boat leaves the pontoon beneath the bridge in half an hour, at thirteen hundred.'

He walked down to the boat, and was carried to the aircraft-carrier in a sad dream. He went on board and went straight to the fore cabin, where he had to wait for a considerable time.

He stood beside an open port, watching the traffic of the Rade. He saw the *Lachine* move from the quayside in the Port du Commerce, watched her as she swung towards the passage through the breakwater, as she came out into the Rade. He watched her as she passed along the shore, as she grew smaller in the distance, heading through the Goulet towards Canada.

The flag-lieutenant said: 'Mr Corbett!'

He went through the steel door into the inner cabin. The admiral, seated writing at his desk, did not look up. He said:

'Well, young man, what can I do for you?'

Corbett said: 'I've got rid of my wife and family. I came to see if I could still have that commission, sir.'

EPILOGUE

To the people of Southampton.

This book it a work of fiction. None of the characters have any existence except in my imagination, barring one, and he is not in your part of the book.

I think you will ask, with some reason, why I have to write about your city. Why, if I can write about imaginary people, can I not write about an imaginary city – or at any rate, about a seaport city in the south of England called Northendton, in the county of Rampshire. My answer to this is, firstly, that I don't think much of the Northendton convention, however good the precedents for it may be. And secondly, although I have written fiction, I have written what to me are very real forecasts of what may be coming to us. I wanted to make them real to you, and so I have laid them in real places.

I have never lived in your city. As a boy I had great kindness from one of you; since then I have visited your city from time to time, poked about in it, and I have admired its virility. But I do not know it as you do, and so it may be that in writing about it I have made mistakes.

Very likely by the time you read these words I shall be in trouble with your chief officials. Your Mayor and your Town Clerk will be grieved with me, your Chief Constable will be indignant, your Medical Officer of Health will be a very angry man, and your engineers of Electricity, Gas, Sewage, Telephone, and Water – especially Water – will be considering what action they had better take.

But I don't care. If I have held your attention for an evening, if I have given to the least of your officials one new idea to ponder and digest, then I shall feel that this book will have played a part in preparing us for the terrible things that you, and I, and all the citizens of the cities in this country, may one day have to face together.

NEVIL SHUTE.

Nevil Shute
Beyond the Black Stump £1.95

In the red dust of the Australian outback an American geologist and an English immigrant find themselves rivals for the daughter of a tough, wealthy, and very Irish family. Nevil Shute's special genius for characterization moulds this very human triangle of personal conflicts and racial contrasts into a tender and gripping story.

'A vivid piece of work' SCOTSMAN

A Town Like Alice £2.50

A magnificent, moving and invincibly readable story of bravery and endurance, of enterprise and love – in war and the aftermath of war. Out of an English girl's faith in humanity and an Australian POW's quiet courage comes 'a harrowing, exciting and very satisfying war romance'. HARPER'S MAGAZINE

An Old Captivity £1.75

In the shelter of a Greenland fiord an elderly Oxford don and his daughter come under the spell of a romance that began a thousand years ago.

The Far Country £2.50

A young English girl and a rugged Czech doctor become caught up with the rawness of life in an Australian timber camp.

The Chequer Board £1.95

Inescapably readable, a powerful novel of four soldiers and the woman they love.

Fiction

☐	**The Chains of Fate**	Pamela Belle	£2.95p
☐	**Options**	Freda Bright	£1.50p
☐	**The Thirty-nine Steps**	John Buchan	£1.50p
☐	**Secret of Blackoaks**	Ashley Carter	£1.50p
☐	**Lovers and Gamblers**	Jackie Collins	£2.50p
☐	**My Cousin Rachel**	Daphne du Maurier	£2.50p
☐	**Flashman and the Redskins**	George Macdonald Fraser	£1.95p
☐	**The Moneychangers**	Arthur Hailey	£2.95p
☐	**Secrets**	Unity Hall	£2.50p
☐	**The Eagle Has Landed**	Jack Higgins	£1.95p
☐	**Sins of the Fathers**	Susan Howatch	£3.50p
☐	**Smiley's People**	John le Carré	£2.50p
☐	**To Kill a Mockingbird**	Harper Lee	£1.95p
☐	**Ghosts**	Ed McBain	£1.75p
☐	**The Silent People**	Walter Macken	£2.50p
☐	**Gone with the Wind**	Margaret Mitchell	£3.95p
☐	**Wilt**	Tom Sharpe	£1.95p
☐	**Rage of Angels**	Sidney Sheldon	£2.50p
☐	**The Unborn**	David Shobin	£1.50p
☐	**A Town Like Alice**	Nevile Shute	£2.50p
☐	**Gorky Park**	Martin Cruz Smith	£2.50p
☐	**A Falcon Flies**	Wilbur Smith	£2.50p
☐	**The Grapes of Wrath**	John Steinbeck	£2.50p
☐	**The Deep Well at Noon**	Jessica Stirling	£2.95p
☐	**The Ironmaster**	Jean Stubbs	£1.75p
☐	**The Music Makers**	E. V. Thompson	£2.50p

Non-fiction

☐	**The First Christian**	Karen Armstrong	£2.50p
☐	**Pregnancy**	Gordon Bourne	£3.95p
☐	**The Law is an Ass**	Gyles Brandreth	£1.75p
☐	**The 35mm Photographer's Handbook**	Julian Calder and John Garrett	£6.50p
☐	**London at its Best**	Hunter Davies	£2.90p
☐	**Back from the Brink**	Michael Edwardes	£2.95p

☐	**Travellers' Britain**	} Arthur Eperon	£2.95p
☐	**Travellers' Italy**		£2.95p
☐	**The Complete Calorie Counter**	Eileen Fowler	90p
☐	**The Diary of Anne Frank**	Anne Frank	£1.75p
☐	**And the Walls Came Tumbling Down**	Jack Fishman	£1.95p
☐	**Linda Goodman's Sun Signs**	Linda Goodman	£2.95p
☐	**The Last Place on Earth**	Roland Huntford	£3.95p
☐	**Victoria RI**	Elizabeth Longford	£4.95p
☐	**Book of Worries**	Robert Morley	£1.50p
☐	**Airport International**	Brian Moynahan	£1.95p
☐	**Pan Book of Card Games**	Hubert Phillips	£1.95p
☐	**Keep Taking the Tabloids**	Fritz Spiegl	£1.75p
☐	**An Unfinished History of the World**	Hugh Thomas	£3.95p
☐	**The Baby and Child Book**	Penny and Andrew Stanway	£4.95p
☐	**The Third Wave**	Alvin Toffler	£2.95p
☐	**Pauper's Paris**	Miles Turner	£2.50p
☐	**The Psychic Detectives**	Colin Wilson	£2.50p

All these books are available at your local bookshop or newsagent, or can be ordered direct from the publisher. Indicate the number of copies required and fill in the form below   12

....

Name_____
(Block letters please)

Address_____

_____

Send to CS Department, Pan Books Ltd, PO Box 40, Basingstoke, Hants
Please enclose remittance to the value of the cover price plus:
35p for the first book plus 15p per copy for each additional book ordered
to a maximum charge of £1.25 to cover postage and packing
Applicable only in the UK

While every effort is made to keep prices low, it is sometimes
necessary to increase prices at short notice. Pan Books reserve
the right to show on covers and charge new retail prices which
may differ from those advertised in the text or elsewhere